THE GREAT CRIME
OF GRAPPLEWICK

Also by Eric Sykes

UFOs Are Coming Wednesday

THE GREAT CRIME OF GRAPPLEWICK

Eric Sykes

My friends live in this book –
Hattie Jacques, Tony Hancock, Dermott
Kelly, Terry Thomas, Spike Milligan,
John Le Mesurier and Noel Murphy.

ONE

On a typical cold damp winter's morning in the middle of August as nine o'clock boomed out over the complex of one of His Majesty's Prisons, the little door in the massive gate opened and 416236 became a person again. Terence was his name, Raffles to his colleagues, and he was known to the police as Pillock Brain.

With casual elegance he fitted a badly made cigarette into an ebony holder and applied a match.

'Be seeing ya,' said the warden behind him.

He raised an eyebrow and turned to make a witty riposte.

Bang! The little door slammed shut, and the badly made cigarette exploded in a shower of sparks. He quickly looked over his shoulder to see if the incident had been observed, but apart from a dog who shied away on hearing the slam of the door, and two spotty urchins, there was nobody to embarrass him. However, even two spotty urchins are an audience to a born actor, as Terence undoubtedly was. A bad actor, but nevertheless a compulsive one, he drew himself up to his full 5 feet 11½ inches on the Beaufort scale and brushed himself down with a pair of old kid gloves. He knew he was an imposing figure – black Homburg, long black overcoat with a half belt at the back and spats, which will give you some idea of how long it had been since he'd had a chance to go shopping.

The two Herberts giggled and nudged each other. There wasn't much entertainment in the immediate post-war years, and suddenly out of the blue here was this tall thin idiot, a brown paper parcel under his arm, and what looked like a smouldering daisy sticking out of his mouth. Even the dog came back to have a look.

Terence winked at the kids and took a match from his pocket, then he flicked his thumbnail against the head. It was a trick he had learned during his stay inside – it was nonchalant and had the effect, especially on new inmates, that here was one cool hombre. However, and perhaps because he was outside his environment, it didn't quite work out. The head of the match ignited and flew onto his Homburg, while some of the phosphorus stuck to his thumbnail. There was a burst of laughter from the audience. Terence dropped his parcel and hopped from one foot to another, sucking his thumb.

'Hey, mister,' gurgled one of the kids, 'your hat's on fire.'

Quickly he snatched it from his head and the wig came with it. This was the end for the spotty urchins. They were holding each other up, tears streaming down their cheeks – it was better than a Laurel and Hardy film. Terence snatched up his parcel and threw it at them. They ran off a few yards and stopped to watch the next bit. They didn't get a treat like this every day. Terence stuffed his wig in his overcoat pocket, then put his hat back on. Without the wig it came right down over his eyes, but at least it hid some of his embarrassment. He bent down to pick up his belongings, and as he did so his braces went. Typical, he thought – if this is freedom I'm going back in. Not only that, the parcel had come adrift, and there were all his worldly goods for everyone to see – shaving gear, carpet slippers and a sock – not a lot to show for the most brilliant criminal brain in the business.

He straightened up and shuffled off down the street, clutching his parcel and his trousers, head well back so he could see where he was going. In high glee the kids skipped after him, pointing out his braces which were hanging down below the hem of his long black overcoat. The dog enjoyed the braces too, and kept darting in, trying to grab them.

A little way up the street a pavement artist watched him approach from the corner of his eye and continued chalking his picture, which might have been a sunset over the sea, or it could have been a fried egg on a lawn. Whatever it was it didn't enhance the pavement – had he been a dog his owner would have been fined on the spot. However, he was waiting for Terence, and whenever he had time to spare – which meant most of his waking hours – he drew or sketched or doodled. In fact his work was on exhibition on the walls of several County Courts, police cells and public lavatories – thus he was known to anybody in authority and anybody against it as Rembrandt.

Terence stopped by the chalking scruffbag and turned round to the kids, who hovered at a safe distance.

Rembrandt didn't look up and continued chalking.

'So dey let you out all right, sorr?' he said, addressing the spats.

Terence looked casually about him and spoke, hardly moving his lips. 'Did you find Helliwell?'

'No sorr, oi did not and dat's a fact.'

'Did you get round to all the old places?'

'Definitely, sorr,' Rembrandt deftly applied a touch of purple chalk and surveyed the effect. 'Oi went round to all de old places, and if he'd been dere oi would have found him.'

He was about to shade the purple bit when the brown paper parcel fell on it, and in a blur he was yanked to his feet by the lapels of his raincoat.

'You've had eight months,' said Terence in a quiet voice.

'Yes, sorr, oi know dat. Oi tink he must have died, sorr. A bomb could have done it in de war.'

'If Helliwell was dead, I would have heard about it.'

The lads looked on silent and wide-eyed. Here was this tall thin idiot with his trousers round his ankles, holding the little man against the wall. It should have been funny, but it didn't seem laughable. The dog growled.

'Eight months, you great steaming Irish bog!'

'Dat's roight and don't you worry, sorr. If he's aloive oi'll foind him, and when oi do, oh yes sorr, oi'll mark him all right.'

Terence, head back so he could see, looked into the dirty, unintelligent face and spoke slowly. 'I don't want him hurt.'

'Oh no, sorr, oi wouldn't hurt him. Oi'll mark him where it doesn't show. De police do dat, and when you come to court you're doubled up in agony and not a mark to show for it.'

A sudden gust of cold wind hit Terence's thin bare legs. He looked down, saw his trousers in a heap round his ankles, and glanced quickly at the kids. 'You managed a car, I trust?'

'Roight behoind you, sorr,' said Rembrandt.

Terence had already seen it, but thought it was derelict. However, he shuffled himself into the passenger seat and the kids moved a little closer, while the dog added a neat touch to Rembrandt's masterpiece. Terence settled himself in and slung his parcel in the back seat. 'Not exactly a Rolls, is it?'

'No, sorr, a Rolls is much bigger dan dis. Oi did tink of getting a Rolls and dat's de truth, but dey always have somebody watching dem.'

The engine coughed into life and Rembrandt rubbed his hands together. 'Roight, sorr, where to first?'

Terence extracted another badly made cigarette from an old tobacco tin. 'Grapplewick,' he said.

'Roight, sorr.' Rembrandt was about to let off the brake when he stopped. 'Grapplewick?' he said. 'Dat's de one place oi've niver heard of, but it sounds a divvil of a long way to me. And why should we be after going to Grapplewick, sorr?' He leered across at Terence. 'Oi know Big Alice wouldn't mind having a look at yez.'

Terence shuddered at the thought of Big Alice – seven years was a long time, and she'd be bigger now. 'Helliwell was born in Grapplewick,' he said.

Rembrandt shook his head. 'Oi wouldn't go back to de place where oi was born – no sorr, if oi had money you wouldn't get me going to dat place. In any case oi tink Helliwell's probably dead.' A new thought struck him. 'Dat's it, why don't you ring de War Office, dey'll be able to tell if he's dead or not.'

Terence wound down the window and flicked the end of his cigarette at the two urchins. They dodged to one side, but the smaller of the two pounced on it and had a couple

4

of quick drags. 'I may have been under lock and key for seven years, but I still maintain my sources of information. Oh yes, Helliwell got himself a nice cushy number in the Ministry of Supply during the war.'

Rembrandt's eyebrows went up. 'Oh, so dat's why de war took so long.' He chuckled at his own witticism. 'Oi'll bet a lot of dose supplies didn't get to de lads at de front.'

Terence sniffed. 'Quite correct. A large percentage went to Ikey the Fixer.'

Rembrandt sucked in his breath. 'Dat's a cliver man, Ikey. Dey'll niver be able to put a finger on him – he's got a chief inspector who runs errands for him.'

'Correct again.' Terence smiled thinly. 'I met them both in the exercise yard a week ago.'

Rembrandt's mouth dropped open. 'He's inside?'

'Snug as a bug in a rug,' he drawled smoothly, 'and incidentally it was our old mate Helliwell who shopped him.'

Rembrandt's mouth fell open again – Terence turned away in disgust. 'Holy Mother! We'd better foind him before Ikey gets his hands on him.'

Terence lit another cigarette. 'There's no rush. Ikey won't be available till about 1965.'

'Dat's all very well, sorr, but he's got influence. Some of his boys'll be looking for him.'

Terence raised an eyebrow. 'I've no doubt of that, but they'll be looking in the wrong place.' He blew a cloud of smoke through the window. 'You see, my little Irish derelict, I took the liberty of telling Ikey that Helliwell's home town was Tunbridge Wells.'

Rembrandt nodded sagely. 'Dat's good tinking, sorr.' But he was uncertain. 'And how far away is de other place – er – what was de name again?'

Terence was arched forward, trying to knot his braces round his waist. 'Grapplewick,' he grunted.

'Dat's de one, sorr. How far is it?'

'About 250 miles as the crow flies, but with your sense of direction, God knows.'

'Dat's a long way, sorr. I'll need to see a mate of mine,

5

he's got some cheap petrol, but it'll cost a bit.' And with that he let off the brake, but before they could move off a new Rover swerved past and squealed to a stop in front of them. The driver leaped out and rushed across the road to disappear down the gents' toilet. Terence and Rembrandt looked at each other, then Terence collected his parcel from the back seat, Rembrandt switched off the engine, and they both made themselves comfortable in the brand-new Rover.

The two urchins watched silently, not understanding, then decided the best place for them was somewhere else, so they ran off. But the dog knew, and, barking furiously, chased the car for a little way towards Grapplewick.

TWO

It is hardly surprising that Rembrandt had never heard of Grapplewick. It is marked on the map as Gwick, because the full name is too long for the dot it represents – a typical northern town splotched on the moors like a handful of goat droppings. Two tall factory chimneys make it a good landmark for pilots, and many a weary traveller on the moors, spotting the two chimneys, knows it is Grapplewick, which gives him a chance to avoid it. It is a town where nobody seems aware of anything, but everybody knows what is going on – in the town, that is, anything over 20 miles away being foreign and suspect. Of course, they bought newspapers – newspapers were useful for lighting fires or wrapping up fish and chips, and most children had the job of cutting it up into neat squares to hang on the nail in the lavatory at the bottom of the yard . . . quite a few of the men actually read the newspapers, but only the sports page.

The majority worked in the two cotton mills, married somebody they'd known all their lives, supported Grapplewick Athletic, and took their wives to bed every Sunday afternoon. Their women brought up the results, supported their husbands, generally hated Sunday afternoons, and, once married, gave their brains a long holiday from which most of them never returned. The younger people, learning nothing from their elders, prepared to go the same way, spending Sunday afternoons parading up and down the High Street, known as the chicken run. The girls, arm in arm, followed by the boys, would go up to the Odeon, then back to Burton's, then up to the Odeon again, the girls

7

giggling and glancing over their shoulders, while the boys played football with anything that happened to be loose, or indulged in a little mock wrestling, seemingly oblivious, always keeping their distance from the girls – as the light decreased, so did the distance between them.

The well-to-do and the bosses lived on the Binglewood Estate, situated on high ground and sufficiently wooded to block out the view of Grapplewick. The only workers to set foot in this exclusive area were tradesmen, gardeners, servants and one or two keen ones from the factory who hung about the golf club on Sunday in the hopes of carrying a bag around for sixpence, and to say 'Yes sir, no sir.'

Even as Terence was emptying his last slop bucket prior to his release the streets of Grapplewick were bustling, echoing to the sound of thousands of clogs on their way to the mills, the foggy gloom illuminated by the glowing ends of countless Woodbines, Park Drives, Craven As and dubious concoctions of all brands salvaged from the gutter. Hawking and coughing accompanied the steady clockering of feet, dwindling and then quickening as the factory hooter wailed its mournful note. The last few footfalls became frantic, and then Grapplewick went back to sleep again until it was time for school.

Near the town centre, at the corner of Leslie Street and Featherstall Road, the men of the Fire Brigade turned up for duty at the station. A red brick eyesore, erected in 1882, it was approached across a cobbled yard, swept and hosed down each day – the old stables were still in use, although now tenanted by the two Clydesdales belonging to Hoskins' Brewery, and they ate well. The main building housed the ancient fire engine, more of a collector's piece than functional, which was hardly surprising because, apart from two engine changes, it was the original tender that had replaced the horses – a fond, familiar sight in the streets. The old 'uns still maintained it would get round faster if they'd kept the horses. However, since the inception of the Brigade there had only been one noteworthy fire, a warehouse on Featherstall Road, and to everyone's embarrassment, although it was only 500 yards from the station, the ware-

8

house would have been completely gutted had it not been for the timely arrival of the Blackburn Fire Brigade. Apparently, on hearing the alarm, the Grapplewick lads collected their gear and helmets and flung themselves onto the engine. Unfortunately, however, nobody could find the driver, and although he wasn't the only one possessing a licence he'd taken the starting handle home with him for safety, and, to complicate matters, he was keeping two homes going, although neither woman was aware of the other. Unable to locate him, the lads endeavoured to push the great engine, applauded, jeered and urged on by a great crowd of townfolk, and to their everlasting shame everything was under control by the time they arrived.

People still recounted the story, with embellishments, and the present Brigade still bore the brunt of the taunts. Fortuitously from that day Grapplewick seemed fireproof, unfortunately giving the lads no opportunity to vindicate themselves, and Aggie, as the appliance was affectionately known, was as yet unblooded.

Leading Fireman Ned Bladdock entered the station. He was round and pedantic, carrying with him an air of authority. He nodded at Barmy Chronicle, accepting a mug of hot, sweet tea. Night shifts had long since been abandoned, and Barmy, although not now on the official strength, looked after the station at night. But then Barmy was not official on any list – officially he didn't exist, even at Somerset House there was no record of a Mr and Mrs Chronicle having any offspring, but somebody must have had fun, because one summer morning the result was found abandoned in the station yard, wrapped in a copy of the *Grapplewick Chronicle*, and legend has it that the fireman who was cleaning the yard swept the bundle along quite some distance before little Barmy rolled out. The poor fireman was so shocked he promptly dropped down dead. According to the story, in order to make up the numbers the Brigade enrolled the little mite as apprentice Chronicle, and the name stuck – Barmy was added later when it became obvious. He stirred the thick tea, leaning forward at a dangerous angle. The front of his long coat was already steaming from the heat of the great pot-bellied stove, which he kept going winter and summer. He gave Ned a wide, toothless grin and put his thumb up.

'OK?'

'It'll do.'

Barmy nodded and swaggered to the door, with his thumb ready to greet the next arrivals.

Ned smiled affectionately after him. 'Silly sod!' He wondered, not for the first time, if Barmy had ever been outside the gates. The fire station was his home, in fact his whole world, but he seemed happy enough, and what chance would he have outside – big boots, long johns and an old First World War greatcoat that had originally belonged to someone who was at least a foot taller. No, it was probably better that he didn't set foot in the street – they'd have him in an asylum before he could say 'OK?'

Cyril Chadwick was the next arrival. Ned nodded to him and dragged out his heavy pocket watch. Young Cyril ignored the gesture – it happened every morning but it was merely habit. The mainspring had long gone, and it only had one hand, so it was permanently at quarter to . . . but to what hour was anybody's guess.

One by one the others rolled up and, as usual, Jack Puller was the last to report – a giant of a man with a Kitchener moustache and a black tobacco line etched round his bottom lip. He squirted a stream of brown juice into the yard.

Barmy grinned. 'OK?'

Jack tossed him a warm greasy bacon sandwich wrapped in a sheet of newspaper. 'Get that down you.'

Barmy took the paper off as if it was his twenty-first birthday present. 'Ooooh, bacon,' he said.

They took it in turns to bring Barmy food. Being an unofficial citizen he didn't have a ration book, but then the lads had little need for ration books either. Every Thursday the Brigade made the rounds of the outlying farms, ostensibly to deal with drainage, flooded fields, burning ricks or whatever. And in return for these courtesy visits the farmers supplied them with eggs, meat, butter, sides of bacon etc. It was considered a sound investment – who knows, perhaps

10

one day their fields might well be flooded, their ditches stagnant, or even, God forbid, there might be a fire.

By the time Jack had helped himself from the dixie the sandwich was gone. The only sign that there had ever been a bacon sandwich was the fat glistening on Barmy's chin.

Jack shook his head slowly in admiration. 'Enjoy that, did you?' he said.

Barmy gave him his eternal grin and stuck his thumb up.

Jack winked. 'It'll make you randy, will that.'

Barmy pursed his lips like the neck of a balloon and slapped the back of his neck.

'Did you have droopy Nellie in here last night?'

Barmy spluttered with delight and some of the lads sniggered – although this was a regular exchange.

'Leave him be,' said Ned Bladdock, getting into his overalls. Droopy Nellie'd have him for breakfast, then spit out his braces.'

Nellie, something of a local celebrity, was a big Irishwoman – eighty-six convictions for being drunk and disorderly and didn't mind putting herself out for a couple of pints of Guinness. The lads of Grapplewick said they wouldn't touch her with a bargepole, but all the same she seemed to get through an awful lot of Guinness.

Jack winked again. 'I'll bet you 'ave a different one in 'ere every night and two on Sundays, eh, Barmy?'

Barmy chortled, pleased with everything. He hadn't the foggiest idea what Jack was on about, but it made him feel he was one of the lads.

'Why do you have to keep having a go at him?' spluttered Ned into his Woodbine. Jack hauled himself up into the driving seat of the huge, antique engine.

'He don't know the difference, do he? If Betty Grable walked in here wi' nowt on, he'd think it were a bloke who'd walked into a bacon slicer.'

Everybody laughed except Cyril, who blushed and snatched the starting handle from under the seat. Trust Jack Puller to make a coarse remark about Betty. Betty was an angel and he loved her with a shining white purity. Every Saturday he wrote to her, c/o Hollywood – he'd even sent

11

her a photo of himself in his fireman's uniform, but so far she hadn't had a chance to reply. His grasp tightened on the starting handle and for one fleeting moment he had a mad urge to clout Jack Puller round the mouth with it. The urge, however, was short-lived as logic asserted itself. In order to defend Betty's honour he would first have to step up onto the running board. Then the handle was unwieldy and weighed a ton. By the time he got into a position to strike, Jack would have killed him.

'Are you going to crank her up or not?' Jack asked patiently. Cyril pulled himself together as he realised Jack was speaking to him.

'Eh?'

Jack leaned down so his face was almost level. Cyril could smell the acrid tobacco juice on his breath.

'I said, are you going to give us a crank, or are you waiting for me to stuff it up your jacksi?'

Cyril looked at the handle as if he'd just realised it was there.

'Oh,' he said. 'Start her up now?'

'Bloody 'ell!' exploded Jack. 'I'm not sitting up here to have my picture took.'

'Give it 'ere, Cyril,' said Ned kindly, and with two strong turns the big engine roared into life.

A flock of pigeons strutting in the yard rose instantly in a solid flap of panic and settled on the roof. The lads in the station watched the throbbing tender anxiously in case something fell off.

'As you are, come on, come on.' Ned guided the engine out into the yard with beckoning arms. Jack eased the choke as it rolled out. He never once glanced at Ned. There were at least two yards to spare on either side, but if Ned wanted to play silly buggers every morning it was up to him. Massive and gleaming, the thundering juggernaut was deafening in the confines of the station, but once outside it seemed to shrink as if fearful of the open air. The pigeons returned to the yard to mock, and some of them pecked arrogantly under the trembling engine. Jack swung himself down and hurried back into the warmth of the station.

'Bloody 'ell,' he shuddered. 'It's enough to freeze t'bloody taters off a polar bear.' Ned joined him at the stove and the yard was left to the pigeons.

''Oo's on the gate?' he said.

Fireman Helliwell slammed his mug down.

'Not yet. He won't be 'ere for hours yet.'

Jack looked at him steadily.

'If it's thy turn on t'gate, then bugger off. Tha knows what t'Chief's like, 'e's unpredictable. 'E might not be 'ere for hours, he might not come at all today, and then again 'e might just now be standing in t'yard, wondering if 'e's on t'*Marie Celeste*.'

Helliwell went.

Ned looked into his steaming mug. ''E's going through a bit of a rough patch at the moment, is Mr Thurk.'

The lads nodded slowly in agreement. Jim Cork spoke up. 'If you ask me, he's not getting all his own way at the Town Hall.'

Ned smiled. 'Don't worry about Mr Thurk. It'll take a bloody landmine to shift him.'

It was another of the vagaries of Grapplewick. The Mayor was not elected annually – in fact he was not elected at all. Mr Thurk's father had been Mayor and his father before him, so, as with Royalty, the Mayoralty was handed down to the eldest son – likewise the position of Fire Chief, and, as the Grapplewick Prize Band was mainly composed of Brigade personnel, Thurks ascended naturally to the role of Bandmaster. The walls of the station were lined with yellowing pictures of various Grapplewick brass bands – stern moustached faces, smartly turned out in uniform, each man holding an instrument, and sitting front row centre of each photograph was a Mr Thurk. Sadly, there were no records on the walls of Grapplewick bands since 1932. Smart uniforms don't remain in one piece forever, and musical instruments deteriorate, so that now, although the keenness was still there and band practice was conducted every Thursday by Mr Thurk, he was the only one to retain a full uniform – three-quarter-length tunic, red sash, gloves and peaked cap. There was no money in the Band Fund –

13

in fact, they didn't even possess a big drum. In order to practise they had to hire one from the scout troop for half-a-crown a week. This always stuck in Jack's craw. He could never get over it.

''Alf a crown a week for a big drum . . . no wonder they can afford to go to camp every bloody year.'

Fireman Helliwell leaned against the gate. He wasn't thinking about music. He was watching the struggling buttocks of a young woman as she hurried down the street. A medium-sized man in a dark uniform touched the peak of his cap to her as he passed and Helliwell practically swallowed his fag end.

'Bloody 'ell,' he muttered and hurried into the yard, hitting the bell twice with his knuckle. Immediately, hoses were rolled into the yard – four of the lads were polishing the old engine, although the brass plate on the side shone like new and the wording on it had in fact long since been buffed away. Jack Puller had the bonnet open, and was bent deep into the warm engine when Mr Thurk entered the yard. Ned shouted 'Shun!' and everybody stood rigid.

'Morning, Chief,' said Ned.

'Morning, lads. Carry on.'

The lads carried on, pretending to carry on. Barmy hurried out with a mugful of tea. Mr Thurk accepted it gratefully.

'Thank you, Mr Chronicle,' he said, as always one to observe protocol.

'Good practice last night. Especially "Men of Harlech". That was especially good.'

The lads nodded. It was a grand tune, even if it was Welsh.

Ned spoke up. 'It'd sound better if we 'ad something decent to play it on.'

Mr Thurk nodded sadly. Here we go again. All avenues had been explored in order to raise funds. They'd had door-to-door collections, but the proceeds were frugal, and the operation had resulted more than once in actual bodily harm. The Firemen's Ball was another disaster. They'd started with a Paul Jones, to break the ice – men walking

14

round on the outside, women going the other way – then the band broke into a waltz. Either the break into the dance wasn't obvious, or perhaps the tempo was too similar, but the dancers kept walking round in circles. 'Wings over the Navy' made no difference – it was like the exercise yard in a mixed prison. There was only one thing for it – a loud chord in G followed by a cymbal clash. The marchers dispersed and sat round the hall. After a whispered discussion between Mr Thurk and the organising secretary, which every eye in the hall tried to lip-read, the secretary blew twice into the microphone and asked if there was anybody who could play the piano. There was. And as the band shamefacedly packed up their instruments, the couples were swinging round the floor to something like 'An Apple for the Teacher'.

Open day at the Fire Station, another money-making scheme, had grossed £18 15s. 6d., but on the debit side they'd lost two helmets, four axes and a length of hosepipe. Also practising was thirsty work, so the band fund barely covered the bill from the off-licence.

Jack raised his voice over the noise of the engine. 'Any news from Mr Forsythe?'

Mr Thurk looked into his mug before replying. 'Not very helpful, I'm afraid.'

Jack spat and leaned into the warmth again. Forsythe owned one of the two mills and, as Foden's, Bickershaw Colliery, Black Dyke and all the big brass bands were sponsored, Mr Thurk had agreed to approach Mr Forsythe.

'We had a long discussion, and he wasn't actually against sponsorship in toto, there were economic factors involved, er, import of cotton, labour costs, in fact there was a possibility of going on short time, and what with the er. . . .'

He trailed off. The lads weren't listening, and being basically an honest man he hated his own words. He hadn't really had a long discussion. When he had entered Mr Forsythe's office the great man had looked up, then gone back to the papers on his desk and said: 'If it's about that band o' thine, tha's wasting my bloody time.'

15

Mr Thurk had cleared his throat, in fact he had cleared his throat twice. Then he left.

Shamefacedly he handed his mug back to Barmy and rubbed his hands briskly together. 'Well, er . . . tempus fugit.' He walked round the bonnet and tapped Jack on the shoulder.

Jack ducked out of the engine.

'Ready to move?' he asked.

Jack wiped his hands on a piece of waste paper. 'As ready as she'll ever be. Where to?'

'Just drop me off at the Town Hall, and pick me up at the usual time.'

The lads scrambled inside the station for helmets and tunics as Mr Thurk swung himself up beside Jack, and in no time at all they were trundling along Featherstall Road – a schoolboy on a bike pedalling furiously to keep up with them.

A keen young policeman watched the brand-new Rover as it passed him. He was about to move on, then stopped. Apart from the fact that it was progressing in a slightly erratic manner, there was something about the car that seemed odd. He turned quickly but it was fast disappearing. Suddenly he realised what had alerted him – there didn't seem to be anybody in it.

Rembrandt straightened up slowly and glanced furtively in his rear view mirror. 'It's OK, sorr, we've passed him, never saw us at all.'

Terence was almost bent double and cursed as he scraped his head from under the dashboard. He quickly swivelled in his seat to look out of the back window, but the policeman was very distant and didn't appear to be agitated. He grunted down again to pick up his hat and wig.

'We're making good time, sorr.'

Terence looked at him in amazement. 'Good time? What are you talking about? We've been on the road three hours now and we're still in London.'

Rembrandt nodded. 'Oh yes, sorr, oi'm laying a false trail so dat nobody can guess where we're goin'.'

'You're bloody well lost, aren't you?'

Rembrandt was vehement. 'Dat oi'm not, sorr. If oi was lost oi wouldn't know where oi was, but you see, sorr, if oi was to go straight up de A1, dey'd know. Oh yes, dey'd know all right.'

Terence shook his head in despair. 'You're a berk, d'you know that?'

'No, sorr, dey'll all be looking for dis car.'

'Exactly, but if you'd gone straight towards Grapplewick we might have been there before it was reported. In fact, we could have been there while the owner was still in the khazi.'

Rembrandt was unmoved.

'Oi know what oi'm doing, sorr. Oi know all de back doubles in London.'

Terence banged the dashboard in exasperation. 'Well, for god's sake don't keep driving past the nick. It's bad enough being inside – so just move it. Helliwell could be dead of old age before we get to Grapplewick.'

Rembrandt sniffed. 'You're de guvnor.'

And he turned right into another street, hoping it wouldn't bring them past the prison again.

CHAPTER

THREE

The secretary coughed and adjusted his glasses. He was reading the minutes of the last debate which had taken place only two days ago. A Council Meeting was in progress, but then in Grapplewick Town Hall there were plenty of these get-togethers: the regular Council Meetings, and the Extraordinary General Meetings (which took place in the Council Chambers), then, apart from all the official meetings, as long as there was a quorum, they gathered in the Mayor's Parlour. Commander Wilson Brown was the newest member to be elected to the Council and he was appalled at the manner in which these affairs were conducted. There seemed to be no division of parties – when canvassing, all the candidates wore large blue rosettes and were all duly elected. It wouldn't have mattered to the electorate if they'd worn false ears and explodable boots. Nevertheless, due to his fine war record the Commander had been elected with a very impressive number of votes, but once in the Town Hall it counted for nothing, and it hurt. He glanced round the table. What a shower. He had only contempt for his fellow Councillors who had allowed this archaic state of affairs to continue. However, with a quiet word here, and a couple of drinks there, he felt he was gaining ground. It appeared to him that he was the only one who was experienced enough, and qualified to hold office. The others as yet couldn't, or wouldn't, grasp the opportunities, but one thing was certain – there was a lot of gravy about, and he was going to be the first to dip his ladle in. The secretary was still on his feet, squinting at something he'd written – owing to

18

the fact that he took the minutes down in longhand it was never a faithful record, merely a gist.

Councillor Wilson Brown tapped the table irritably. 'Is there much more of this?'

The secretary looked at him over the rim of his glasses. 'I'm doing the best I can.'

Wilson Brown looked at him with distaste. The secretary wasn't a pretty sight – a tall, thin, stoopy man with a huge, beaked, purple-veined nose that overhung his tiny mouth, and no top lip to speak of. Wide-eyed children watched him eat his food, wondering if he was actually stuffing it up his nose.

Mr Thurk nodded to him kindly and he carried on.

'Where was I? Oh, yes. Councillor Wilson Brown proposed a motion that a statue of Winston Churchill be erected in the town centre, but the Mayor suggested a bandstand would be a more popular choice. Councillor Wilson Brown then replied. . . .'

He stopped short and looked round the table. Councillor Wilson Brown broke the silence.

'Never mind what I said, just get on with it.'

Lady Dorothy glared at him. 'It should never have been said. It is a word I am not accustomed to hearing, and I cannot protest too strongly.'

'I apologised, didn't I?'

Mr Thurk broke in. 'I think we can delete that from the minutes. Carry on, Wilfred.'

The secretary nodded. 'Well, that's all there is. After the offending remark, the meeting broke up in disorder.'

With this, he sat down heavily and winced, making a mental note to see Dr McBride about his piles. No sooner was he down than Councillor Wilson Brown was on his feet.

'If I had commanded my ship in the way in which the affairs of this town are conducted, Grapplewick would be under German occupation.'

Lady Dorothy glared at him.

'With due respect, Commander,' she said in an icy tone,

19

'you are not the only man in this room who served his country during the war.'

'Hear, hear,' muttered deaf Crumpshaw. Lady Dorothy thanked him, although she knew he hadn't heard a word.

Councillor Wilson Brown raised an eyebrow. 'I am well aware of the sacrifices made by the citizens of this town.'

Lady Dorothy blushed. She had presented Wilson Brown with an opening and he'd fired a full salvo. Her husband had been killed in 1944, but his name did not appear on the cenotaph. The Mayor patted her hand as he also remembered. His Lordship had managed to stay out of the war until it became obvious that we were going to win, so in 1944 he obtained a commission in the Honourable Artillery Company where he divided his time between his London clubs, the officers' mess and the occasional hunt. From information gleaned from his driver, he discovered that the Second Front was imminent, so he badgered the War Office with requests to be in the first wave on D-Day. On Winston Churchill's personal intervention, his wish was granted and he was transferred to an infantry regiment along with his valet and head groom. Unfortunately, when the invasion force finally sailed he was in London badgering the War Office for permission to take two of his hunters, and on hearing the news that they'd started without him, he had his gear packed and went home to Grapplewick. His personal valet and head groom leaped into France on D-Day, tragically landing on the same mine. His Lordship was never the same after that. A few weeks later he was jogging over the golf course on his favourite mare – he'd had more than a stirrup cup, in fact he'd had a bootful – and was unaware that a well-hit golf ball struck his mount on the backside. The horse staggered, giving him just enough time to hold on, then the mad gallop began, down the fourth fairway, churning up the green, through the rough, over two stone walls, with his Lordship now hanging round its neck like a long-lost relative.

The horse, with the adrenalin of over-confidence and a belly-full of best-quality oats, did an almighty leap to clear an outhouse. It didn't, but His Lordship did, and even his

20

aristocratic skull was no match for the hard cobblestones on the other side. Thus Lady Dorothy, from being a grass widow, became a fully fledged one, and took his place on the Council. As Councillor Wilson Brown had remarked on more than one occasion, this was highly unorthodox, if not downright illegal. However, as he was the new boy he had to accept the situation – for the time being anyhow. Mr Thurk, on the other hand, enjoyed the company of Lady Dorothy and he found himself, not for the first time, wondering if she harboured such feelings for him. He pulled himself together as he became aware that Councillor Wilson Brown was speaking.

'With regard to the brass band, it is the joke of Grapplewick, and to suggest that we encourage it would be a gross misappropriation of the rates, and most certainly would make this Council the laughing stock of the North of England.'

Mr Thurk was on his feet. 'May I remind you, Councillor, that all the well-known bands – Foden's, Black Dyke and Bickershaw Colliery – only achieved greatness because of the financial encouragement they received.'

Wilson Brown shook his head. 'At least they started with a knowledge of music.'

The Mayor said nothing. The Band Fund was a regular topic at these meetings and a little money had always been allocated before the arrival of Wilson Brown.

The door opened and one of the cleaners stuck her head in. 'Are you goin' to be at it all day?' she said with a long-suffering face.

Councillor Wilson Brown glanced at her. 'How long we carry on is no concern of yours, and the next time I suggest you knock before entering.'

She stared round the table. 'Oh, aye, and what about my 'usband's dinner?'

Mr Thurk turned round in his chair and smiled kindly. 'It's all right, Mrs Macclesfield. You needn't do in here today, thank you.'

And with that she sniffed and closed the door behind her.

Immediately Edward Helliwell, one of the younger

members, took advantage of the break and was on his feet. 'If I may intercede, at our last meeting we did not establish what we were going to do with the space in the town centre. Now, having heard the proposals – i.e. a statue in honour of Winston Churchill and the Mayor's suggestion for a bandstand, both of which seem highly controversial and emotive – can we consider transforming it into a Garden of Rest?' He looked round the table and coughed into his hand.

Councillor Wilson Brown went on as if Edward was a ghost. He turned towards the Mayor: 'At the risk of being pedantic, don't you think you have enough on your plate with your duties as Mayor and Chief of the Fire Brigade without spending valuable time on that tuppenny ha'penny band?'

Mr Thurk ignored the remark, but drummed his fingers on his order papers. Lady Dorothy came to his rescue.

'The brass band is entirely voluntary and a spare-time job, and as long as I have been privileged to know the Mayor he has not once allowed it to interfere with his official business.'

'Hear, hear,' said deaf Crumpshaw.

'My dear lady,' said Wilson Brown in feigned astonishment, 'what the Mayor does in his spare time matters little to me. As far as I am concerned he is at liberty to indulge himself in plasticine modelling, he can run with his hoop up and down the High Street or go clog dancing in the evenings for all I care. It is the time wasted in Council Meetings holding out his begging bowl for the band that irks me. . . . Band!' he snorted derisively. 'We might as well spend the money taking a party of blind people to a silent movie.'

Councillor Helliwell was still standing. He coughed again, discreetly. 'We could stock it with flowers in season and in November it could be transformed into a sea of poppies.'

He looked round, but everybody was staring fixedly at the table. He heard a bus pass, and somewhere in the building someone dropped a bucket.

22

'Perhaps we could give it some thought.' He coughed again, and sat down to join the others staring at the table.

At the same time, in Bishop's Stortford, the police received a phone call to the effect that a baker's van had been stolen from the High Street. The desk sergeant made a note of it and put the phone down. It rang again almost immediately. It was a PC Macnamara calling in with the news that a brand-new Rover reported stolen in London was now parked outside Turner's bread shop.

Terence was furious. 'Didn't it get through to your thick Irish brain that a bread van might be conspicuous?'

Rembrandt didn't reply. He was driving with one hand whilst he held a crusty loaf in the other.

Terence tried again. 'Why a bread van, for God's sake?'

Rembrandt swallowed a great lump. 'We have to eat, don't we? It's good bread, dis.'

Terence looked out of the side window. 'Brilliant.'

Rembrandt glowed with pride and took another huge bite.

Terence turned to face him. 'If you see a coal cart, we'll switch. Then we can have toast.'

Rembrandt considered this for a moment, then shook his head. 'It's new bread, dis. You never toast new bread and dat's a fact.'

Some time later the police found the bread van in Boothby Pagnall, and a little old lady came out of the butcher's shop to find a space where her Ford Prefect had been.

FOUR

Fireman Cyril Chadwick had the original idea. One morning he arrived at the station one hour late. Ned opened his mouth to ask for an explanation when he caught sight of the sack that Cyril was carrying, and the mysterious smile on his face. So he followed him into the station. Cyril put down the sack gently and waited till the lads gathered round. Jack was the first to speak.

''As tha brought tha lunch?'

Cyril winked and delved into the sack. The lads moved back a step in case something sprang out, and with the air of a professional illusionist he brought out a gleaming kettle drum. Twenty-three mouths fell open, and one set of dentures and a wad of tobacco fell out. Ned's eyes widened and he moved forward to touch the skin.

'Bai, that's a grand drum is that.'

Cyril preened and took a pair of drumsticks out of his belt. 'Listen to the tone,' he said, and propping the drum between his stomach and the wall he gave a couple of rolls and a paradiddle. Jack brushed his wad of tobacco on his sleeve and popped it in his mouth.

'Where did you pinch yon bugger from?' he asked.

Cyril put the drum back in the sack. 'I got it from Cowell and Bottisford's.'

The lads looked at each other in wonder. Many's the time they'd all stood, noses pressed to the window of Cowell and Bottisford's: drums, euphoniums, big drums, trombones – it was one of the best music shops in the North of England.

'I'll bet that set thee back a bit,' said Ned.

'No it didn't,' said Cyril. 'They took my old 'un in exchange for this.'

Jack spat on the stove. 'Go on, pull t'other one. Thy drum was clapped out, only had one skin and that had a plaster on it. That one there's practically new, snares and all. Aye and bloody white ropes 'anging down.'

Cyril shuffled uncomfortably. 'Well, I, er, had to give 'em something else as to sort of make up the difference . . . and it's only lent, mind you. If anything happens I can get it back in five minutes.'

He stroked the sack and the lads waited. Ned spoke first.

'Come on then, what else did you give him besides that drum of yours?'

Cyril blushed and lowered his eyes. 'My 'elmet.'

Every head swivelled to the rack where the helmets hung. 'Tha's given him thy 'elmet?'

'No, not given, only lent. He promised I could redeem it if it was necessary.'

Ned bridled. 'That's all very well, but that 'elmet doesn't belong to thee. It's Corporation property. What're you going to wear on the engine — a beret?'

Cyril came back quickly. 'We only wear them for show, anyway. We nearly always wear our peaked caps.'

'Mr Thurk's not too happy about that either. Always on about a smart turnout.'

Cyril played his trump. 'All right then, which d'you think he'd prefer — us with caps instead of 'elmets or a smart brass band? Go on, I know which he'd prefer.'

Jack thought about his cornet. It was getting harder to play. If he didn't get a new one, he'd be needing a truss.

Ned looked at the sack again. 'I've seen a grand big drum in that there window, a right bobby dazzler. Got battle honours as far back as the Crimean war.'

Jim Cork nodded. 'Aye, it'll be better than the one tha borrows now.'

'It will an' all,' said Jack. 'And we wouldn't have to pay half a bloody crown a week for the loan of it.'

Ned solemnly took a coin out of his pocket. 'We'll toss

up,' he said, 'and if it's 'eads it's all right, and if it's tails tha takes it back and we'll say no more about it.'

He spun the coin into the air and they all crowded round to see what it was. Ned had to toss it three times before it came up heads.

The following day Mr Bottisford, pottering in his shop, listened absent-mindedly to the approach of the fire bell. He glanced towards the window and was surprised when the fire engine pulled up outside. He was even more surprised to see the firemen leap off, two of them running to a hydrant with a hosepipe, while several more manhandled a ladder to his bedroom window. He stood aside as three of them entered the shop itself, one going into the back room while two of them dashed upstairs. It was all carried out so quickly that before his brain could get round to forming a question, the large fireman was coming slowly down the stairs, helmet in hand, mopping his brow. His companion brushed past him to the door and said, 'False alarm.'

Ned Bladdock walked in wearily. 'Sorry about that, Mr Bottisford,' he said. 'Bloody kids.'

'False alarm, was it?'

'Aye,' said Ned. 'We can't afford to ignore 'em.' He leaned his elbows on the counter with the air of a man called out on unnecessary alarms every five minutes.

Jack Puller joined him. 'Especially this shop,' he said, looking around him with shining eyes.

'Oh, I don't know,' sighed Mr Bottisford. 'Business is terrible. I sometimes think I'd be better off with the insurance. Then again' – he swept his hand round the brass band instruments – 'this lot 'd take a lot of burning. I should have gone into the timber business.'

Jack nodded, and there was a pause. Then he placed a newspaper bundle on the counter. Mr Bottisford looked on curiously as Jack took out his battered cornet. Enlightenment dawned.

'You've seen Cyril, then?'

'Aye,' said Jack, and pushed the instrument tentatively forward.

Mr Bottisford scowled at it. 'How have you ever managed to play on this?'

'It's not too bad,' said Jack.

Mr Bottisford picked it up carefully. Jack watched him apprehensively.

'Don't turn it upside down! One of the stops 'll fall out.'

While Mr Bottisford was examining the cornet, Jack took off his helmet and placed it deliberately before him.

Mr Bottisford took the hint. 'Not another helmet.'

'Biggest we have in the station,' said Jack, proudly pointing to the '7½' on the head band.

Mr Bottisford shook his head sadly, and walked round the counter to a glass case containing half a dozen cornets. He selected one and handed it over. Jack licked his dry lips and took it as if he was about to baptise a new-born baby. He put it reverently to his lips, but before he could blow Mr Bottisford grabbed his arm.

'Dost a want everybody to know what's goin' on?' he bleated. 'Supposin' somebody comes in?'

'That's all right, Mr Bottisford,' said Ned with authority 'Street's roped off as far as Woolworth's.'

'Never mind Woolworth's,' snapped Mr Bottisford. 'They'll hear that.'

Ned agreed, and Jack wrapped it quickly in the paper before Bottisford had a change of heart. Jim Cork joined them with a large object wrapped in a tatty blanket, and Mr Bottisford was hardly surprised to find it was a battered old euphonium. He glanced at it scornfully, then suddenly he took it from Jim and examined the bell closely. He pointed to the scratched initials 'J.B.'.

'This belonged to Josh Barlow,' he said.

'That's right, my Uncle Joshua.'

'Well, I'll go to our 'ouse,' said Bottisford in amazement. 'Josh taught me all I know about music.' He held the instrument fondly, then lifted it to his lips and blew tentatively. Again he blew, but it was useless – not a peep. His lips and his wind had gone years ago. He lowered the euphonium, breathing heavily. 'Well, tha's kept it clean any road,' he wheezed. 'Bai, when Josh blew a note on that, all t'visitors

27

used to get off t'*Queen Mary*.' He smiled nostalgically, then frowned. 'I've got enough helmets, though.'

Jim Cork looked over his uniform, then down at his thigh boots. Ned looked up at the ceiling in exasperation.

Mr Bottisford nodded. 'Well, I can use them on t'allotment, I suppose,' and five minutes later curious onlookers observed a fireman walking out of the shop in his stockinged feet carrying a blanket-wrapped bundle. In half an hour rumour swept the town that a child had perished in the fire.

Ned and Jack were about to leave when Mr Bottisford stopped them. 'They're only on loan, you know.'

'Ah know that,' said Ned. 'Them helmets and stuff's only collateral . . . we can reclaim them any time.'

'Aye,' said Mr Bottisford shrewdly. 'On production of my instruments.'

Ned nodded.

'Or,' went on Mr Bottisford, 'tha paid for 'em in cash, and that'd suit me a lot better.'

'Right,' said Ned. 'Oh, and by the way, if you're ever free on a Thursday, you might like to pop in and listen to a band practice.'

Mr Bottisford's eyebrows shot up in delight, then they slowly went down. He'd heard them once, and that was in the open air. God knows what it would be like in a confined space. 'I always listen to the wireless on Thursdays,' he said. 'But I'll tell thee what, I wouldn't mind coming in one day to have a look at the old photos.' He looked from one to the other. 'They're still on t'walls, aren't they?'

Jack nodded. 'Aye, every year till a few years before the war.'

They were proud of the past Grapplewick bands, but embarrassed and somewhat ashamed that they had not attained the standard to join their illustrious forebears.

'We had a good band in them days,' said Mr Bottisford. 'I was second trombone, you know.'

Jack nodded. 'Aye, we've seen you on the photos.' He was eager to be off with his shiny new cornet, but Mr Bottisford hadn't had much chance to reminisce since Cowell died. He leaned across the counter.

'The old Mr Thurk was Bandmaster in them days, and what a Tartar he was. Couldn't read a note, but what an ear for music,' he giggled. 'Once at a band practice Tommy Burton the double B had had a few pints of brown ale, and during a loud piece. . . .'

Jack broke in, eager to be off. 'You've told me before.'

Mr Bottisford ignored the interruption. 'I could see old Tommy squirming in his seat, holding it back till we got to a crescendo . . . crash went the cymbals, and Tommy's face relaxed. I was right next to him and never heard it, but at the end of the piece old Mr Thurk put down his baton and looked straight at him.'

'Tha'd be better off playing the double B at t'other end,' he said. Mr Bottisford burst into laughter until a cough took over. 'Wonderful ear for music, old Mr Thurk.' Mr Bottisford was wheezing and dabbing his eyes.

Outside, the fire bell dinged fiercely. Jack heaved a sigh of relief. 'Well, another emergency, I suppose,' and he made his way to the door.

Ned dawdled. 'That's a grand big drum you have in the window.' But before he could pursue the matter the engine burst into life, and he hurried out. Jack didn't wait for stragglers. That was the beginning of the exchange of stock between the two concerns. It was a slippery slope.

Three miles south of Grapplewick, Terence and Rembrandt stepped out of a small MG sports car. Terence stretched himself and surveyed the scene. The Pennine Gorge was a well-known beauty spot, frequented mainly in the summer but hardly ever in the winter when a good snow would make the road impassable. Terence blew into his cold hands and walked to the edge of the plateau. The keen wind made his eyes water and almost took his breath away. A few drops of rain spattered the back of his neck and he pulled his collar up. It suddenly occurred to him that there wasn't a cloud in the sky, and he whirled round to see Rembrandt relieving himself against the wheels of the car with no regard for the direction of the wind. Angrily Terence took out his handkerchief and rubbed the back of his neck.

'You dirty little bugger,' he snarled.

'It's OK, sorr,' said Rembrandt, tucking his pitiful manhood away. 'They can't touch you for it as long as it's against the off-side wheel. It's an old law, you see, sorr, from the days when they had horses.' He was about to elaborate when Terence cut him short.

'Just get the baggage out.'

Rembrandt stared at him, perplexed. 'Get the baggage out, sorr?'

'Out of the car.'

'Out of the car, sorr?'

Terence looked up at the heavens with a sigh and back at Rembrandt. 'You suddenly gone deaf or something?'

Rembrandt was uncertain. But when Terence took a menacing step towards him he had the boot open in a flash and two newly acquired suitcases and a carrier bag appeared like magic on the ground at Terence's feet.

'Thank you,' he said with a biting sarcasm that only people of breeding could get away with. He strolled casually to the edge of the gorge and looked down. Then he turned his gaze to the left and in the far distance two tall factory chimneys stood out against the bleak moors. Rembrandt followed his gaze.

'Dat must be Grapplewick, sorr.'

Terence didn't reply.

'We can be there in ten minutes. It's all downhill from 'ere, sorr. 'Tis only the first bit that's up.'

Terence went to the side of the plateau where the ground sloped steeply to accommodate a footpath. He swung to face Rembrandt.

'Bring the car here.'

Rembrandt peered over his shoulder at the grassy slope. 'We'll be better off sticking to the road, sorr. Dat's only a path.'

Terence clenched his fists and it was enough. Rembrandt was in the car like a startled ferret, slowly easing it forward to the edge. Terence waved him nonchalantly forward, then casually held up his hand. Rembrandt snatched the brake and leaned out.

30

'Are you sure this is the quickest way, sorr? Oi don't tink it's a road at all.'

'Out,' said Terence.

Rembrandt couldn't wait. He fumbled with the door handle and shot away from the car. He was about to ask why it was necessary to park so near to the edge, but he was too late. Terence was thirty yards away, scrambling to a piece of high ground in order to survey the road. Satisfied, he held onto his hat and scuttled back down to the plateau. Rembrandt watched him apathetically, hands deep in his pockets, hopping from one foot to the other for warmth – or it could have been a weak bladder. Terence pushed him to one side, leaned into the car and released the brake. Then he strolled round the back, placed his foot on the rear bumper and gave it a contemptuous shove. Nothing happened. In fact the car seemed to bounce back slightly. He frowned and, placing both his hands on the boot, he gave a tentative heave. The car was unyielding. He looked round to see if Rembrandt was watching, but it was OK – Rembrandt was totally absorbed rummaging deep into the litter bin. Checking that the brake was off, Terence went round the back and tried again. This time he was really straining. His face puckered up and reddened, and a vein in his forehead throbbed dangerously. But the bloody car was obstinate. He straightened up, breath rasping in his throat. He didn't have to turn to know that Rembrandt was watching him now. It made him angry – he should have told the little sod in the first place, but it was too late, his pride was at stake. Jamming his hat down, he leaned forward and with a grunt he made an almighty heave. A look of horror crossed his face and he shot upright, clasping the seat of his trousers. Rembrandt clucked sympathetically and shuffled to the back of the car.

'You should let me do dat, sorr.' And with a flick of the wrist he had the boot open. ''Tis easy when you know how.'

Terence's agonised look changed to amazement. He forced himself to speak calmly – he was in no position to rant. 'It's nothing to do with the boot. I was trying to push the car over the edge.'

31

He stopped suddenly as another spasm wracked him. Rembrandt smiled confidently and shook his head. 'You'll not do dat, sorr. No sorr, safe as houses is dat little car. Whilst you wuz up de hill, I put two rocks under the front wheels.'

Terence screwed his eyes shut and turned to face the sky, struggling to contain himself. One thing was certain, had he been mobile with both hands free, the little Irish reject would be on his way down to the bottom of the Pennine Gorge. Realisation dawned on Rembrandt. He looked aghast at Terence, then at the car, then leaned forward to peer over the edge.

'Oi'm not wid you, sorr. If we push de car over, how're we going to get to dat town?' He pointed in the direction of the two factory chimneys.

'We take a bus.'

Rembrandt took a smart step back, shaking his head vigorously. 'No, sorr. Oi'm not takin' no bus. Dey all has de numbers on 'em. Oh yes, sorr, we wouldn't get a mile before dey had de road blocks up.'

'Just get those rocks from under the wheels.'

Rembrandt rarely looked directly into Terence's face, but he did so now and what he saw wasn't encouraging. He scurried round to the front of the car. 'Oh, oi'll do dat for you all right, sorr, but oi'll not take no bus and dat's a fact.'

He leaned on the bonnet, easing the car back a fraction. While he kicked the nearside rock away, muttering useless obscenities, he gingerly made his way to the front wheel, clinging desperately to the headlamp to stop himself sliding down the incline. Terence walked round in a tight circle as if his ankles were shackled, pondered idly what it was about the Irish that made it logical to risk life and limb scrambling round the front of the car when it would have been much simpler to go round the back. He turned away as his stomach contracted. There was a strangled yelp and he looked round just in time to see Rembrandt fling himself clear as the car rolled down the incline, bouncing slowly at first, then picking up speed as it slewed through the wooden safety fence with an ease that didn't say much for its safety.

Rembrandt scrambled to his feet, crossing himself at the same time – it was merely a reflex action. Almost in slow motion, the car tumbled into the gorge. Cartwheeling through the air, it smashed first into one side and a head-lamp flew off. Rocks started to tumble, then in a lazy parabola it careened into the opposite side, gouging a scar. A wheel bounced exuberantly behind it, and finally all the bits and pieces splashed into the tiny stream, followed by a miniature avalanche of rocks, small bushes and anything else that wasn't firmly rooted. Terence was satisfied – nothing at the foot of the gorge bore any resemblance to a car.

Some three hours later the twice daily bus from Blackburn pulled up in front of Grapplewick Town Hall. Rembrandt stepped off with the luggage and stood aside while the conductor gingerly helped Terence onto the pavement. He watched the tall thin man walk stiff-legged, hardly able to put one foot before the other.

'All the best to you, colonel,' he called after him. Terence acknowledged with a slight raise of his hand and shuffled on. The conductor shook his head. The poor devil had had to stand all the way from the Pennine Gorge because of a war wound and, judging from the smell, it was time they changed the dressing.

'Well, we made it, sorr,' said Rembrandt.

Terence didn't reply. He was looking for a gents.

FIVE

'And the roof is still leaking?'

Mr Thurk made a note in a little black book and took a sip from his half of bitter. Elsie rang the till and handed out some change to a small, well-dressed man, then came over to Mr Thurk and leaned on the bar. Mr Thurk blushed. Elsie was one of those barmaids that made pubs a viable proposition, and when she leaned over the bar to talk it was a personal favour. She had, without doubt, the finest upper bodywork in Grapplewick, and hindquarters to match.

'Sorry about that, Mr Thurk.'

'That's all right, Elsie. I just made a note that your roof is still leaking.'

Elsie nodded. 'It's worse than ever. We put a bucket under, but when it rains it keeps us awake.'

Mr Thurk had a quick vision of her husband, a strapping lad when he married her not too long ago, now slightly bent with dark rings under eyes that stared out of a white face – it must be a hell of a leak.

'Can you do anything about it? I mean, it's driving my Fred up the wall. When it rains really hard, he's up and down all night.'

I'll bet he is, thought Mr Thurk, then he forced himself to look at her face. 'Pardon?'

Elsie sighed. 'I said, can you do anything about it?'

Mr Thurk took another gulp at his drink. 'Well, it's really not my pigeon, it's more a matter for the Housing Department.'

She pouted. 'Yes, I know, but I thought with you being Mayor and all. . . .'

Mr Thurk glanced at his watch. 'All right, Elsie. I'll have a word with Mr Thomas and ask him to pop round and see you.'

Elsie frowned. 'Oh, him . . . he's been to see me . . . tall feller with a big droopy moustache.'

'That's him – what did he say about it?'

'Well, he agreed that it was bad and said there shouldn't be no difficulty in finding alternative accommodation.'

Mr Thurk finished his drink. 'Well, there you are then. . . .'

Elsie plucked his sleeve and drew him closer. He gulped and hoped he wouldn't have to agree with anything, because if he nodded his face would go smack into that glorious bosom. Elsie didn't appear to notice. In fact if people didn't stare at her chest she thought they were blind.

'There's just one thing,' she said quietly.

'Yes?' said Mr Thurk. He meant to say yes, but it sounded as if someone had scratched a balloon.

'When he said there'd be no difficulty in finding alternative acccommodation, he smiled in a funny way.'

Elsie released his arm and stood back. Mr Thurk straightened. 'Oh come on now, Elsie, he always smiles in a funny way – his teeth don't fit properly.'

Elsie looked slightly disappointed. 'Oh, then you don't think he's expecting a bit of hanky panky, because you know what my Fred's like.'

'Don't worry about that, Elsie. Mr Thomas is a family man, he's chapel.'

'They're the worst,' said Elsie, knowingly.

'No, there's nothing to worry about there,' said Mr Thurk. 'I'll tell him to get on with it as soon as possible.' He buttoned his raincoat.

'Thank you, Mr Thurk.'

'That's all right, Elsie. Give my regards to your Fred.'

And with that he stepped out into the night. Elsie watched him go and wondered idly why he'd never married – although there was a bit of talk about him and Lady

Dorothy. Then she thought about her Fred and all those headaches he'd been getting in the last few months. A rapping on the bar snapped her out of her reverie.

'Good evening, miss. A large whisky and a small Guinness for my friend here.'

Rembrandt frowned.

'I'm sorry, sir, it'll have to be a small whisky, I'm afraid. Our stocks aren't back to normal yet, so I usually save it for my regulars.'

Rembrandt cheered up.

'All right, a small whisky then.'

Elsie nodded, already pulling the Guinness. Apparently engrossed, she was well aware that the scruffy little man was standing on tiptoe to get a better view of her superstructure. She placed the two drinks on the bar and looked directly at Rembrandt.

'If you come in here again let me know, and I'll get you a box to stand on.' Then she turned to Terence: 'That'll be two and threepence.'

Terence slapped half a crown on the bar and smiled. 'Keep the change, my dear.'

Elsie put the money in the till and took out threepence, which she tossed into a pint glass behind the bar. 'You're not from round here, are you?' she said.

Terence sipped his whisky. 'That's right,' he smiled. 'No fixed abode, you might say – commercial travellers.'

Elsie stared at him, intrigued by his moustache. One side was all right, but the other half seemed to flap when he talked.

Terence was quick to notice and pressed his hanky to his mouth to repair the damage.

'We're from London,' piped up Rembrandt, addressing Elsie's chest.

Elsie ignored him. 'Commercial traveller, did you say?'

'At the moment, my dear, yes. A bit of this and a bit of that. After six years in the Western Desert and Burma it's rather difficult to adjust to civilian life.' He laughed deprecatingly. 'Still, it's not an uncommon situation these days.'

Elsie nodded sympathetically. 'I know a lot of 'em are finding it hard to settle down.'

Terence tossed back his drink. 'Well, must be off. Have to find a place to get the old head down tonight.'

Elsie took his empty glass. 'Aren't you fixed up anywhere?'

Terence put on his 'don't worry about me' look. 'It's all right, my dear. Had to do a bit of shopping when we arrived – toothbrush, shaving cream.' He shrugged. Rembrandt finished his Guinness. 'And I had to buy a pair of flannels for him.' Terence glared, but it was lost on Elsie.

'Well, you've left it a bit late now,' she said.

'You wouldn't happen to have a first-class hotel in the area?' asked Terence.

Elsie put her hand to her cheek. 'Well, not first-class hotels. But if you're stuck there are usually one or two rooms vacant here.'

Terence brightened. 'That would be excellent, my dear. I don't fancy wandering around on a cold night like this.'

Elsie frowned. 'There hasn't been anybody staying here for ever such a long time, and I don't know if he still lets them.' She thought for a moment. 'Wait here. I'll ask Mr Helliwell to come down.'

Terence's eyes widened and he stared at her without focus. She wondered if he was an epileptic.

'Did you say Helliwell?'

A broad grin spread over Rembrandt's face. 'Oi allus said you were lucky, sorr. Bulls-eye first time aaargh....' He finished the sentence with a yelp and hopped round the room.

Terence looked at Elsie. 'He gets it every so often. I think it's the cold weather.'

Rembrandt sat at one of the tables and massaged his shoe. 'You bloody near broke my foot. You do dat again and oi'll, oi'll ... an' you'll be sorry.'

Elsie smiled uncertainly. 'Mr Helliwell is the landlord.' She edged away to the foot of the stairs and called 'Mr Helliwell'. She put her head on one side and listened, then called again. An unintelligible reply came from upstairs.

Elsie looked across at Terence and Rembrandt. 'There's two gentlemen enquiring about rooms.'

Again an undecipherable answer, but Elsie was satisfied and she came back to the bar. 'He'll be down in a minute.'

Terence leaned on the bar, outwardly calm, but his stomach was churning again. He was trying to decide how to handle the situation, but one thing was certain – he'd have this pub for a start. It wouldn't cover the debt Helliwell owed him, but then again there might be more stashed away in a bank or something.

'Another whisky, and make it a large one.'

Elsie was about to say something, but Terence's face didn't encourage a refusal.

Rembrandt limped to the bar. 'And oi'll have a pint of Guinness.'

Terence took the whisky and gulped half of it down. On an empty stomach he was already feeling light-headed. Oh, yes, Helliwell owed him all right, driving off with the loot while he was only halfway down the ladder. Seven years of his life Helliwell owed him. His heart skipped a beat as he heard footsteps clomping down the stairs. Terence leaned back, elbows on the bar. He intended to turn slowly round and catch the expression on Helliwell's face.

Elsie spoke. 'These two gentlemen wondered if you had any rooms to let.'

Terence turned slowly and his face fell. If this was Helliwell he'd had very poor plastic surgery, and his legs had been amputated at the knees.

Rembrandt stepped into the breach. 'Are you Mr Helliwell?'

'I am.'

The landlord looked at the two of them suspiciously. 'I haven't let rooms for a long time.' He shook his head. 'How long would you be likely to want them for?'

Terence pulled himself together. He should have known there'd be more than one Helliwell. If he'd had any idea just how many, he would have been on his way back to London and Big Alice. 'Shouldn't be more than a few days – all depends on what the business is like.'

38

Helliwell nodded. 'Two pounds ten a week bed and breakfast . . . each.'

Terence slapped the bar. 'Done!' He pointed to the bags and nodded to Rembrandt to gather them up. Terence smiled at Elsie. 'Oh, put the drinks on my bill will you?'

Helliwell looked sharply at Elsie, then shrugged. 'Follow me, gentlemen.' And they did.

Two weeks later they were still in residence and Elsie had taken to wearing high necked dresses.

SIX

Commander Wilson Brown walked briskly into Helliwell's tobacconist's shop in the High Street.

'Morning, Commander. I haven't seen you for some time.'

'That's true. Been trying to give it up.'

Mr Helliwell sucked in his breath. 'Don't do that, you'll put me out of business . . . the usual?'

Wilson Brown nodded, and the little tobacconist took down a tin of Navy Cut and pushed it across the counter. 'Good film on at the Odeon this week – about a Yankee destroyer. You'd think they won the war without us, wouldn't you? Well made, though – destroyers going in against the Japanese. . . .'

The Commander pocketed the tin of tobacco. 'Didn't serve in destroyers, I'm afraid. Fleet Air Arm.'

They both turned towards the window when they heard the fire bell, and watched the old engine lumber slowly past.

'Wonder where they're off to?'

The Commander snorted. 'Chip shop, I shouldn't wonder.'

Helliwell chuckled and handed over the change. 'Good day to you.'

The Commander touched his cap and left. A grand man, the Commander, thought Mr Helliwell. Didn't go round spouting off about his war experiences like some people, but he'd bet his bottom dollar that the Commander had seen plenty of action. The doorbell tinkled and interrupted his thought. He greeted the tall bearded stranger – the little man he ignored.

'Ten Park Drive and a box of matches.'

He slid them across the counter. 'There you are sir, that'll be twopence ha'penny – anything else?'

'Yes, there is, as a matter of fact. I caught the name "Helliwell" on the window and I wondered if I might have a word with him?'

'You're speaking to him.'

Terence nodded. 'Yes, I'd half gathered that.' He took out his wallet and extracted an old faded newspaper clipping. He proffered it. 'I wonder if you're any relation to this Helliwell?'

The tobacconist pushed his glasses onto his forehead and squinted closely. 'Not very clear, is it?'

He didn't notice Rembrandt edging behind Terence.

'It's about ten years old, taken before the war – Joseph Helliwell.'

The tobacconist handed the clipping back. 'There's something familiar about him, but he's no relation of mine. Mind you, Grapplewick's full of Helliwells.'

Terence put the paper carefully back into his wallet. 'Yes, so I'm beginning to realise. Well, thanks anyway.' He looked round, but Rembrandt had already gone. 'Be seeing you.'

And Terence left. Helliwell rubbed his jaw and pondered for a moment, then, shaking his head, he tossed the coins into the till and slammed the drawer shut. He turned to go back to his fire in the other room, then stopped dead. He whirled back to the till and thumped the key. The drawer flew open, but all it contained was the tall bearded man's twopence ha'penny.

Just around the corner Terence caught sight of Rembrandt shuffling along and hurried to join him. Rembrandt was absorbed, counting out a few one pound notes, and at first didn't notice Terence walking alongside. Terence watched for a moment in amazement, realising where the notes had come from, and then with a snarl he took hold of Rembrandt's lapels and pinned him against the wall. The little Irishman took it stoically – it seemed that never a day went by without Terence hauling him up by his lapels. He once wondered, idly, if he shouldn't cut them off, but he

41

quickly dismissed the idea – it was better than being lifted by the throat. Terence was livid.

'You stupid little Irish git, do you want to get us arrested?'

Rembrandt looked at Terence's adam's apple. 'We can't live widdout money, sorr.'

Terence stared at him for a moment, then released him, snatched the notes from Rembrandt's hand and stuffed them into his own pocket. After a quick glance round, he ripped off his beard and put on a pair of dark glasses.

SEVEN

Mr Thurk stood in front of the pot-bellied stove, tapping his empty mug against his leg impatiently. Barmy hopped forward and took it from him, dipping it into the dixie.

'No more, thanks,' said Mr Thurk, and looked at his watch.

Then he walked to the door and gazed over the empty yard. He looked at his watch again and turned to the stove. Barmy pointed to the mug, but Mr Thurk shook his head.

'Didn't they say where they were going?'

Barmy grinned. 'Nope,' he said and giggled with delight at being able to help.

Mr Thurk looked at him for a moment, then strode back into the yard, just in time to see the labouring old tender turn into the gates. He walked alongside as Jack turned the engine round in a wide circle. When it came to a stop Ned smiled.

'Morning, Chief. Parky this morning.' He rubbed his hands vigorously together.

Mr Thurk glanced at the red nose shining under the big brass helmet. He noticed too that some of the lads were wearing peaked caps, but this wasn't the moment – he'd get round to that later. He put one foot on the running board. 'Where the devil have you been?'

Jack switched off the engine. 'We ran out of tea.'

Mr Thurk spluttered. 'You ran out of tea . . . there's enough tea on that stove to have a bath in.'

'We ran out of sugar as well.'

Mr Thurk stepped down, raised his arms and let them fall against his sides in exasperation. Ned cleared his throat.

43

'It's all right, Chief. We had the grid up in the road and checked the drains while Cyril nipped in like.'

Mr Thurk raised his eyes to heaven and Barmy put his thumb up. 'OK?'

He looked at the faces staring at him with bovine expressions. 'That's all very well,' he said, 'but you can't keep using the tender as a delivery van. I mean, people notice these things.' He paused. 'And look at the time – I'm supposed to be at the Town Hall twenty minutes ago.'

'Sorry, Chief. It won't happen again.'

Ned got down to sit with the lads on the back and Mr Thurk hauled himself up next to the driver. Jim Cork was already cranking the engine. It was still hot and sparked immediately. Jack crashed it into first gear with a noise like a bad train smash. He hauled on the wheel and, as they rolled out of the gates, a tall, middle-aged man with a big parcel under his arm dodged to one side and shouted something. Jack put his foot down and they trundled along Featherstall Road. Mr Thurk leaned over to Jack and yelled in his ear.

'Wasn't that Mr Bottisford's lad?'

Jack didn't take his eyes off the road. 'Who?'

Mr Thurk was about to say something else, but changed his mind, and the lads on the back looked at one another in relief.

The Mayor's Secretary, however, was far from happy. Stoop-shouldered, hands behind his back, he was pacing agitatedly up and down between the pillars on the Town Hall steps. Eyes watering in the wind that had reddened his nose, he looked for all the world like a turkey at the beginning of December. The Mayor was rarely late – and to be so on this day of all days! Three large crates had been delivered first thing, and Councillor Helliwell had had them carried into the Mayor's office. Wilfred followed like a dog watching his breakfast put into the bowl, but Helliwell had told him to leave. It was as if the dog biscuits had been given to the cat – after all, he had been the Secretary when Helliwell was still wetting the bed. Wilfred sniffed in disgust as the thought crossed his mind that by the looks of him he

44

was probably still doing it. He stood behind a pillar to keep out of the wind, when he felt, rather than heard, the rumble of the old fire engine before it came into view in the High Street. He was down at the foot of the steps before Mr Thurk alighted.

'Morning, Your Worship.' He wiped a few drops from the end of his nose with the back of his hand.

Mr Thurk looked at him, then glanced quickly at the Town Hall. 'What's all the panic, Wilfred?'

The Secretary was trying to hurry him up the steps, another droplet appearing on the end of his nose.

Mr Thurk looked away in disgust, and when he looked back it had gone, but another one was forming. He shuddered. If that was blood he'd be dead in ten minutes. They were now striding briskly through the Main Hall.

'What's to do, then, Wilfred?'

Wilfred shook his head. 'Summat's up but I don't know what it is. I was asked to leave.'

Mr Thurk stopped suddenly and Wilfred cannoned into his shoulder.

'They asked you to leave?'

Wilfred looked furtively over his shoulder. 'They did an' all . . . mind you, there was only Councillor Helliwell there at the time, but now Lady Dorothy's in and the Commander and quite a few others. There were these three big boxes delivered about nine o'clock.' He lowered his voice. 'They're in your office.'

'Boxes? What kind of boxes?'

'Big 'uns.' He spread his arms out. 'Any road, we'll soon find out, won't we?'

Mr Thurk nodded and stood aside to allow Wilfred to open the door. They didn't hear him enter because they were crowded round the table giving all their attention to what appeared to be a model of some kind. Wilfred ahemmed 'His Worship the Mayor' and they all whipped round. Mr Thurk surveyed the tableau. It was rather like a headmaster walking in on a dormitory feast. Lady Dorothy smiled uncertainly.

'Good morning, Anthony.'

45

He looked at her inquiringly. 'Morning, Dorothy.'

Then he approached the table – his apologies for being late forgotten as he saw the model. He took out his specs, which he only used in order to give himself time to think, and surveyed the table. It was a fine-looking effort, no doubt about that. Tiny buildings, large areas of green to represent grass and four high blocks of flats like double-blank dominoes surrounded by tiny trees – it was very impressive. The Members of the Council examined it in silence, or perhaps it was a way of avoiding Mr Thurk's eyes. After what seemed an age, the Mayor took off his glasses.

'Did you know anything about this?' he enquired of Lady Dorothy.

She looked at him sharply. 'I'm afraid I know as much as you do.'

Unaccountable relief flooded through him. He nodded at the model. 'May I enquire what this is?'

Councillor Helliwell rose to his feet and licked his lips. 'I accept that it is highly unorthodox, but I took the liberty of having it constructed, and I may add, at no expense to the Council – that is, after consulting various members. . . .' He glanced quickly at Commander Wilson Brown. 'We decided that, er. . . .'

Mr Thurk broke in. 'Yes, but what is it?'

Helliwell looked at him in amazement. 'It's Grapplewick.'

The Mayor put on his glasses again and bent forward to look closely. 'That's never Grapplewick,' he said. 'Not my Grapplewick – that's more like a Yankee mental home.'

Councillor Helliwell blushed and looked round the table for support. Lady Dorothy put her head on one side. 'I recognise the Town Hall, but it seems to me that this building, here, is situated where the Fire Station now stands.'

Helliwell ran a finger round his collar. 'Yes it does, but then again, something has to go if we are to modernise the town.'

All eyes turned to Mr Thurk's stony face.

Lady Dorothy was aghast. 'But that's the Fire Station! We can't have a town without a Fire Brigade.'

Councillor Wilson Brown smirked. 'Well, my dear lady,

46

that is a matter for debate. With Blackburn and Bolton within close reach and, may I add, better equipped, we may have to disband our Brigade in the interests of economy.'

Mr Thurk looked at the Commander, then at Helliwell. He pointed to another impressive model building. 'And this . . .?'

Councillor Helliwell wrung his hands together nervously. 'That's the hospital.'

The Mayor's eyes widened.

'The hospital . . . you expecting a plague?'

Helliwell blew his nose, then dabbed his forehead. He'd be cleaning his ears out next unless someone came to his rescue. Dammit, the Commander was in this too and so were Taylor and Winterbottom – why for God's sake didn't they speak up? He glanced at the Commander, who was examining his little finger. He blew his nose again.

'Well, er, naturally . . . this is purely exploratory. The first stage, so to speak.'

'Aaaah,' said Mr Thurk. 'The first stage . . . last night in bed you had this wonderful idea for a new Jerusalem, so you got up early and dashed off this magnificent model before breakfast.'

Lady Dorothy saw the red spots on the Mayor's neck and tried to ease the situation. 'May I ask where all the money for the new development is to come from?'

The Commander looked at Helliwell, and Helliwell stood up as if hypnotised.

'Well, the government are making grants to Town Councils with a view to er. . . .'

The Mayor turned to Lady Dorothy. 'He's a bit of a live-wire, is our Helliwell. He's not only been busy with fretwork, he phoned Mr Attlee in Downing Street this morning and enquired about a state grant.'

Old Crumpshaw missed most of the exchange but he wasn't exactly senile. He waved his hand to encompass the high-rise flats.

'And these skyscrapers, aren't they situated on the area where Coldhurst Street and Sheepfoot Lane are now?' Crumpshaw looked from face to face. There was silence

47

round the table. 'Never mind that,' he said, in case some-body had said anything. 'What's going to happen to all the houses at present in this Ward?'

The Commander decided it was time he took a hand. 'With due respect, Mr Crumpshaw. . . .'

'Eh?'

He sighed and leaned over the table. 'With due respect, Mr Crumpshaw, they're practically slum dwellings and should have been condemned years ago.'

'Condemned!?' Crumpshaw slapped the table. 'Condemned? I live in Coldhurst Street and so did my father before me, and you'll not get a cleaner street in Grapplewick.'

The Mayor nodded. 'I agree. They're not slum dwellings, and they're not exactly palaces either, but they're something that many palaces are not, they're homes. . . . Bricks and mortar don't make homes, it's what goes into them – the loving, the marrying, the children, the dying, a sense of family. Streets where all the doors are open, and troubles and happiness are shared, and at the same time privacy is respected – all this will be destroyed the minute your models become a concrete reality.'

Lady Dorothy fumbled in her handbag. She was moved.

Crumpshaw glared round at his colleagues. 'Every Monday regular as clockwork, the wife black-leads that hob and you can see your face in it, and woe betide anybody who walks in without wiping his feet.'

The Commander smiled. 'That's all very well, but you can't keep Grapplewick in the nineteenth century.'

The Mayor looked at him steadily. 'I'm not against progress, Commander, but above all else it is my wish to keep the people of Grapplewick together, to maintain family unity, to keep their faith in right and wrong and to respect authority which we represent. All this will be turned to rubble when you bulldoze homes and pile them on top of one another in these concrete ghettos.'

Old Crumpshaw tapped the table with a weird bony finger. 'When the wife's finished stoning that front step, you could have your dinner off it.'

The Commander sighed. 'I'm not suggesting that they are dirty – in fact, they are a credit to the householders – but they don't have bathrooms, they don't have indoor toilets. . . .'

Mr Thurk leaned forward. 'And those flats of yours won't have fireplaces.'

'Of course not. The flats will be centrally heated.'

'But, no fireplaces.'

A flicker of annoyance crossed the Commander's face. 'Of course not.'

'I've visited that fine house of yours on the Binglewood Estate, Commander, and you have a fireplace – a big 'un too.'

'I fail to see what that has got to do with it.'

'I think you do. The fireplace is the focal point of the home. A cheery glow to greet you when you come in from the cold, where the family can sit and discuss and plan, or just sit, content . . . you can't suddenly uproot them and put them in your buildings. What will they do – arrange the chairs round the radiator?'

Wilson Brown smiled condescendingly. 'With due respect, Mr Mayor, quite a few householders possess television sets, and in a short while most houses will have one, perhaps even two.'

'I'm afraid you're right, Commander, and a sad day that will be. Every television set carries the same picture, but there's a picture in every fire that's different, and it's your own picture, not one that's concocted for mass consumption.'

Mr Thomas got to his feet. 'As one of the Housing Committee, I would like it put on record that although I had some inkling of the proposed plan, I was not aware that it had proceeded to this length and I feel that some Members of this Council are definitely out of order.'

He sat down and made a tick on the notepaper in front of him. Mr Thomas was a great one for sitting on the fence – as more than one Councillor had remarked in the past, he must have a backside like a hot-cross bun.

Wilson Brown rose slowly, as if he was about to announce

the end of the world. 'Fellow Councillors, I have not been privileged to sit in these Chambers as long as any of you, and have not yet acclimatised myself to the tempo of the post-war years. Fighting ships at sea is an occupation far removed from discussing the merits of fireplaces – and, incidentally, the only fireplaces on His Majesty's ships are in the boiler rooms, and we had very little time to sit round these discussing the price of meat.'

It was a cheap jibe and only Helliwell started to laugh, which he quickly changed to a cough. Wilson Brown continued.

'Whilst I respect the Mayor's view and his superior knowledge of the town, I feel he must agree that I have seen more of the world and that the world is changing. In fact it has progressed to such a degree that Grapplewick is in danger of being left behind in the great new opportunities that are before us.' He squared his shoulders as if he was addressing the quarter deck. 'I'm not suggesting that we demolish buildings for the sake of erecting new ones, but better ones. The Town Hall with its fine architectural features will remain and so will the church, but why shouldn't we have a modern hospital, a shopping mart, recreational centres? The main road through Grapplewick is hardly a modern highway.'

He paused while Crumpshaw adjusted the whistle on his hearing aid.

'Now I agree that presenting this model before you this morning was unorthodox and a shock tactic, but some of us on this Council have given months of serious thought and discussion to the project. It may appear to some of you to be a rather clandestine mode of conduct, but I think you will concede that, had we pursued the normal channels, we would not have progressed much further than an item on the agenda.'

He looked round the table and, with the knowledge that he had made his point, he sat down. Mr Thurk gazed unseeing at the model. He had had the same cold, sick feeling in his stomach when he realised his father was dying. He felt suddenly weary – he had his finger in the hole but Wilson Brown was hammering away at the dyke. Lady

50

Dorothy slid a note across the table to him. It read, 'It's only the first round'. Without expression he put it in his waistcoat pocket, got to his feet, and addressed himself to Wilson Brown.

'Congratulations on a very fine speech. I think you covered the whole of Grapplewick except for one small item, the one ingredient that makes a town, a village, a country . . . the people.

The Commander fidgeted impatiently.

The Mayor pressed his point. 'Oh yes, the people, the one quantity that appears to be missing from your equation.' He leaned forward. 'Do you know Jimmy Lees?'

The Commander frowned, taken by surprise. 'Jimmy Lees? I don't think I've heard the name.'

Mr Thurk's eyebrows went up a notch. 'Then you're the only one in Grapplewick who hasn't.'

Crumpshaw glared across. 'Jimmy Lees, the bellringer. Everybody knew Jimmy Lees.'

Mr Thurk nodded. 'Before the war we had a peal of bells at St Mary's. Every Wednesday they practised, and they rung them twice on Sundays and at special services. On a fine night people used to stand at their doors and listen. "Jimmy's in fine fettle tonight," or "Jimmy's had a few," they'd say, and at the end of each peal straight into the Dog and Partridge, regular as clockwork, went Jimmy. Twelve pints of Guinness and in each one he broke a raw egg.'

Crumpshaw chuckled. 'He did an' all, a raw egg – and they were good eggs in them days. Twelve pints, no more no less, and you should have seen him. Six foot four of him striding home with raw egg hanging off his moustache like icicles on a polar bear's belly. A grand lad . . . built like a brick chicken house but wouldn't hurt a fly.'

Wilson Brown sighed impatiently.

Mr Thurk tapped the table. 'One night they were ringing a peal of Grandsire Caters. They got the peal – over six hours – and the conductor called "stand", and it was only then they realised that Jimmy's bell was still going. He was dead as a doornail – eyes wide open, going up and down, up and down, still ringing.'

51

Crumpshaw shook his head sadly. 'Aye, and to this day nobody knows how long he'd been dead. It took three of them to prise his fingers off that rope.'

Wilson Brown spread his palms. 'Very macabre. But what's the point of the story?'

'The point Commander, is this. The whole of Grapplewick turned out to Jimmy Lees' funeral, and bells all over the North of England were muffled on the Sunday as a token of respect.'

The Commander looked as if he were about to say something.

Mr Thurk held up his hands. 'Just a minute, I haven't finished yet. Since the war the bellringers have disbanded, and we now have a carrillon. Some man presses a button and the bells play. Who is this man? I doubt if anyone in this room knows his name, and when he dies I doubt if there'll be many people of Grapplewick following the cortege.'

The Commander shrugged his shoulders.

'It's people that breath life into a town, Commander – Josh Arkwright. . . .'

Crumpshaw knuckled the table. 'Aye, what about Josh Arkwright, then? There's another one – went to London and back in twelve days on his bike.'

Mr Thurk shook his head. 'No, Mr Crumpshaw. He walked to London and back in twelve days with a petition for the cotton workers.'

Crumpshaw nodded. 'That's right. He cycled to London with a petition from the cotton workers. . . .'

The Secretary tugged his sleeve. 'He WALKED to London with a petition.'

Crumpshaw looked blank for a moment, then his face cleared. 'That's right. I tell a lie. He walked to London and handed the petition to Lloyd George.'

The Secretary tapped his arm again. 'You're wrong, Emmanuel. He didn't actually hand it to Lloyd George – Lloyd George was in Scotland at the time – but he did give it to the policeman at the door.'

Crumpshaw nodded. 'Oh, aye, I knew he handed it in.'

'What matters is,' said Mr Thurk, 'that many children born after that were christened "Joshua".'

'That's right,' broke in Crumpshaw. 'And for months afterwards his boots were on display in the Co-op window, worn down to the welt. And I'll tell you something else. There was allus a queue every Saturday, filing past to have a look at 'em . . . there were that.'

Wilson Brown snorted. 'In bygone days every town had its characters. If you go back another fifty years you'll probably be able to dig up a man who walked to Blackpool with a horse under each arm, balancing a barrel of ale on his head.'

Mr Thurk was in quickly. 'All right, then, let's be more recent. What about Mother Nicholson's corner shop on Ripon Street? No child ever leaves empty-handed, nobody goes without. If they don't happen to have any money on them, it'll always do another day. Always a loaf of bread and some dripping for any tramp or down-and-out who happens to pop in. Where's all that going to go when you knock it down and build your shopping mart, or whatever you call it?'

Crumpshaw nodded, but he might have been asleep.

Mr Thurk looked round the table. 'Everybody in Grapplewick knows the lads in the football team, because they work alongside them and pal up with them, see them in the pub after a match. But there'll come a day when that team will be strangers – and that's the black day I'm trying to put off as long as possible. Dr McBride still goes round in a pony and trap – he's brought more than half of Grapplewick into this world, and he's treated more people than you've had hot dinners. He knows everybody's ailments, and in many cases what they're going to get next. Eighty-two years old but they'd rather go to him than the whole of the Royal College of Surgeons. Matty O'Toole, the policeman – everybody knows Matty and the kids love him, except when they misbehave, and they only do that once. How can he walk past all the houses chatting to the folks and drinking cups of tea with 'em if they're stacked twenty deep in your wonderful tower blocks?' He wagged his finger at Wilson Brown.

'And make no mistake. Once we get a barrier between the Matty O'Tooles and the people, there'll be locked doors and nobody'll want to venture out at night. Oh yes, Grapplewick is still breathing and we are still a family town.'

Wilson Brown snorted. 'Don't forget the workhouse – old men in one side of the building, and their wives in the other, separated, allowed only to walk out together on Saturday afternoons – children with rickets, consumption, the district nurse visiting the schools every month to de-nit the kids, the means tes. . . .'

Mr Thurk slammed the table. 'We also had the gibbet, and we deported men to Australia, and we shoved little boys up chimneys. Of course it wasn't a perfect system, but the change was gradual. What you are proposing is to change the whole structure of Grapplewick in one clean operation because the means are at your disposal . . . a tree takes two hundred years to grow, but you would have it chopped down in order to prove the efficiency of your new machine saw.'

Old Crumpshaw chuckled. 'We used to call her Nitty Nora.'

Mr Thomas rose to his feet. 'If I may intercede . . . it seems that neither side has had sufficient time to prepare a case. I suggest that this debate be postponed till some further date.' He sat and began to scribble furiously.

Wilson Brown rose to his feet, but before he could speak there was a discreet knock on the door and Ned Bladdock leaned in, holding out Mr Thurk's white helmet. 'Excuse me,' he said. 'Alarm call, Chief.'

The Mayor rose, and with a final glare at the Commander he was gone.

Wilson Brown sat down and lugged out his pocket watch. 'What a coincidence . . . opening time.'

Lady Dorothy slapped the table, and two miniature trees fell over. 'I object in the strongest possible terms to the remarks made by Commander Wilson Brown.'

The Commander was unmoved. 'My dear lady, we have not had a fire in Grapplewick since before the war – fortuitous, perhaps, because I doubt if our illustrious Brigade has the expertise to deal with one.'

Lady Dorothy was on her feet. 'Again I object to these scurrilous and unfounded remarks.' She looked round the table, and her heart sank, for there was no support.

EIGHT

'Here we are, sorr. Number 26, Waterloo Street.'

Terence nodded and adjusted his eyepatch. It wasn't much of a disguise, but his changing rooms, better known as the gents' toilet at the top of Union Street, were all engaged and he couldn't stand at the urinal forever. The attendant was a doddering old fool, but the less he saw of Terence undisguised the better, so the only change in his appearance was an eyepatch. Still, it wasn't bad. People always remember an eyepatch and ignore the height, weight – or even if the suspect only has one leg. Rembrandt eyed the peeling door and the scuffed window and the half a drab curtain that could have been sacking.

'If he's livin' here, sorr, oi tink he must have spent it all . . . if oi had dat kind o' money he owes you, oi wouldn't be living in dis pigsty.'

Terence was inclined to agree. This was his fifteenth Helliwell. Why couldn't Helliwell have an uncommon name like Joe Aristotle or Joe Archimedes, but then, knowing Helliwell he'd be hiding away in Greece somewhere. If it wasn't for Elsie at the Dog and Partridge he might have given up weeks ago. He brightened at the thought of her. Nothing definite had happened yet, but she was back with her low-cut dresses, and as soon as he entered the bar she poured him a whisky without him having to ask – a large one, too. But he had to find Helliwell first. Then he'd have money and a big car, and he felt sure she wouldn't take much coaxing – off to Blackburn for a slap-up meal in the best hotel and then . . . Rembrandt broke the spell with a smart rat-a-tat on the door. The dingy curtain twitched and a moment later the door opened six inches and a big woman in curlers peered out.

'Yes?' she asked.

Terence touched his peaked cap. 'We've come to read the gas meter.'

Curler-face looked from one to the other. 'Again?'

Rembrandt took a notebook from his raincoat and leafed through a few pages. 'Mrs Helliwell, 26 Waterloo Street?'

She stood there for a moment, undecided, then she opened the door wide. 'You'd best come in then. It's under the stairs.'

'Tanks very much,' said Rembrandt, and moved along the small corridor to the meter. Terence followed her into the room. She turned and stared at him. He smiled – it had once been a winning smile, but years on a prison diet hadn't done him any favours. She took a step back.

'Do you want summat, then?' she asked anxiously.

'Well – I was wondering, Mrs Helliwell, if you are related to a Joseph Helliwell?'

She folded her arms and looked at him suspiciously. 'Yes, he's my husband.'

Terence's heart sank. He hadn't really wanted to find Helliwell in a dump like this. He looked round the room and wondered if they had a dog, because if they did it certainly wasn't house-trained. The great lump in the torn pinny was waiting for him to speak. Terence noticed that one of her stockings was down by her ankles and didn't even match the other one. He almost felt sorry for Helliwell, but he abandoned the thought quickly. His old partner had a glib tongue and if Terence didn't watch himself he'd be lending him money.

Her eyes narrowed. 'You're nowt to do wi' Rugby Club are you, because if you are you're wastin' yer time. Joe had nuthin' to do with those funds.'

Terence's heart sank even lower. If Helliwell was down to fiddling a few bob from the till, he couldn't be sitting on a fortune. However, he'd come this far and he might as well see it through. . . .

'No, madam. It's nothing to do with the Rugby Club, but I would like to see him again.'

She looked at what was left of the carpet. 'Well, I don't know where he'll be now, he's a long-distance lorry driver. 'E could be anywhere, he goes to the docks a lot. . . .'

She stopped suddenly and looked at him. 'Again?' she said. 'Have you met him before, then?'

Terence nodded. He didn't believe her for a moment. The thought of Joseph driving a lorry was ludicrous. 'Yes, we met some time ago and I borrowed a fiver off him.'

He took a fiver from his pocket. Her hand almost flashed out, then changed direction and rested on her cheek.

'A fiver from my Joe?'

Terence opened up the crinkly note casually. Her mouth opened and closed, but the fiver was burning her eyeballs.

'Oh, well,' she floundered. ' 'E might be in the other room. 'E just comes and goes and . . . er. . . .' She tailed off and turned her head to call Joe, but her eyes never left the money.

A door opened and a small black man entered the room. 'What's up now, Florrie?'

Terence stared at him, then at the woman. 'Your husband?'

'Yes.' She pointed at the note, which was already disappearing into Terence's pocket. 'This gentleman says 'e borrowed five pounds off you and 'e's come to pay it back,' she added hopefully.

Terence put his hands up to halt her. 'No, madam, there's been a mistake. The, er, Joseph Helliwell I know was . . . er. . . .'

She broke in like a whiplash: 'Was white – that's what you were goin' to say, wasn't it?' She took a step towards him. 'My Joe was born in England, but because 'e's a blackie 'e doesn't count.' Her voice was rising dangerously.

'It's nothing to do with his colour. It's just not the same person.'

'Oh, aye. I've 'eard that one before. If 'e was white you'd 'ave paid up like a man, but because 'e's a blackie it's different.'

She was trembling with self-righteousness, and the other stocking gave up the struggle and sank gratefully over her slipper. The black man put his arm round her shoulders but she shook him off. He smiled at Terence apologetically.

'Don't fret yourself, Florrie. I never lent him any money.'

She was slightly mollified. 'You'd better not, an' all. You're never off your backside long enough to earn any.'

Terence was glad of the change of attack. 'Well, madam. . . .'

She whirled back at him. 'Don't you "madam" me. I know your sort, borrowing money all the time an' never paying it back.'

At that moment Rembrandt shuffled in. 'Are you sure you have gas in dis house, missus, 'cos dat machine is empty.'

She looked quickly at her husband and he looked at his feet.

Terence took the opportunity of backing towards the door. He had a feeling that poor black Joe was going to be lifting bales and towing a lot of barges as soon as they'd gone. He was almost at the door when she turned on him.

'Go on – clear off, the pair of you! And if you cut off the gas again, I'll be down at that place of yours and I'll cripple you.' With that she turned suddenly and picked up the poker.

Terence didn't wait to take his leave. He was running up the street with Rembrandt a few paces behind old black Helliwell, and the way he was going he wouldn't slow down till he reached Africa.

NINE

Ordinary folk, wearied by the war, were disillusioned by the peace. The wave of euphoria that seemed to have gripped the rest of the country on the advent of the Labour Government was greeted by a wave of indifference in Grapplewick. Austerity – clothes rationing, food rationing, not even any sweets for the kids – meant they had no desire to be the masters now. They didn't want British Railways. They still thought fondly of the LMS and the LNER and with native shrewdness could not understand the logic of smashing monopolies in order to create a bigger one. They didn't mind the fact that some people were rich – without the rich there'd be no poor, and then where would they be?

Politics had never been a major topic of conversation in Grapplewick, but a couple of years ago men had come to hand out leaflets, and in some cases to speak in the factory yard during the dinner hour. As the older ones used the break to get their heads down and the younger ones kicked a football around, the speakers had never got past 'Comrades' or 'Brothers', and one unfortunate had been used as a goalpost, so the visits ceased. But all the same, the townspeople were unsettled. A herd of wildebeest sensing the approach of lions . . . Mr Thurk felt the mood of the town. Grapplewick needed a victory, a shot in the arm, something to unite them. First prize in the brass band competition, or second prize – even getting to Bellevue would be enough. Grapplewick Athletic to win the FA Cup – but no, on second thoughts he had a better chance with the band. The 'Latics had only scored four goals all season – one an own goal and three in a charity match against the scouts (the scouts won ten-three). Mr Thurk was worried, and Lady Dorothy was worried about Mr Thurk. The lads in the Fire Brigade were worried because, although the band was getting stronger, fire equipment was causing a severe shortage of space at Cowell and Bottisford's. It was only due to Mr Thurk's preoccupation with other matters that they'd got away with it so far, and, although they didn't realise it at the time, troubles are like people – it only takes one person to stand outside a closed shop door and in no time at all there's a queue.

It happened one afternoon when they were standing round the fire engine trying to decide which bit should go next, when he swung arrogantly into the yard on a heavy-duty bicycle, rattling on the hard cobbles, which didn't seem to bother him at all. He swung his leg expertly over the saddle and stood on one pedal until he brought his machine to a halt against the wall. The lads watched this display of bikemanship in grudging admiration. He was medium-sized in a brown trilby, scarf, grey-belted raincoat and heavy boots. That was the uniform of rent collectors, debt collectors, bailiffs – in fact, trouble. He carefully took off his gloves, then his bicycle clips, and put them in his raincoat pocket.

'Morning,' he said to everyone in general.

Ned pinched out his Woodbine and put it behind his ear. 'Dost tha want somethin'?'

'Aye,' said the man's back as he unstrapped a thin brief-case from the rack behind the saddle. 'Can we go inside out of this bloody wind?' And without waiting for an invitation he strode into the station.

Cyril tugged Ned's elbow and whispered, 'Shall I go and fetch Mr Thurk?'

Ned thought for a second. 'Nay, it could be about anything. Let's find out what's to do first.' Then he looked round at the lads and with a jerk of his head he indicated they should all go inside.

'Right,' said the man as they surrounded him. 'I'm Neville Burtonshaw, Fire Brigade Union North-west Branch.' He paused to let this sink in. 'Now, who's your representative?'

The lads looked at each other and shuffled uneasily.

'Well, come on,' he said testily. 'You must have a representative – it's a Union matter.'

'Oh, aye?' said Ned guardedly. 'What's up then?'

The man looked at them all incredulously. 'What's up?' he repeated. 'Where've you lot been hidin' for the last fifty years? I'll tell you what's to do.' He spread out the fingers of one hand then started to tick off the items. 'One: you've never paid your Union dues. Two: you've never been represented at any Branch meeting. Three: we've had no reply to any of our directives. . . .'

Ned broke in, 'That's because we're not Union members.'

Burtonshaw ignored him. 'Shall I go on?'

'No,' said Jack nastily. 'Tha's made thy point. Now if you don't mind, we've work to do.'

'Work?' the man snorted. 'Never mind your bloody work. I've heard about this station. It's organisation you want, not work.'

Ned tried to ease the situation. 'I think you'd better wait till the Chief gets here.'

The man turned on him. 'I'm not 'ere to talk to bosses. I'm talking to you lot as Brothers.'

Jack spat on the hot stove with a sizzling crack. 'If I'd wanted a brother I'd 've picked a better bloody model than thee.' He turned and walked into the cold sunlight. A couple of the lads went with him.

The man pointed after them. 'That's typical, that is! We sweat our guts to get better pay and better working conditions, and that's all the thanks we get.'

'We don't do too bad,' said Ned. 'We've always managed.'

Harry Helliwell at the back of the group piped up nervously, 'What if we don't want to join?'

Burtonshaw turned slowly towards him, but Harry had edged behind Lofty Butterworth so he addressed himself to Lofty's collar stud.

'Don't want to join?' he mimicked. He glared round the wall of impassive faces. 'You'll bloody well join all right and there'll be no ifs and buts. . . .'

The lads shuffled their feet but avoided his eyes. He sensed his advantage and went on. 'Now before I leave 'ere you'll elect a representative. I've not cycled all the way from Blackburn for the good of me health.'

Ned put his hands deep in his trouser pockets, studied his belt buckle for a second and then looked directly at him. 'Oh, aye,' he said, 'and if we do get a representative, what'll his job be, then?'

'His job, Comrade, will be to collect Union dues, list any grievances and complaints, attend Branch meetings and keep you up to date on developments and any instructions the Union might deem it politic to issue.' While he was talking he extracted a sheaf of papers from his briefcase which he now proffered like a conjuror asking someone to take a card. But nobody stepped forward, so he moved to the desk and slapped them down forcefully.

Helliwell had another go. 'There's no law says we have to join. . . .'

Burtonshaw bared his teeth. 'Not yet there isn't, not yet. But there bloody soon will be, Brothers, you mark my words. Our lot are in power – we're the masters now. The bosses 'ave 'ad their day. We're givin' the orders, and the sooner that sinks in the better for all of you.'

Jack Puller appeared at the door, a dark silhouette against the winter sunshine. 'Are you goin' to be at it all day, or is somebody goin' to give us a hand out 'ere?'

The lads turned towards him, uncertain. One or two of them started moving towards the door, then more of them edged away. Burtonshaw worked swiftly round like a sheepdog.

'Where the bloody hell d'you think you're all going? This is an official meeting.'

Jack was incredulous. 'It's 'itler, it is. We've all been thinking 'e's dead and 'ere 'e is as large as life without his 'tache on.'

A couple of lads sniggered and the spell was broken. They started to move positively into the yard. Burtonshaw floundered about, his face a deep red with embarrassment and fury. He turned in time to see Ned stuffing the papers

63

into the pot-bellied stove. He rushed forward and grabbed Ned's arm, but it was too late.

'Right,' he squeaked. 'Right! You've bloody done it now.' He slammed his foot on a chair, his hands shaking with rage as he put his bicycle clips on.

Barmy grinned at him. 'OK?'

'Bugger off, you,' he snarled, pulling on his gloves with trembling hands. Then he pointed a grey woollen finger at Ned. 'Tha's been warned. Make no mistake about it, you'll not get work in any Brigade in the country when I've finished with you.'

Ned observed him calmly. 'So that's the way the wind blows, is it?'

'Aye, that's the way the wind blows.' And with that he hurried out into the yard to where his bike should have been. He looked uncertainly along the wall, then at Jack Puller. Jack was sitting on the running board of the old engine. He squirted a stream of tobacco juice at a pigeon. ''Ave you lost summat?' he asked.

Burtonshaw glared at him. 'You know bloody well what I'm looking for. Where's my bike?'

Jack stood up and looked around the yard. 'Your bike?'

Burtonshaw pointed to the ground. 'I left it here against the wall.'

Jack shook his head sadly. 'That was a bloody silly thing to do, wasn't it? Leaving a bike unattended. That's asking for trouble that is, especially in this town. Open your mouth too wide 'ere and they'll 'ave your teeth.'

Burtonshaw was already striding towards the main gate. Jack shouted after him. 'I'll give thee a lift to t'bus stop if you like.'

The tension was gone. The lads jeered and mocked and swaggered behind Jack to the gate. Chadwick lifted his arm in the Nazi salute and shouted, 'Heil Hitler!' Ned watched from the door. He was uneasy and couldn't quite pinpoint the reason, but he knew that somewhere a beetle had entered the woodwork.

Terence and Rembrandt weren't exactly worried, they were

Just sick of Grapplewick. The pavements were worn and uneven, hardly conducive to Rembrandt's sunsets and landscapes. In any case, Terence had forbidden it and he was tired of being hauled up by the lapels. However, he hadn't been totally frustrated. The walls in his room at the Dog and Partridge were covered with exotic murals – not the usual sea, sand and palm trees that were normally his trade mark, but ladies in all kinds of recumbent postures, all nude. He could never quite get the legs right, but then again he'd only seen Elsie over the top of the bar.

Unfortunately the landlord happened to be passing the room just as Rembrandt was leaving, and caught a glimpse of the exhibition. He pushed the door wide open and strode in, dumbfounded. He didn't recognise Elsie – after all, Rembrandt was only an amateur – but he knew a great pair of bristols when he saw them. After a perfunctory examination he whirled on Rembrandt, white-faced and furious, and told him to pack his things and get out, screaming that Grapplewick was a decent place and that he ran a respectable hostelry. Terence appeared at the door and joined Helliwell in his tirade against Rembrandt, adding that a few years ago he would have had him court-martialled. Rembrandt seemed oblivious, slowly gathering together his meagre possessions, 50 per cent of which appeared to be Guinness. Terence ordered him to clean up the walls before he left, but Helliwell hurriedly overruled him, and moments later Rembrandt found himself on the pavement with his ever-clinking carrier bag. Later that day the landlord moved all his own belongings into Rembrandt's vacant room. Terence stayed on as a guest. A glimpse of those nudes reminded him of Elsie, and his leg twitched most of the morning. He was worried that it was only his leg – had prison life robbed him of his manhood? It would be acutely embarrassing to leap into bed with her, and find only his leg twitching. He couldn't very well put it down to an old war wound, because there'd have to be a mark. He stamped his foot heavily and the twitching ceased, but only until he saw Elise again.

That same evening Rembrandt found himself in the public

bar of the Weavers Arms. He was on his second pint when the barman said, 'Go on, 'op it! We don't want you in 'ere.'

He pulled himself out of his glass to ask what he'd done, when he realised the barman was addressing someone over his shoulder.

'Oh? And it's not de loikes of you dat's goin' to stop me.'

Rembrandt brightened. Here was an accent he understood. He turned, but the big woman was already alongside him at the bar.

'Go on 'ome, Nellie. We don't want no trouble.'

She leaned over the bar and the man stood back. 'An' who's goin' to put me out, oi'd loike to know? You're not de man to do it. Now are you going to give me a Guinness or not?'

He held his hand up, pleading. 'You know what t'boss is like, Nellie. It's not me. 'E says not to serve you.'

'Oi'll buy her a drink. Give her a Guinness and fill me up as well.' Rembrandt surprised himself. He'd never bought anyone a drink in his life. Perhaps it was the sound of the brogue that reminded him of his loneliness, but with the luck of the Irish and that one quixotic gesture he now had accommodation at a reasonable rent, but then a couple of Guinnesses had always been the going rate for Droopy Nellie. Her house, sagging and weary with age, was by the old rubbish tip where the gypsies lived, but it had a roof – well, most of it . . . there was a hole in the bedroom ceiling the size of a football. Rembrandt said he'd mend it, but Nellie said she liked to lie in bed and look at the stars, for which he was grateful, as he had no intention of scrabbling about on top of that house. However, she was delighted when he whitewashed a wall and chalked up a flamboyant sunset over a lagoon with palm trees in the foreground. She stared at it for a long time, and said he was her little genius. She said it was so realistic it made her feel homesick. That flummoxed him for a moment, and he wondered if she was coloured – actually she was quite dark, but that was only lack of soap and water. So he stoically accepted the fact that it wasn't everybody who could appreciate art, and chalked under it 'Dublin Bay'. He was as contented as he'd

66

ever be, if only he didn't have to meet Terence every morning in the gents' lavatory with a fresh list of Helliwells.

They were also worried at the police station. In the past few weeks the crime rate had doubled – all petty theft. The other constables kept clear of Matty O'Toole, who took this thievery as a personal affront. He was sure it wasn't any of the regulars – they, in fact, had complained to him that somebody was giving them a bad name. Also he hadn't seen Droopy Nellie for over a week now, and he wondered if she was ill – however, when he paid her a surprise visit she was having a stand-up wash in an old tin bath. He closed the door hurriedly – he hadn't realised she was that droopy. It wasn't a pretty sight – a weatherbeaten fountain in a garden of empty Guinness bottles. In any case, Droopy Nellie cleaning herself up? She always made a rumpus at the station when a bath was compulsory – Nellie washing herself in her own time didn't make sense. The whole world had gone mad.

It was a worrying time, but the sun still shone on Barmy, the stove glowed and the tea was always hot. Also Jack Puller's father had died, and Jack – more as a joke than anything else – had given Barmy his father's false teeth. It wasn't funny to Barmy, though. He struggled with them for a few days, but they were either upside-down or back to front, or else they simply didn't fit. It didn't bother Barmy – they were now permanently in a glass of water by his bed of sacks. Always cheerful and smiling, hour upon hour Barmy sat facing them, often holding desultory conversations. The teeth just grinned back at him, and eventually Barmy would rise, put up his thumb and say 'OK?'

TEN

If Terence and Rembrandt were beginning to despair in their search, Ikey the Fixer was frantic. He was not a vindictive man, but could not reasonably accept the fact that he was tightly locked away in a north London prison, while Helliwell was free to enjoy the wealth that had been largely accumulated with Ikey's connivance. He had been transferred from the laundry, even though he was actually in the exercise yard when the head warder inadvertently fell into one of the boilers. After a short spell in the machine shop he was transferred to the hospital, having contracted a mystery virus causing excruciating pain to his bank balance. The treatment prescribed was lots of rest and special food brought in at great expense. The prison doctor, old and wise, diagnosed his condition as a wasting disease, and when Ikey thought of the money he was having to fork out he was inclined to agree. Quite a few bob was outgoing in order to keep the doctor sweet, but the fine balance lay in not overdoing it in case the old fool decided to retire.

Ikey received visits from many doctors, none of whom had been through medical school, although most of them were adept at cutting people up. Everybody knew they were Ikey's mob, but none were brave or foolhardy enough to complain, and today it was the turn of Ballantine, better known to staff and inmates as Jimmy the Hat. A big, florid man, he sported a livid scar down his cheek, the result of a second opinion. He stood at the foot of Ikey's bed looking down at his feet, so that the brim of his bowler hid most of his face. Ikey, propped up by pillows and smoking a huge cigar, ignored him, apparently engrossed in the *Financial*

Times. The door opened and the warder poked his head round. Ikey snatched the cigar from his mouth and said, 'Piss off.'

'Sorry,' said the warder, and withdrew. But the spell was broken and Ikey lowered the paper.

'Well?'

Jimmy the Hat shrugged his shoulders helplessly.

Ikey examined the ash on his cigar. 'You bring me nothing? The money I pay you, and you bring me nothing?'

The big man shrugged again. 'He ain't there, boss . . . there's only one Helliwell in Tunbridge Wells, and 'e's not Joe, 'e on'y 'ad one leg.' Ikey looked at him sharply and Jimmy held up his hands. 'It was blown off in the war.'

Ikey nodded for a time, then addressed his cigar. 'Thanks for coming all this way to tell me nothing.' He sank back in the pillows. 'My life, here I am a sick man yet, and all the time you do nothing except steal me blind.'

''Ang about,' started the big man.

'Shut up . . . eight of the boys I have, and not one of you has come up with something.'

Jimmy fidgeted. 'Joe Helliwell could be dead.'

Ikey slapped his forehead. 'Joe Helliwell could be dead,' he repeated. 'What a brain! He could be dead. Yes, he could be dead. But it would be on a piece of paper. When you are dead, you have to have a piece of paper which says you are dead. When you are born it's a piece of paper. When you are married it's a piece of paper. You cannot have a crap without a piece of paper, eh?' He held out his hands.

Jimmy put his head down again. He had to admit he'd never thought of checking the records – a quick flip through the telephone directory and a few questions – but then thinking wasn't one of his achievements. 'I'll go back and check that out,' he mumbled.

Ikey didn't appear to have heard. He knocked the ash off his cigar and applied a large gold lighter. In between puffs he said, 'Find . . . Pillock Brain.'

Jimmy frowned. 'Oo?'

'Terence. He got out a few weeks ago.'

'Oh, 'im. That ponce.'

69

Ikey blew a cloud of blue smoke upwards. 'That ponce has more brains in his little finger than you got all over your body. And I'll tell you this, he needs Helliwell as much as we do.' He pointed his cigar at Jimmy. 'You find Terence, and Helliwell will not be far away . . . you got it?'

Jimmy shuffled uneasily, then nodded. 'OK.'

Ikey's eyes widened. 'Is that all you got to say? You tell me OK . . . what is OK? You are some kind of magician that you can pull Terence out of a hat. How you gonna find him? You go out of here and say "OK", then you come back in three weeks later and say where is he.'

'I'll put the word out. If he's in the smoke I'll 'ave 'im.'

Ikey slapped the bed in exasperation. 'If he was in London, I could have him without your help.' He was about to light the cigar again, but stopped as a sudden thought struck him. 'Wait a minute,' he said. 'A piece of paper, you gotta have a piece of paper.' He stared unseeingly at the wall opposite, his brain almost audible.

Jimmy glanced surreptitiously at his watch. He never liked making these visits – he had an uneasy feeling that one day on his way out he would feel a heavy hand on his shoulder, and somebody would be saying, 'Where do you think you're off to, sunshine?'

'Got it!' Ikey applied his lighter and puffed furiously. Jimmy watched him enviously. He was dying for a cigarette but he knew it wasn't allowed. 'That's it,' said Ikey. 'You got a piece of paper . . . Helliwell was in the Ministry of Supply in the war.'

Jimmy nodded. 'That's right.'

Ikey spread his arms wide. 'Well,' he said, 'you don't get a job in a government office without a piece of paper. Somewhere there is a piece of paper – Joe Helliwell, when he was born, where he was born.' He leaned forward eagerly. 'Listen, and listen good. There is a man called Thomas Reece – you got it? Thomas Reece, he's in the phone book. You tell him to go through the records, tell him it's for Ikey, he owes me . . . you got it?'

Jimmy nodded vigorously. 'Thomas Reece.' He gathered

his overcoat round him, eager to be off. 'As good as done, guvnor.' He touched his hat and hurried away.

'Here.' Ikey's voice stopped him as he reached the door. 'You see the screw outside – you tell him I'm ready for my tea.'

Jimmy nodded and was gone.

Ikey put his head in his hands, biting viciously on his cigar, angry at not having thought of it before. The money he could have saved! Then he relaxed. A week at most and he would have the information he was after. Sadly, however, it wasn't Ikey's day. He had overestimated Jimmy's capabilities. Thomas Reece was not at the address in the phone book – he had in fact emigrated five months previously – but that wasn't going to stop Jimmy the Hat. He had a job to do and, with the doggedness of a backward pack mule, he booked passage on a flying boat to Australia. Ikey did not see him again for six weeks, when he returned to the prison triumphantly bearing a photostat copy of a piece of paper stating that one Thomas Reece had died in Sydney aged forty-eight.

Later that same day a government office in Whitehall was burgled . . . a heavy axe, where Ikey would have preferred a rapier.

ELEVEN

October laid down its burden and November roared in from Siberia, heralding a hard winter to come. For ten days the weather was the main topic of conversation. Winds swirled the smoke back down the chimneys, scattered tiles, rattled the window panes and whistled malevolently through the Grapplewick keyholes.

The eleventh of November blustered over the moors with no respite and a cock, judging it to be dawn, gathered itself to wake the neighbourhood. A sudden gust blew it off the fence before it could open its beak, and another blew it slap against the barn. That was enough. To hell with reveille! It scuttled back inside while it still had feathers.

In the town centre, impervious to the weather, the great clock on the Alliance building disdainfully boomed out the hour, and Grapplewick stirred. Mrs Waterhouse lit the fire and bustled to the stove to prepare Mr Thurk's breakfast. Normally she would have been in an hour later, but today was Remembrance Day, a big day for the Mayor and all the local dignitaries.

'Morning, Mrs Waterhouse.' Mr Thurk padded to the sink in his woolly vest, braces dangling over his striped trousers. 'Don't worry too much about breakfast. I'm not that hungry.'

'You're having breakfast and that's that. It's cold this mornin' and you'll want something 'ot down you.'

Mr Thurk didn't argue – it would be useless anyway. He tucked the towel in the top of his trousers and ran the tap. She elbowed him out of the way and poured some hot water from the kettle.

72

'Thank you, Mrs Waterhouse.'

'Hark at that wind,' she replied. 'It'll carry a few of 'em off, will that. There'll be some drawn blinds next week.'

He shuddered. Of one thing he was certain – the wind wouldn't shift Mrs Waterhouse. It would take a direct hit from a Junkers 88 to do that. He glanced sideways at her as he lathered his chin, and wondered idly whether a moustache would suit him.

Commander Wilson Brown hadn't slept well. Branches had been flicking the window all night, and he was fearful that the great beech would come crashing down onto the house. He could well do without the day before him. For the last two years he'd enjoyed Remembrance Day. He was proud of his uniform with its gold braid and medal ribbons, a fitting reminder of the debt that the people of Grapplewick owed him. Unfortunately he lived too well and, while his girth had expanded, his uniform hadn't. Glancing furtively towards the bedroom door he unlocked a drawer and took out a brown paper parcel. He quickly shed the wrapping and stared distastefully at the corset, holding it between finger and thumb as if it were a dead cat. In the distance the factory hooter wailed, and he thought of the poor devils who had to be up and about at this time every morning. It was an ordinary working day for the millhands, although the machinery did shut down at two minutes to eleven to observe the silence.

By ten o'clock even the weather seemed to respect the dead. The wind abated in an uneasy truce, helping to swell the congregation in Grapplewick parish church. Lady Dorothy, one of the first to arrive, stood to allow the golf secretary and his wife to pass along the pew. He acknowledged with a slight nod. Remembrance Day for him was an embarrassing reminder of one pitch-black night in 1945. A landmine, jettisoned in panic, had floated gently towards Grapplewick. Luckily it exploded on the golf course and the only casualty was the club secretary's wife, who was found wandering dazed and stark naked. She claimed she was walking the dog before going to bed when the blast blew all her clothes off. It really was a remarkable escape, and, such are the vagaries of explosions, that her clothes were found neatly folded on the second tee. The head greenkeeper, whose trousers had been blown off by the same freak blast, was able to corroborate her statement. The dog presumably was blown to smithereens, and to this day the club secretary still wonders whose dog it could have been.

The Reverend Leadbetter, carried away by the size of his flock, droned on. He paid tribute to the young men and women who had willingly laid down their lives for King and Country. Mr Thurk squirmed uneasily in his seat. He had a sudden vision of a long queue of khaki-clad men shuffling slowly forward to lay down their lives. It was ludicrous – nobody willingly laid down their life. They kicked and screamed and clawed to hang onto it, no matter what the cause. If the old fool didn't wind it up soon, they'd miss the Last Post round the Cenotaph. Somebody was sobbing quietly, and he turned his head slightly. It was old Mrs Helliwell, and he couldn't help thinking it was always the survivors who suffered. A grand lad, Walter Helliwell, and Grapplewick's first war casualty. Corporal Helliwell, one of the last to be taken off at Dunkirk, had come home on leave. The train pulled into Grapplewick Central in the black of night and, full of navy rum, Walter stepped out of the wrong door. As he was picking himself up, the down train hit him. It took them three days to collect it all together – in fact one of his boots was on the station roof and part of his kitbag was discovered just outside Blackburn. Poor Helliwell!

Noticing a shuffling and uneasy throat clearings the Reverend Leadbetter glanced at his watch, and in almost indecent haste wound up the service. As they moved slowly outside to assemble round the pitiful little Cenotaph Jack Puller, on the battlements of the old church, blew the Last Post. Even Jack's faltering efforts could not conceal its haunting quality. Now, at the eleventh hour of the eleventh day, silence was observed, broken only by the soft keening wind and the church clock striking three. Cold pinched faces looked on – old young faces with new medals, and worn-out faces with medals from earlier campaigns.

74

Mr Thurk was glad of his thick mayoral robes as the wind freshened. He bowed his head and remembered – he thought of Lady Dorothy and her soft skin, then quickly gathered himself together, staring guiltily at the Cenotaph: SERGEANT W. THURK RAF 1943. Poor Willie! A warm flush of shame passed through him as he recalled the envy he felt for his younger brother when he came home on leave with his three stripes and the magical half brevet of an air gunner on his chest.

Willie had no interest in music and preferred to work in the mill rather than join the Fire Brigade. Yet despite this heresy Father, who was normally a strict disciplinarian, treated him like a puppy dog, always had a toffee for him on Saturday and smiled at his escapades – and there were plenty of them, even the time Willie broke his ankle jumping out of Mrs Tatlock's bedroom window when her husband came home unexpectedly. Mr Tatlock was no fool and guessed immediately who it was, especially as Willie left his trousers on the bedrail.

Twenty minutes later Dr McBride, roused by a frantic knocking, was attending to Willie and listening to his explanation. But Dr McBride wasn't that old – if Willie had fallen off his bike, what was he doing riding round at three in the morning in his shirt and socks? Anyway Willie was Willie, and as he only lived down the street he helped him home. Willie stopped dead when he saw a light on downstairs, and the doctor agreed to come in with him in case of emergency. He hopped pitifully into the room, and had it not been for the doctor blocking his exit he would have hopped out again – to Australia. Mr Tatlock and Father were sitting together in the cold front room drinking whisky. Nobody moved for what seemed an eternity, then Mr Tatlock rose slowly and held Willie's trousers up accusingly. Willie, a pathetic sight in his long shirt, hobbled forward, took them, and then stepped back. It was all done in silence, carried out with a solemnity more fitting to a masonic initiation ceremony. Anthony remembered shivering at the top of the stairs, puzzled by the quiet, his nerves taut, waiting for the inevitable explosion. As the silence lengthened he took a step

75

down, then froze as he heard his father chuckle. Then Dr McBride sniggered, and then the three of them were all laughing like lunatics. Anthony crawled back to bed, glad in a way because he hated violence, but lonely and jealous of Willie. Had the position been reversed he wouldn't have dared to come home at all. Then again, he could never visualise himself with Mrs Tatlock. He shuddered – no wonder Mr Tatlock worked nights. He pretended to be asleep when the three of them helped Willie in to bed beside him, and from under his slitted eyelids he saw his father ruffle Willie's hair.

'You little bugger,' he said, then blew the candle out. As they went downstairs Anthony heard Mr Tatlock asking Dr McBride if he wouldn't mind looking in on his missus on the way back – she'd accidentally walked into a door. And now all that remained of Willie was his name on the Cenotaph. Anthony suddenly loved his brother and tried to visualise what it must have been like on that last fateful raid – enemy shells buffeting the aircraft, searchlights probing and blinding, Willie blazing away with his hot guns, a flash of white light, then oblivion. Anthony fumbled for his handkerchief and hoped it had been quick. Had he known the truth it would have given him little comfort. Willie had never fired his guns in anger. In fact he'd never even seen the enemy coast. His first operational flight was his last. The light flashed from the control tower the pilot released the brakes and G for George was rolling. Willie, sitting dry-mouthed in the rear turret, was mesmerised by the runway unwinding beneath him faster and faster and faster, and his last panic-stricken thought had been, 'Shouldn't we be up in the air by now?'

Anthony remembered when the 'We regret to inform you' telegram arrived. Father read it slowly. Then placed it on the mantelpiece. Then he shook his head sadly and sat down heavily. 'Good job his mother isn't alive, this would've killed her.'

Anthony looked at the poppies, and he was back with Lady Dorothy's lips. He leaned slightly forward to catch a glimpse of her, but she was hidden by Commander Wilson

Brown, a very imposing figure in his naval uniform, stiff as a ramrod. But it was his profile that stirred Mr Thurk, the look of anguish on the strong grey face staring unseeingly ahead. Again Mr Thurk felt compassion, and wondered what poignant memories were causing such pain. The Commander, however, was not stirred by memories at all – he was convinced that his corset had drawn blood, and his bowels were moving. If this damned farce didn't end soon, he was going to have a nasty accident. He winced as another spasm gripped him – my kingdom for a nice warm toilet! Lady Dorothy, misreading his inner torment, sympathetically squeezed his arm and he almost lost control. 'Silly bitch,' he thought.

Remembrance was over.

Outside the Gaping Goose, waiting for opening time, Rembrandt replaced his cap. 'Terrible things, wars – oi've been through two of 'em and oi don't want another, and dat's a fact.'

Terence looked at him as one would at a bad accident. 'You amaze me, do you know that?'

'No, sorr, oi don't know dat.'

'You've been through two wars?' repeated Terence incredulously.

'Yes, sorr.'

'In the First you were sucking gin at your mother's breast, and you spent the Second World War in southern Ireland making it illegally.'

'Dat's what you tink, isn't it?' Rembrandt jiggled the matches in the tray he was carrying and sniffed. 'Oi would have been in the Commandos but oi didn't have the height.'

'You'll have the height in a minute if I put my toe up your backside.'

Rembrandt edged unobtrusively against the wall, but he wasn't giving up. He pointed with his chin to the impressive row of medals. 'Dey don't give you dem for nothing, sorr.'

Terence looked away, noticing that the crowd around the Cenotaph was beginning to disperse.

'Oi've never claimed me pension for dees medals, sorr – never once.'

'Why don't you shut it, you Irish ratbag. Those medals were attached to the raincoat when you stole it from blind Albert.'

Rembrandt shuffled his feet. 'Oh, dat's what they all say, but there's not a bit of truth in it. Oi never stole it. Blind Albert definitely promised it to me when he'd gone, God rest his soul, and oi was de only one there to hold his hand when he finally passed away.'

Terence fitted the Park Drive to his cigarette holder. Rembrandt struggled to light it, and as he did so Terence looked directly at him and spoke in measured tones. 'Blind Albert died of pneumonia because you nicked his raincoat.'

He was about to refute this when a little old lady fumbled in her purse and put sixpence in the tray. Rembrandt held out a box of matches but she shook her head.

'No, thank you. That sixpence is for you.' And she shuffled away.

'God bless you, mum,' murmured Rembrandt.

Terence looked away. 'Pathetic.'

'Der's a lot of money in selling matches if you go de right ways about it, oh yes, sorr. An iceberg is nine-tenths under the water.'

Terence missed this obscure bit of philosophy as the bolts slid back behind him, and the Gaping Goose opened its doors. With an ingratiating smile he stepped inside. Rembrandt was about to follow when something caught his eye. A large, heavy man stopped in the street, struggling vainly to light his pipe, but what took Rembrandt's eye was a large gold watch chain across his waistcoat. Rembrandt jiggled his matchboxes. The one-tenth of the iceberg was slowly floating towards him.

'Here y'are sorr, take a box wid de compliments of an old soldier.'

The large man stopped. 'Not from an old soldier. I'll take a box but I'll pay for it an all.'

'God bless you, sorr.'

A plane passed overhead and Rembrandt looked up. 'Dat'll be the Dublin plane.'

The man looked up, and it was his undoing. The gold

78

watch was in Rembrandt's pocket. It was a brilliant piece of manipulation, and it subsequently proved to be a costly mistake.

TWELVE

Grapplewick proceeded without incident into the No Man's Land between Remembrance Day and Christmas, but in the Station Yard Fireman Bladdock paced anxiously up and down. Jack Puller was always the last, but he was never this late. Ned lugged out his watch for the umpteenth time and shouted to Helliwell on the gate, 'Any sign of 'im yet?'

Helliwell took his hands out of his trouser pockets long enough to make a 'no' sign at him.

Ned shook his head in exasperation. 'Where the bloody 'ell is 'e, then?'

Barmy held out another pot of tea. 'OK?'

'Not now, Barmy, it's coming out of me ears.'

Jim Cork sauntered over. 'Can't you drive 'er into t'yard?'

'I will if he isn't here in a minute.' He looked at the great old engine and licked his lips. He didn't relish climbing into the driving seat, but if Mr Thurk arrived with Aggie still in bed there'd be hell to pay. He stepped into the yard again, looked towards the gate, and as he did so Helliwell staggered in, half supporting Jack. Ned hurried forward to help, shocked at his appearance. One eye was closed, shot with the colour of the sky before a tropical storm, blood was trickling from his mouth, and there was a nasty cut on his chin trickling onto his torn uniform.

'Bloody 'ell, Jack, did you fall under a train?'

Jack straightened up and brushed the back of his hand gingerly across his chin. 'I'll get the bastard, and when I do I'll wrap that bloody bike round his neck.'

Barmy hurried over with a pot of tea. 'OK?' he grinned.

Jack ignored him. 'Four of 'em. Big buggers an' all, but

80

'e waon't there himself. They never are – allus get somebody else to do it.'

Barmy edged round the front of him, still proffering the tea.

'Bugger off, Barmy,' snarled Jack.

'OK,' said Barmy, grinning, and went inside to pour it back.

'Who're you talking about, Jack? Who did this?' asked Ned.

Jack winced and felt his eye. 'That union bugger from Blackburn – 'e wasn't there, but they kept calling me scab and blackleg.' He tried to smile. 'Any road, there's one of 'em 'll be on t'operatin' table now, and another bugger won't be havin' any more children.' He walked slowly to the tap in the yard and let the cold water run over his head.

Ned stood at his side. 'We'll report this to Mr Thurk.'

Jack jerked round. 'You bloody well won't,' he hissed. 'This is nowt to do with Mr Thurk, it's my problem.'

Ned shrugged helplessly. 'Well, you can't let him see thee like this, 'e's bound to ask questions.'

Jack didn't appear to have heard – he was gazing into the distance. Ned followed his gaze but there was nothing to see. It was all in Jack's mind, and Ned wouldn't have been in that union official's shoes for all the brass and medals in the world.

'Burtonshaw, that's the name.'

Ned nodded. 'Aye, that's the name: Neville Burtonshaw.'

Jack pulled himself together. 'Well, I'd best get this bloody engine into t'yard.' He swung himself carefully up into the driving seat. By the time Mr Thurk arrived, Jack had gone home, ostensibly with the flu.

'There's a lot of it about,' said Mr Thurk absent-mindedly, and as he didn't trust Ned at the wheel he took the bus to the Town Hall. As soon as he was gone the lads hurried back into the warmth. They stood in a semi-circle round the big pot-bellied stove, and nobody spoke for a time. Then Jim Cork cleared his throat and said, 'Bloody 'ell.'

Barmy dipped a pot into the dixie and offered it, but

there were no takers. They needed a good shot of whisky, not stewed tea.

Ned jangled some loose change in his trousers pocket and spoke to the stove. 'Well, that's put t'cat among t'pigeons.'

'It has that,' said Helliwell. 'It could 'ave been any one of us.'

There was another silence, then young Turner fidgeted. He was the newest recruit – tall, red-faced, pimples, and always had a boil going on his neck. 'There's nowt wrong wi' bein' in a Union,' he said.

Ned looked at him. 'No, there's not, but they're not goin' the right way to get new members.'

Turner went even redder. 'What I meant was. . . .'

But Ned cut in. 'What tha meant was, you're scared to bloody death.' He looked round. 'All of you.' Nobody contested this, so he went on. 'Well, I tell you this. Nobody from Blackburn's comin' 'ere and duffing up my lads. I don't care 'oo they are.' He looked round the group. 'Now get your helmets on, and climb on that tender. We're going to see this Neville Burtonshaw.'

Nobody moved. They were uneasy.

'What's the matter with you? There'll be no violence. I'm only goin' to have a few well-chosen words with 'im.'

Helliwell coughed. 'It's not that, Ned. 'Ow long is it since you drove that thing? You'd never get it out of t'yard for a start.'

Ned looked at the engine, then back at the lads. He squared his shoulders. 'Listen,' he said, 'I was driving that thing when your mother had to wipe your nose.'

Helliwell came back straight away. 'Aye, I know, but it was easy in them days. You had a man in front with a red flag.'

Nobody laughed – they were still shocked by what had happened to Jack Puller, and had Neville Burtonshaw walked into the yard at that moment they would have been Union members to a man.

Ned, however, was committed. 'Get that crank handle out, and I'll show you whether I can drive or not.'

They collected their helmets and wandered unwillingly

into the yard. Ned sat high up in the seat, tight-lipped, gripping the wheel as if to hold the whole thing together. Helliwell, red-faced, swung the great handle for the third time, to no effect, and stepped back to catch his breath.

'Give it 'ere,' said Jim Cork, and spat on his hands. 'Right!' And he swung fiercely – but the old engine squatted stubbornly, quietly mocking their efforts. Jim tried again. He swung it round and round in a mad frenzy, but he might as well have been mangling washing. Ned, sitting up in the driving seat, was staring as if mesmerised, and young Helliwell had to tap him twice on the knee.

Ned looked down at him. 'What's up?' he said.

'Is it switched on?'

Ned looked blankly. 'Eh?'

'Switched on.' And Helliwell mimed switching on.

'Oh, aye,' said Ned, embarrassed, and he scanned the dashboard. 'Oh, aye,' and he turned on the ignition.

Jim Cork stood back in disgust. 'That's marvellous, that is! Bloody marvellous! Nearly bloody well ruptured meself.'

Barmy sauntered up. 'OK?'

'Bloody marvellous,' said Jim, and gripped the handle tightly. 'Is it switched on now?' he shouted.

Ned put his thumb up.

'Are you sure? Little red light on and everything? I'm not a bloody organ grinder, you know.'

Ned put his thumb up again. 'It's OK now.'

With an ear-splitting roar the engine caught. Everybody ducked instinctively. Pigeons clashed together in a hurry to get out of the way. The engine jerked forward like a cantankerous bullfrog and stalled.

Barmy stepped forward and patted the side. 'Whoa, whoa,' he said. Then, sure that it was calm, he grinned. 'OK.'

Jim wasn't amused. He was flat on his back by the wall, afraid to move in case he couldn't. Some of the lads hurried over to him, but mainly they were concerned for Ned whose head had gone straight through the windscreen. 'Stay still, Ned,' said one of them, while they gingerly picked the shards

83

of glass from the frame. 'Steady, now. Ease back, that's it.' And Ned was free.

He took off his helmet carefully, his face white. 'By the bloody centre,' he said. 'If I hadn't been wearing this.'

Walter Buckley picked a large piece of glass off the bonnet and put it back again. 'I'd just cleaned the bugger, too,' he said, and strolled inside. The rest of the lads joined him, and in no time at all they were back at their favourite positions round the pot-bellied stove, each aware that changes were coming and, whether they liked them or not, they would be forced to accept them. The trip to Blackburn was thankfully postponed.

'Right, lads,' said Ned briskly. 'Who's goin' to nip down to Hepworth's Garage?'

'I'll go,' said Smelly Watkins. 'What do you want?'

Ned raised his eyebrows. He'd rather it hadn't been Smelly. Smelly wasn't too bright – in fact he sometimes made Barmy look like a scholar. 'We'll want a new windscreen, won't we?' said Ned slowly.

'Oh, aye.' He pondered a moment. 'Will I take the old one with me?'

Ned looked round at the other lads. 'It's like being in a bloody lunatic asylum.'

Smelly came to a decision. 'I'll tell him we want a new one.'

Ned nodded. 'You do that.'

Smelly was about to leave when Ned called after him, 'Oh, and get me five Woodbines while you're at it.'

Smelly took the proffered shilling and shambled off.

Helliwell watched him go. 'You should have written it down for him. He'll never remember that lot. And if he does what's the betting 'e comes back with a Woodbine and five bloody windscreens.'

Again nobody laughed. They weren't listening – too much had happened and they were all staring fixedly at the stove.

Half to himself, Ned said, 'I'll tek morning off tomorrow and go and see Burtonshaw on't bus.' And there the matter ended.

Surprisingly enough, Jack turned up for band practice

that night and seemed in a better frame of mind. Ned marvelled at the way he played the cornet – it wasn't brilliant, but with his cut lip it was downright miraculous. He must have been in agony – but then that was Jack, and Ned felt a great pride in knowing him. Mr Thurk had been so preoccupied that he didn't seem to have noticed the newness of some of the instruments. Ned had taken the precaution of draping an old mac over the big drum to hide the battle honours, but Jim Cork's euphonium, right under his nose, gleamed and glistened like a crystal chandelier. Also the shrinkage in Fire Station property seemed, astonishingly, to have escaped him – after all you'd think he'd have missed the bell by now.

Due to strike action there was no *Grapplewick Chronicle* the following morning, and very few people read the Blackburn paper. Even so they would probably have missed a small item at the bottom of page three, captioned 'Hit and Run': 'Neville Burtonshaw, a Union official, was found in a ditch near his home unconscious, and is suffering from multiple injuries. The police had difficulty in freeing him from the remains of his bicycle, and it is believed he was the victim of a hit and run driver.'

Burtonshaw, lying in the Infirmary, accepted the story, although he couldn't recollect hearing a car, and certainly – if there was a car – it couldn't have had headlights.

Terence took in the three brass balls, then surveyed himself in the pawnshop window. He rather fancied his little moustache and goatee beard, and wondered idly how long it would take him to grow his own. He winked at himself and entered the shop. Almost as soon as the bell tinkled, old Mrs Hellingoe appeared from the inner recesses. Terence raised his homburg. 'Bonjour, Madame.'

She stared at him uncomprehendingly.

Terence smiled apologetically. 'I am vair sorry, Madame, I speak not good ze Anglais.' He lifted his shoulders – it was vintage Charles Boyer. 'Alors, I am desolate. My baggage, vis all my papeurs, my monee, stole . . . how you say? Stole?'

She nodded and spoke to him as if he was deaf. 'STOLEN.'

'Ah so . . . yes, stolen.'

She clucked her tongue. She knew the drill – always a hard luck story, then the stuff that had to be pawned. The better the hard luck, the more they hoped to gain. She leaned towards him. 'HAVE YOU BEEN TO THE POLICE?' When she said 'police', she held her hand up high to depict a tall man.

Terence pretended to be mystified, then his face cleared. 'Ah oui, the police . . . I have been, yes, but, alors, they can do nothing.'

She decided to move things along. 'If everything has been stolen, how can I help you?'

He sighed. 'Not everything, Madame. I have my watch.' He took the heavy gold chain out of his pocket and placed it on the counter. 'I am desperate, compris? But I must be in Paree tomorrow, otherwise I would not part with ziz for a million francs.'

She picked it up and glanced at him sharply, then she took it to the window where there was more light. Terence watched her. 'It was a present for me from an English capitaine, I ide heem from the Germans in the war. Three times the Gestapo question me, but I do not break down, so at the end of the war the capitaine, e say, "Henri . . . you must ave zis." "I do not want it," I say, "as head of the resistance I only do . . ." '

She broke into his reminiscences. 'I'll see my husband, he'll say how much.' She took the watch into the back room. Terence gave her a Gallic bow. He examined one or two objects in her absence, humming the Marseillaise. With a few pounds in his pocket he might take the bull by the horns and ask Elsie out for a meal tonight. There must be some place in Blackburn and he'd be able to afford a taxi – that would impress her. He wished he'd thought of being a Frenchman long ago, it always got 'em going. 'Darling, je vous aime beaucoup.' He heard the firebell in the distance getting closer, and looked out of the window to watch the old engine lumbering by. It was going so slowly he thought

for a moment it was going to stop outside, and he smiled –
not a bad idea at that, it must be worth a bob or two on
the antique market. He turned just as Mrs Hellingoe sidled
up.

She gave him a tight smile. 'My husband,' she pointed to
her wedding ring, 'is looking at it now.'

'Merci.' There was a long and awkward pause, and he
heard a ting as if the telephone receiver had been replaced.
Then a large, heavy man in a velvet smoking jacket came
through. Terence smiled and touched his hat, but the man
ignored the courtesy and leaned his elbows on the counter
while he examined the watch. Terence felt a tickle of cold
sweat run from his armpit down his side. Suddenly uneasy,
he mumbled, 'In 'alf an 'our, I must board on the train. . . .'

The man was in no hurry. He looked at Terence. 'The
wife tells me you got this during the war.'

Terence nodded quickly. 'Oui, a capitaine.' He wiped the
palms of his hands down his overcoat 'Now I must make
haste.'

The large man clicked open the watch. 'It's got his name
engraved inside the back.' He tapped the inscription with a
finger like a Wall's pork sausage. 'Samuel Hellingoe.'

Terence's lips dried. 'That is correct, Monsieur. Capitaine
Sammy, as we used to call him, always he look at the watch
and say, "One day the war will be over, Henri, and this will
be yours," . . . ha ha.'

The man's eyebrows went up slightly. 'My name also
happens to be Samuel Hellingoe.'

Immediately Terence knew the game was up. He snatched
forwards, but with amazing speed for such a big man Hellingoe stepped back. His wife yelped. All pretence gone now,
Terence glared at him. He should have bolted then, but he
wasn't going without the watch or the money. His mind
raced – physical violence was out of the question for Hellingoe was all of eighteen stone and the watch was like a
penny in a fist that was as big as a sheep's head. Terence
put his hand in his overcoat pocket and thrust forward two
fingers. 'Hand over the watch or I shoot.'

Hellingoe's face went white, then his eyes flickered over

Terence's shoulder and he relaxed. The shop bell jangled and Terence swung round. Matty O'Toole and a much younger constable were blocking his exit.

'He's got a gun,' shrieked Mrs Hellingoe, but Terence quickly held up both arms to show he wasn't armed. He had a feeling that an anti-tank gun wouldn't stop O'Toole.

Hellingoe mopped his brow, and with a malicious little smile he tapped Terence on the elbow. 'Would you like me to contact the French Embassy, Monsieur?'

'Bollocks,' said Terence, and joined the policeman.

THIRTEEN

Every Thursday Mr Thurk arrived at his office early, Thursday being the day the Fire Brigade made their goodwill tour of the farms. As he wasn't supposed to notice where the meat and eggs came from it was his way of turning a blind eye, but in any case there was always plenty for him to do at the Town Hall, and round about half past ten Lady Dorothy called in, and sometimes a few others. If there was a quorum they'd have a meeting, but if not he and Lady Dorothy popped across to Whitehead's café, over the billiard hall, to take coffee and biscuits.

The plump little waitress put down the biscuits and asked if there was anything else.

'No thanks, Florrie.' He smiled up at her. 'When's that sister of yours due?'

She blushed. 'Any time now, Mr Thurk. She's at the hospital.'

He patted her hand. 'Well, let me know when it happens and I'll be round to see her.'

Florrie took out a tiny handkerchief, and put it to her nose. 'Thanks,' she said and hurried away.

Lady Dorothy watched her go. 'She doesn't look too happy about it.'

Mr Thurk spooned sugar into his cup. 'She isn't. She's very fond of Emmie, but the trouble is Emmie isn't married. There's been hell to pay . . . her father's threatened to chuck her out. It's not just that she's having a baby – she won't tell who's responsible, and that takes a special kind of courage in this town.' He sipped his coffee contemplatively.

'Mind you, if it's black that'll narrow the field. We've only got one blackie here at the moment – Joe Helliwell.'

She looked at him. 'Why should the father be Joe Helliwell?'

He smiled. 'Sorry, my dear. It was a joke in very poor taste. They live next door, you see, in Waterloo Street.'

She took a biscuit off the plate. 'Strange, isn't it?'

'Strange?'

'Yes. Well, how did Joe Helliwell come by his name, and how did he come to live here in the first place? I mean, didn't he have a family?'

He chuckled. 'It *is* strange,' he said. 'They reckon old Fred Helliwell brought him home from the Boer War in his knapsack. I don't know whether that's true or not, but in any case Fred raised him. Anyway, he's married now. He married Florrie Dyson – or rather she married him. I think she wanted him as some kind of ornament.'

Dorothy smiled at him fondly. 'You know, Anthony, that's why it's so right and proper for you to be Mayor. To you Grapplewick isn't just a town, it's your family.'

He nodded absently. 'I suppose so,' he said, 'but for how much longer?'

She looked at him sharply.

'Well, Dorothy, you can see how things are going, how things are changing. . . . First the war, then Wilson Brown being elected to the Council – he's the one stirring things up.'

She frowned. 'If only he'd go back to the Navy, or retire or something.'

He looked at her over the rim of his cup. 'Oh, I can get rid of him all right,' he said. 'I could get shot of him tomorrow if I wanted.'

Her eyes widened. 'Well, for goodness sake do it.' She waved her hand searching for words. 'Do it . . . get rid of him before it's too late.'

He shook his head. 'Not yet, Dorothy . . . he's flushing them out for me . . . there are some good Councillors, and some bad ones, and he's pointing them out.'

She put down her cup. 'Yes, young Helliwell's suddenly sprouted wings.'

He nodded. 'Yes . . . I've noticed that too. For years he's been tentative about the Garden of Rest in the town centre – not a bad idea – but now, with Wilson Brown's backing, he wants to uproot the whole of Grapplewick and plant acres and acres of trees . . . shrubs . . . grass . . . flowers.'

Dorothy traced a pattern on the tablecloth. 'He could be sincere,' she said.

'Oh yes, he could be. But there's Ormroyd's Garden Equipment.'

'I know it, yes,' she said, but she wasn't any wiser.

He spoke deliberately. 'Ormroyd's son is married to Helliwell's sister.'

'Aaaah!' She sat back. 'I didn't know that.'

'Oh yes,' he said. 'Before the war they were big. Lawns and stuff on the Binglewood Estate – well, they practically started it. And the park . . . then came the war and the park was used to grow vegetables . . . sectioned off into allotments and so forth . . . and still is. Now the Garden of Rest in the town centre would have helped. In fact Ormroyd came to see me, and dropped the wink that if it went ahead he would as good as finance the band. Young Helliwell doesn't know this, but that's one of the reasons I've been lukewarm to the idea. In any case, if the new Grapplewick project goes ahead that will put old Ormroyd in the big league again, and Helliwell won't go short either.'

Her mouth tightened primly. 'Nor will Commander Wilson Brown.'

He put his cup down. 'No,' he said, 'I don't think so. That's the funny part. I don't think he knows about Ormroyd's. He's never concerned himself with the people of Grapplewick. I don't suppose he'd even recognise one of my lads out of uniform – you see. . . .' But he stopped short as she looked over his shoulder. He turned to see Ned Bladdock approaching, helmet under his arm like an emissary bringing the good news from Ghent to Aix.

He bowed to Lady Dorothy, then turned to his Chief.

'Beg to report a fire, sir, at the offices of the *Grapplewick Chronicle*.'

Mr Thurk shot up. 'I'll come at once.'

Ned puffed out his chest. 'It's all taken care of, sir. Everything's under control. His eyes were shining with the story he had to tell – after all this was his first actual fire. He swapped his helmet to his other arm, and Mr Thurk, feeling conspicuous, sat down again. 'You see, sir, apparently the fire had gone out once, before we arrived, and when we dashed in we collared two of 'em sprinkling paraffin over the machinery.'

Mr Thurk was on his feet. 'Paraffin?' he repeated.

Ned calmed him. 'It's all right, sir. The police have them now – two of the printers.' He looked round him, proud of his smoke-blackened face. There hadn't been much smoke at all, but a bit of axle grease had helped.

Mr Thurk sat down again. 'That's all very well, Ned,' he said. 'You've done well, but you know the regulations – on receipt of alarm I am to be informed immediately. I should have been there,' he ended lamely.

'There wasn't time, sir.' Ned leaned one knuckle on the table. This wasn't for public consumption. 'You see, sir, we were on our way to collect the . . . er' he looked round ' . . . the usual Thursday stuff, and we were just passing the *Chronicle* building when one of the pickets outside the gates flagged us down and shouted "Fire!" There was a bit of smoke at one of the windows, then a face appeared and said, "It's gone out again." Then, they tried to stop us goin' in, said it didn't concern us, but Jack Puller takes a bit of stopping. Well, you know Jack . . . any road, that's how we managed to catch 'em red-handed.'

Lady Dorothy looked up at him. 'Did you say pickets?'

Mr Thurk sighed. 'They're on strike.' He stood up wearily. 'Well, Dorothy, if you'll excuse me I'd better be getting along to the Station.'

A flash of alarm crossed Ned's face. 'No, sir. Well, I think it's better if we clear things up first . . . tidy the appliance and that. I'll make out a full report . . . er . . . give us an hour, sir.'

The Mayor looked at him steadily for a moment, then sat down again. 'All right, Ned, I'll be over in an hour.'

'Thank you, sir.' Ned bowed slightly to Lady Dorothy, and made for the exit.

Lady Dorothy leaned over. 'He didn't seem too keen to have you back at the Fire Station.'

He smiled. 'I'm not surprised.' He stirred what was left of his coffee absently. 'For some time now they've had a deal going with Cowell and Bottisford's for musical instruments, and, not to put too fine a point on it, the fire engine is somewhat lacking in equipment.' He paused. 'Still, the little episode this morning might give their consciences a bit of a jolt,' he chuckled. 'Mind you, if they'd had a bell it would have given the fire raisers ample warning!'

She didn't appear to have heard him. 'How long have they been on strike?' she asked.

'Eh? . . . Oh, the printers. There's been no *Chronicle* for three days now.' He shook his head sadly. 'I'm afraid it's a sign of the times.'

'Strikes, you mean?'

'No,' he said. 'There's been strikes before, but mainly they were justified and used only as a last resort. Now this one. . . .' He passed his hand wearily over his face. 'What happened was, one of the printers opened a window in the machine shop, said it was too hot. Then the chap who worked under the window said he was in a draught and closed it again. Then the other fellow walks over and opens it again. Then the shop steward was called in, and he suggested they have it half open, but neither of them would agree to that – it had to be fully open or fully closed. Then the man who was working by the window closed it and cut the cord so they couldn't open it at all, by which time a sub-editor walked in and asked what the trouble was, and when they told him he said they were acting like a bunch of kids. That really put the cat among the pigeons. They shut down their machines and walked across to the Star to convene a meeting which went on till closing time. It was too late then to get out next day's edition.'

'And that was three days ago?'

'Yes. They demanded a written apology from the sub-editor which they got, then they immediately convened another meeting to decide whether to accept it, and when they came back it was coupled with a demand for protective clothing and a wage increase. Anyway Arthur Taylor, the owner, said he wasn't going to be blackmailed and threatened to sack the lot of them, and this morning was the result.'

Her eyes widened. 'But this is ridiculous – if they had burned down the building they wouldn't even have a place to work anyway.'

'Ah, yes,' he said. 'But I don't believe that would worry the politically motivated men behind this strike. They'll just move on.'

She looked at him quizzically. 'You're not against Unions, are you, Anthony?'

'Me?' He laughed. 'Before the war, I was one of the most active Union supporters in the North. Speak anywhere, I would, and I still believe that we need good strong Unions. But their main aim should be the welfare of the members, and that's what it was in the old days. . . .' He pushed his coffee cup away and leaned forward. 'During the Bolshevik Revolution the mobs were running wild, burning and looting, and Lenin nearly went potty. "Don't burn the palaces, you fools," he said. "If you want to burn something, set fire to your own hovels." '

Dorothy smiled. 'Was it Lenin or was it Marx?'

'Whoever it was, that's what they're doing here now. Well, they're not actually burning palaces, but they're doing their damnedest to tear down existing values and standards.

She looked at him quizzically. 'Yes, but things are vastly different in Russia.'

'For the moment,' he replied darkly, 'a new philosophy is being preached in this country, a philosophy based on dissatisfaction, hate, envy – this in itself is evil.' He leaned forward. 'The only antidote is love.'

Dorothy's eyes flickered but Mr Thurk didn't appear to have noticed.

'Love has no class barriers, and if there was a choice

94

between love and hate I know what most people would choose, and you don't have to be a millionaire to experience it.'

This time Dorothy put her head down and busied herself in her handbag. Mr Thurk became suddenly embarrassed as he realised that what he had just said sounded like a proposal. He looked round the café, flustered, and his eyes lit on a portrait of the Royal Family. He chuckled. 'Did I ever tell you of the time before the war, when the King and Queen came to Grapplewick?'

Dorothy shook her head and Mr Thurk laughed. What a day that was! The old King George V was due in Grapplewick at eleven thirty. Well, we were all up at five o'clock, Mother fussing around – Dad was Mayor, you see – and it was a beautiful morning, promising to be a scorcher.' He paused. 'We used to have some real hot summers when I were a lad.... Anyway, Mother was arguing with Dad because he wasn't going to wear anything under his robes of office, and she kept saying suppose you get knocked down, and what if a sudden gust of wind springs up. But when Dad made up his mind – that was that.' He leaned back to let the waitress replenish their coffee cups. 'Thank you, Florrie.'

She smiled and teetered off.

'Just after ten Dr McBride called for Dad in his pony and trap and took him to the Town Hall, and we followed on foot. What a sight – flags and bunting everywhere, all the scouts and guides lining the route, St John Ambulance strutting up and down – they had their hands full later on with the heat and everything. And the crowds ... I don't know where they all came from, but they'd been there for hours. Every window was full of faces, every lamp-post was festooned, and the little streets had flags across from window to window.' His eyes narrowed as he looked back over the years. 'When we arrived at the Town Hall a great cheer went up, and I was proud for my father until I saw what had happened ... as he was stepping down from the pony and trap his robe got caught, and of course everybody saw more than they bargained for!' He laughed. 'He was lucky really – if he'd taken one more step forward he'd have walked out of it altogether – my mother didn't speak to him again for a week.'

Dorothy laughed. 'I wish I'd been there,' she said.

'It didn't bother my father. "They cheered, didn't they?" he said. "At least they know they've got one man in the Town Hall." Anyway, the band was playing a selection from something or other – and it was a good band in those days – and Dad was upset because he wanted to conduct them, but it wouldn't have been dignified in his mayoral robes.'

Dorothy chuckled. 'It would have been even more undignified without them.'

He smiled. 'Anyway, the time came nearer to eleven thirty and we all assembled on the Town Hall steps. You could feel the atmosphere . . . you could almost reach out and touch it. Everybody was straining to look towards the high point at Pennine Gorge. Arthur Buckley was up there keeping watch, and as soon as the cars came in sight he was to fire a rocket. Then we'd be prepared, you see.'

She nodded.

'Anyway, half past eleven came and went, and no sign of the rocket. Then suddenly we heard cheers at the bottom end by Linney Lane, and we realised that either the rocket hadn't gone off or Arthur was drunk and he'd missed them. As a matter of fact it turned out he was drunk, and as he went to light the rocket the bottle holding it fell over, and the rocket shot through Sag Bottom fields, and what with the drought and everything the crop caught fire, and when the King drove past Arthur was flapping with his coat trying to stop the blaze, so he never got to see the King. . . .' He laughed. 'Oh, my word! Ten acres and three barns went up. Poor old Arthur. He's dead now, you know . . . he had a polypus.' Anthony touched his ear by way of explanation, and she nodded. 'We all saw the smoke, mind you, and as Dad was Fire Chief as well it was his duty to get the Fire Brigade to it. But as he said after, his first duty was to the sovereign. Anyway, the three cars came slowly up Union Street and the crowds were going mad . . . every window in the cotton mills full of waving people, though they couldn't have seen much from where they were. On a signal from my father the band struck up the National Anthem, and as the cars drew level my father took off his hat and the King bowed his head. It was a magic moment. They looked marvellous, just like . . . well, just like a King and Queen. . . .' He took his handkerchief and blew his nose.

Dorothy smiled at him. 'Did they stay long?'

Mr Thurk shook his head. 'Oh, they didn't stop. Straight through and off to Blackburn. But what a day that was . . . the factories closed down at dinner time, the tables were brought into the street, and all afternoon the kids had races and games on Grapplewick Edge. Every door was wide open, and there were great barrels of beer outside every pub, and this town was welded together with such a bond . . .' He leaned back. 'Such a bond. Such love.'

She sighed. 'I wish I'd been there, Anthony.'

He lugged out his watch. 'Bai jingo, look at the time.' He signalled for the bill, and as he turned towards Lady Dorothy a bread roll hit him on the back of the neck. At the same moment a large woman came out of the ladies' toilet and stared, aghast. Then she swept towards a young lad sitting innocently at one of the tables, and gave him such a wallop that his cap went flying.

'That'll teach you,' she said, as she dragged him towards the door. 'That's the Mayor, that is.'

'Well, I didn't know, did I?' he snivelled, and they were gone.

Lady Dorothy pressed the serviette to her mouth to stifle a laugh, but Mr Thurk wasn't too pleased. Then he too began to laugh, brushing the crumbs from the back of his collar. They were still laughing when they walked up the street, in fact tears were streaming down his face and he had to hold onto the bus stop to steady himself.

Lady Dorothy stopped and looked at him seriously for a moment. 'D'you know, Anthony, I can't remember the last time I saw you laugh . . . *really* laugh.'

'Nor I you.' And they started to giggle again.

FOURTEEN

Commander Wilson Brown had a hangover, and he was trying not to let it interfere with his duty as Magistrate. Normally he enjoyed his days on the bench, and felt that he dispensed justice with a sure, deft touch that roused both respect and even admiration in his colleagues, the police, and even the defendants. The truth, however, was sadly different. The police scornfully referred to him as Admiral Pinhead, and would go to great lengths to avoid having to attend his sessions, while the villains knew they were more likely to be treated leniently in a collar and tie, and a row of medals virtually guaranteed an acquittal. The Commander was blissfully unaware of these sentiments, and was proud of his position. He could be harsh, sometimes witty, even jocular, especially when Droopy Nellie was up before him, but it never occurred to him that nobody ever seemed to laugh. This morning, however, his head was throbbing and three aspirins had made very little difference. He struggled to concentrate – it would hardly be appropriate if the drunks that sagged in the dock realised that, while they were drinking themselves into trouble, the man lecturing them had been dancing on the billiard table in his underpants. A flush of shame engulfed him as he remembered, but then it wasn't an everyday occurrence to get a hole in one, and it had been a costly affair.

There had only been one or two members at the bar when he had entered the club house, but a hole in one goes round the golf grapevine quicker than greenfly. In no time at all the members' lounge was packed, and half-a-bitter men suddenly developed a taste for scotch, Binglewood golf club being the only place in Grapplewick with an abundant supply. Luckily most of them had left by the time he struggled onto the table to give his impression of a belly dancer, but word would get around.

Lady Dorothy leaned towards him and whispered, 'It's his first offence.'

The Commander tried to collect his scattered thoughts, and looked sternly at the miserable creature in the dock. Then he leaned towards old Brierley on his left. 'What do you think, Walter?'

Walter eased back a little as the stale whisky hit him. 'A caution, I think.'

'Right.' Wilson Brown leaned forward. 'As this is your first offence, you'll be let off with a caution.'

The little man gave a great sigh of relief. 'Thanks, Your Honour.'

Wilson Brown nodded. 'And next time I suggest you take more water with it.'

The little man looked at the policeman and the PC shrugged. In fact everybody was wondering what taking more water had to do with stealing clothing coupons.

Another sorry creature was hustled into the court, and while the usher was mumbling the formalities Wilson Brown cast a red eye towards the dock, Terence was examining his nails disinterestedly. For some unaccountable reason this nonchalance sent a surge of unease through the Commander. He palmed a couple more aspirins to his mouth, and gulped a tumbler full of water, then looked carefully at the man in the dock. Terence looked up and returned his stare. For a moment it looked as if they were trying desperately to hypnotise each other, then Terence slapped the rail in front of him.

'I don't believe it,' he gasped. 'It's too good to be true. Helliwell!'

The policeman was about to caution him when Wilson Brown gave a large belch and slumped down in a dead faint.

FIFTEEN

The *Grapplewick Chronicle*, now back in uneasy circu-
lation, made it a front-page blockbuster: 'Commander
Wilson Brown Has Heart Attack', followed the next day by
'Commander Off Danger List'. This was pure conjecture as
the hospital had given them no information, which was
hardly surprsing as the Commander hadn't even been there.
After being helped from the bench, he'd revived himself with
a stiff brandy, and the only visible sign of his heart attack
was a plaster on the bridge of his nose where it had come
in contact with the bench – but then a bloody nose doesn't
sell newspapers. Under normal circumstances the front-page
pictures of himself in a naval uniform would have pleased
him, and indeed he would have ordered half a dozen, but
with the advent of his old partner the charade was over.
Terence was relieved. With all the attention focused on the
Commander he never even got a mention, and he was having
a field day. From his crummy little room at the Dog and
Partridge he now had the run of Wilson Brown's magnificent
house on the much sought after Binglewood Estate, and he
was in no hurry to move on. Actually he'd never been inside
a place like this in daylight. He helped himself to a large
whisky and settled comfortably in an armchair by the great
fireplace. Wilson Brown watched him wearily. 'Suppose I
give you £10,000 – and I'll have to struggle to get it, mind
you – but would that do?'

Terence raised an eyebrow. 'Do what?' he asked.

Wilson Brown gave a sigh of impatience. 'You know what.
Will that settle things?'

Terence pondered a while. 'Moneywise, I suppose it

sounds reasonable. But what about my seven years? There must be compensation for that, wouldn't you say?'

'I had no choice.'

Terence swilled his whisky round the glass. 'Perhaps not, dear boy, but to drive off as you did, leaving me halfway down the ladder, was hardly cricket.' He paused. 'And with a sackful of goodies over my shoulder, it was difficult to convince the law that I was merely cleaning the windows . . . especially at three in the morning.'

Wilson Brown sprang to his feet. 'Oh, come on now, it wouldn't have helped you if I'd stayed, and there wouldn't be any money, just remember that.' He looked pointedly at Terence to let this sink in.

Terence didn't appear to understand the significance of this – he was idly scratching his crotch. The Commander frowned: after all, they were his trousers. He made a mental note to have them cleaned, or better still his gardener could have them. He'd be overwhelmed, and word would get round ('Always looks after his men, does the Commander'). Then he recalled that the gardener had asked for a raise only last month, and his jaw hardened. That's all everybody wanted nowadays, money money money. Well, OK, but he wasn't having the trousers as well. The bloody cheek of it! It was bad enough having to pay him two pounds twelve and six a week, but he wasn't going to clothe him into the bargain.

'You're right, it wouldn't have helped if you'd stayed.'

The Commander grunted. 'What . . . oh, yes. I'd have been in the same boat as you.' He waved his hand round the room. 'And don't run away with the idea that all this comes from the proceeds. Oh, no. I made most of my money after that, when you were inside.'

Terence smiled. 'Of course you did. Ikey told me about it.' A momentary flash of panic crossed Wilson Brown's face, and he took a gulp from his glass. Terence beamed. 'Incidentally, he sends you his regards . . . he's doing quite well in the laundry.'

Wilson Brown hurried to the sideboard to replenish his

drink. 'He's taken care of for a few years anyway,' he muttered.

Terence held out his empty glass. 'His boys aren't. They're sniffing about for you, Joe.'

Wilson Brown poured from a height so that the decanter wouldn't rattle against the glass.

'Nervous, Joe?' asked Terence. 'You know, your best bet is a monastery. Or better still have an operation and be a Mother Superior – you wouldn't be happy as an ordinary nun.' He stood up and sauntered round the room. 'We might get a billiard table in here.'

Wilson Brown's eyebrows went up. 'We?' he said. 'How long do you intend to stay here?'

Terence was examining the ship's bell. 'You seem to be under a misapprehension, old boy. The question is, how long do *you* intend to stay here?'

Wilson Brown stared at him for a long moment, then dashed off his drink and poured another one.

Terence was now looking closely at a wooden ship's crest. 'Interesting,' he murmured. 'Where did you pick up all this nautical?'

'It was here when I bought the place.'

Terence swung round to him. 'I see . . . yes, so you promoted yourself to Commander.' He nodded round the room. 'The mind boggles, Joe,' he said. 'Had the fixtures and fittings included gothic arches and a picture of the last supper, you might have been a bishop.' He pursed his lips. 'On balance, I think you did well. Commander Wilson Brown sounds right.'

'Wilson Brown *is* right,' snarled the Commander. 'It happens to be my real name.'

Terence's jaw dropped. 'Well, I'll be damned.' He moved towards him. 'I thought we had no secrets, Joe, and in all those years you never told me.'

There was a discreet tap at the door, and they both turned. 'Yes,' barked the Commander.

His housekeeper peered timidly into the room. 'A gentleman to see you, sir.'

Wilson Brown looked sharply at Terence. 'I'm not expecting anyone . . . who is he?'

Mrs Farley flustered. 'He did tell me, but I couldn't quite catch it. It sounded Italian, but I think he's Irish.'

Terence relaxed. 'Ah, yes. Rembrandt. Show him in please, Mrs Farley.'

She looked at her master for confirmation and he nodded. As soon as she'd gone he whirled round to Terence. 'Is he still alive? What's he want?'

Terence shrugged. 'That is something I've never been able to ascertain. However the question is academic . . . I want him here.'

Wilson Brown looked as if he'd just stepped into something nasty. 'Here . . . in this house?'

Before Terence could reply the door opened and Mrs Farley ushered in Rembrandt from a safe distance, then edged round him to escape. Rembrandt's gaze slowly swept round the room. 'Ah, dis is more like it, sorr.' He swaggered over to the fire, his carrier bag jinking and clinking as he walked. 'Oi could settle down here, and dat's a fact.' He took off his cap and stuffed it into the bag, extracting a bottle of Guinness in return. Fascinated, Wilson Brown watched the little Irishman as he fiddled beneath his long dirty raincoat. For one awful moment it looked as if he were undoing his flies, then he brought out a bottle opener attached to a scruffy piece of string.

Wilson Brown sighed audibly. The little ratbag was unpredictable, and could quite easily have put the fire out as a token gesture.

'Good health . . . here's to the old firm all together again.' As he put the bottle to his lips Wilson Brown was mesmerised by the hairy grey adam's apple bobbing up and down to accommodate the Guinness. Finally Rembrandt took the bottle from his lips and gave a huge belch. 'That'll keep the dust down,' he muttered, and placed the empty on the mantelpiece next to a silver cigarette lighter. Then he wiped his mouth with the back of his hand. 'Oi wouldn't mind a couple of eggs and a bit of bacon, and a sausage if der's one goin'.' As he talked he picked up his bag and made his way to the door.

Terence snapped his fingers, and Rembrandt stopped. 'The lighter.'

Rembrandt made a good attempt at being puzzled for a moment, then he took the lighter from his raincoat pocket. 'Oi was going to light the gas, sorr.'

'Never mind the gas, you stunted peat bog. Put it back.'

'Yes, sorr.' He replaced it on the mantelpiece and shuffled out.

Wilson Brown spread his hands. 'You saw that. He can't stay here . . . I mean, well, he'll attract attention.'

Terence nodded. 'Oh, yes, but he'll attract more attention wandering the streets of Grapplewick. That's why I want him where I can keep an eye on him.'

Wilson Brown tried again. 'You don't understand. If he's seen wandering round the Binglewood Estate he'll be run in purely on suspicion.'

'Oh, I agree,' said Terence. 'So I'll keep him in during the day and exercise him after dark. There's quite a few places on the estate I wouldn't mind seeing myself.' He heaved himself out of the chair. 'You don't have a map of the disposition of the dwellings on the estate, do you?' he asked innocently.

Wilson Brown gazed into his glass. 'There's a map at the gates . . . well, there's one at every entrance to the estate and. . . .' He stopped suddenly, and his eyes widened. 'You're not thinking what I'm thinking, are you?'

Terence looked at him levelly. 'Probably,' he said.

Wilson Brown stared at him aghast.

Terence smiled. 'After all, it is my profession, and this is right up my alley. Here I am, a bear in a honey garden.'

Wilson Brown stood back, shaking his head vigorously. 'Oh, no. You're not messing on my front door step. I've finished with all that rubbish. I'm straight now,' he snickered. 'Binglewood Estate – you wouldn't stand a chance. The police aren't all idiots, you know. They'll soon trace you to me. Oh, yes. I stuck my neck out last week when I gave you a suspended sentence. The houses on this estate

104

are pretty well looked after with burglar alarms and dogs. . . .' He trailed off, unable to meet Terence's scornful gaze.

'You know, Joe, you're pathetic. You really are quite pathetic.'

Wilson Brown took the poker and hacked away at the fire. 'It's you who's pathetic. You're the one who got nicked trying to sell a watch back to its owner.' He laughed. 'That's pathetic, isn't it? The great Raffles hauled into a provincial court with cardboard in his shoes and the arse hanging out of his trousers.'

It was Terence's turn to feel embarrassed. He moved away from the fire, for the gum holding his wig was beginning to run down his forehead. 'What about you, *Commander*? That's a laugh! *Commander* Wilson Brown – you wouldn't recognise a battleship if one sailed up the drive,' he chuckled. 'Hardly a master stroke, promoting yourself to Commander. I mean it only takes one phone call to the Admiralty and you're up the spout.'

Wilson Brown was unperturbed. 'Really? That's all you know, my friend. I've still got a little bit up here.' He tapped his forehead.

Terence looked at him quizzically, then he shrugged. 'Come off it, you fixed yourself up in the Ministry of Supply during the war.'

'Wrong again. Joe Helliwell worked in the Ministry of Supply.'

Terence felt uneasy. If he wasn't careful he was going to lose game, set and match. Then his brow cleared. 'You still owe society seven years for that abortive little job in '39.'

Wilson Brown turned away. 'You'd still have to prove it,' he said.

'Oh, I've got proof,' said Terence. 'There's no problem there. In any case, all the publicity connected with the trial wouldn't do your career much good.'

Wilson Brown said nothing, but glared at him. Terence relaxed – he was back in the game. He laid his head back and stretched out his legs. The whisky and the fire gave him a marvellous sense of wellbeing, and with so many aces in

105

his hand he almost felt sorry for his old mate. A whiff of frying bacon reminded him he hadn't eaten since breakfast, but his eyes were heavier than his need for food and he dozed.

The slam of the door jerked him upright and Rembrandt glided in with his everlasting carrier bag. 'Dat's filled a corner up,' he said. 'The sausages could have been done a bit more. Dey take a lot of doing, a good sausage.' He took a half-full bottle of wine from his pocket and took a deep swig.

Wilson Brown winced. Along with the house he'd inherited a very finely stocked wine cellar, and here was this ratbag knocking back a Château Lafite as if it was meths – 1933 and all.

Rembrandt put the cork back and stuffed it into his raincoat pocket. 'Not bad, dat. Oi tink oi put too much sugar in it.' Terence knew Rembrandt was enjoying himself, although one couldn't tell from his expression. He only had two expressions in his repertoire: mouth open and mouth closed. He slapped his cap on his head. 'Where is the car keys?' He held out a greasy hand towards his host.

Wilson Brown stared at him for a moment in astonishment, then his jaw tightened and he started to go red.

Terence saved him from apoplexy. 'All right, you've had your fun and you've been fed. Now shoot upstairs and get your great empty head down for the night.'

'Oi'm goin' into town to see my girlfriend,' said Rembrandt stubbornly.

Terence looked at him steadily. 'If you're not in that pit in ten minutes, I'll cut it off. Then you'll have nothing to play with.'

'Yes, sorr.'

Terence relented a little. 'In any case the car doesn't belong to you. You just can't go round appropriating other people's property like that.'

Rembrandt didn't move. 'Oi was goin' to bring it back. In any case, it's not doin' the car much good sitting der in a damp garage, and nobody's using it tonight.'

'Ah, that's where you're wrong,' said Terence. 'I'm taking

it.' He didn't particularly want to go out, but the mention of a girlfriend had twanged a chord, and Elsie would be impressed when she caught sight of the car.

Wilson Brown wasn't giving in that easily. 'Just a minute. I might want to go into town tonight.'

'Splendid,' said Terence. 'I'll give you a lift.'

'You haven't got a licence.'

Terence waved his hand. 'A mere technicality,' he chuckled. 'I'm not sure if I can still drive the damn thing . . . never mind – if anything happens, we can always get another one, eh?' And with that he whistled himself upstairs to select something from Wilson Brown's wardrobe.

Elsie looked bored. It was quiet in the Dog and Partridge – there'd only been one couple in all evening, and when the woman caught sight of Elsie she had her boyfriend out of the bar so fast it was difficult to remember if they'd had anything. Now Elsie surveyed herself in the mirror behind the bar. She prodded her hair, then leaned forwards to examine her lips – satisfied, she turned sideways and tucked her stomach in.

'Aphrodite rising from the water.'

She jerked round at the voice. 'Oh, it's you. Good evening, Major. You're quite a stranger.'

'Yes,' said Terence, inserting a professionally manufactured Player's cigarette into his holder. 'I had to motor down to Manchester, to clinch a deal, and I just thought I'd drop by to say hello.'

Without the asking, Elsie was busy pouring him a large measure of whisky. 'Oh, that's why you're all dressed up to the nines,' she said.

'Thank you,' he smiled at her. He'd always fancied himself in a dark blue pin-striped suit, and this was good material – although the sleeves could have been longer, and he had a choice with the trousers, which either finished four inches above his shoes or else he lengthened the braces, showing a considerable expanse of shirt below the waistcoat. He had opted for the former, since the shortness didn't show behind the bar.

107

'Where are you staying now?' she said. 'Found somewhere nice?'

He sipped his whisky. 'I'm staying with an old friend of mine . . . met him during the war. Commander Wilson Brown – know him?'

'Oh, yes. Comes in here now and again.'

'Good man,' he said. 'He took me off the beach at Dunkirk.' He looked down at his glass. 'One of the last.'

She looked down in sympathy. 'Nasty, that,' she said, then she brightened. 'Walter Helliwell, he was at Dunkirk,' she said. 'Walter Helliwell used to live in Sheepfoot Lane.'

'Never met him.' He gave a rueful grin. 'Too busy trying to save my batman.' He raised his glass. 'Here's to you, Taffy, wherever you are.'

Elsie frowned. 'I thought the little Irishman was your batman, the one who used to stay here with you.'

'He was, after Taffy bought it . . . four batmen died under me.' He sighed. 'I often wonder why all those good lads went, and an old reprobate like me was spared.'

'Oh, you're not that old,' she said coyly, and poured him another large whisky.

Terence smiled at the compliment. 'Well, that's enough about me. How's that husband of yours?' Her face clouded. 'Oh, Fred.' She began to wipe the bar. 'The doctor's put him on iron jelloids.' She bent forward to rinse the cloth under the bar and his leg twitched. 'There's nothing organically wrong with him,' she went on, 'it's just that he needs a holiday.'

He smiled sympathetically. 'We all need that,' he said. His brain was racing, and he had to make his pitch while the bar was empty. 'I'm thinking about going back into films,' he said.

She stopped rinsing the cloth, and he was sorry. 'Films,' she said. 'Have you been in films?'

'Not *in* them. Before the war I was a producer.' Her face told him that he'd scored. 'I was on the phone to Ronnie yesterday, and he's keen to make a sequel to *Shangri La*.' He drained his whisky and put the glass down, but she was too overawed to fill it again.

'Ronald Coleman?' she said in a hushed voice. 'Did you meet him?'

He laughed. 'Meet him? Ronnie wouldn't move a step without me. "Terence, old boy," he used to say. . . .' As he said this he gave a passable imitation of the Coleman voice. ' "Terence, old boy, if anything happens to me in this picture, you could take over and no one would know the difference." '

Her eyes were wide. 'Have you made any other films?'

'Ooooh. . . .' He pursed his lips. '*Life of a Bengal Lancer*, that was one of mine.' He pushed his glass slightly forward and she took the hint. 'Gary Cooper and I,' he went on, 'when we weren't actually shooting the film, we used to go horse riding together.'

She poured the whisky into his glass as if it was communion wine. 'Gary Cooper?'

'Yup,' he said, and laughed. 'Anyway, to change the subject, do you know of any good restaurants in Blackburn? I mean a good one, a really tip-top restaurant?'

'Blackburn,' she said, as if he'd just mentioned Rangoon. 'Well, I don't know offhand, but I could find out for you.'

'No, no,' he said quickly. 'It's just that after all your kindness to me, you know, when I first arrived, I thought perhaps you'd allow me to take you to dinner one evening.'

She stared at him. 'Well,' she said, 'that'll be nice, but I'll have to ask my Fred.'

Bugger Fred, he thought. 'Of course,' he said. 'When are you free?'

She shrugged. 'Well, the evenings are no good. I'm here, you see.'

He brightened. 'Tell you what,' he said, 'it's Saturday tomorrow. Why don't I pick you up after you finish at lunchtime, and we'll go for a spin?'

'Not tomorrow,' she said. 'I go to football on Saturday afternoons.'

'Football,' he said, trying to keep the distaste out of his voice.

'Oh yes, can't miss tomorrow. It's the first round of the

109

FA Cup. . . .' She leaned towards him. 'I've got a good idea. Why don't you come as well?'

The proximity of her chest was too much for him. If she'd said 'Let's jump off the roof with an umbrella,' he'd have been halfway up the stairs with his brolly. 'Right,' he said, and peeled a crispy fiver off a sizeable wad. 'I'll be in tomorrow lunchtime.' He slid off the stool.

'Just a minute,' she said, 'you want some change.'

'Keep it,' he said, 'and buy yourself something nice.'

She stared at the money uncertainly. 'Well, if you're sure . . . that's very nice of you.'

'Nothing, my dear.' He took a couple of steps, then turned. 'Oh, by the way, I'd rather you didn't mention anything about the films – me being a producer and everything.'

She was disappointed, but agreed to say nothing.

'Thank you. Only if it ever got out that I was up here, the press would be on, the film companies would be on, and I wouldn't have a moment's peace.'

'I shan't say nothing,' she replied.

He nodded, then left hurriedly before she caught sight of his too short trousers. A football match was a small price to pay for two hours of her company, and he passed a feverish leg-twitching night.

Grapplewick Athletic, known fondly as t'Latics, weren't brilliant – in fact they were even more widely referred to as 'them clowns'. Nevertheless it was the dream of most young lads one day to don the blue and white shirt, and run out of a little wooden shed every Saturday afternoon. Terence was hardly aware of the stamping supporters. He was content to sit huddled on the cold wooden bench next to Elsie – it purported to be Stand E, although it was the only covered bit on the ground. Fred shivered on the other side of Elsie, but Terence felt no compunction about that. With a bit of luck he'd be dead by half time.

It was easy to spot the home team. They ran onto the field like fathers at the school sports, and two of them didn't join in the kick about because they were too heavily winded and had to put their hands on knees to get their breath back. The star of the 'Latics' was the goalkeeper, which was surprising. He was humpbacked for a start, and scurried from side to side in the goal mouth like a hermit crab. He was dressed all in black, and, unable to afford shinpads, two copies of the *Grapplewick Chronicle* were stuffed down his stockings, giving his legs an odd, misshapen look. The way he crouched it wouldn't have surprised anyone to hear him declaim 'Now is the winter of our discontent. . . .' However, appearances were deceptive, and had it not been for his agility Grapplewick would have been considerably more than six down at half time.

Terence enjoyed the first half, or to be more accurate he was fascinated by the goalkeeper and wondered if he was human. He didn't mention this to Elsie, because she obviously thought the whole team was marvellous.

'Do you like it?' she said.

'Very good.' He smiled, and took a flask from his overcoat pocket.

'That's nice,' she said and took it, examining the gold Wilson Brown monogram.

'WB,' she said.

'Warner Brothers,' he whispered.

'Oh.' She hadn't the foggiest idea who Warner Brothers were, but it was obviously expensive.

Terence poured a jigger of whisky into the cap and handed it to her.

'Lovely,' she said, and proffered it to Fred.

He shook his head sullenly and looked away. He wouldn't have minded a drink, but it was too much effort to take his hands out of his pockets.

'Cheers.' Elsie sipped and held it out to Terence.

'No, my dear.' He pushed her hand back gently. 'Get it all down, there's plenty more.'

She knocked it back and gasped.

'That's the style,' said Terence. 'It'll warm you up.' He looked at her rosy face and the smiling lips. God, he thought, I'd warm her up given half the chance. A drum roll broke his thoughts, and he looked towards the field.

Mr Thurk raised his baton, and the band edged into the 'Marche Lorraine'. For football lovers the band was usually the highlight of the match, and for music lovers there was always the second half, and there were the regular wags with raucous, carrying voices: 'Give us "Nellie Dean".... When's the last waltz?' And the kids tried to lob pebbles in the bell of Herbert Barlow's double bass, unless Matty O'Toole was on duty – he wasn't today, and Herbert was twitching and ducking, but never missed a note.

Mr Thurk, however, was oblivious, totally absorbed in the music – 'Sons of the Brave', and now 'Three Jolly Sailormen'. He glanced round at the band, and he was proud. Many's the time they'd marched off the pitch bloodied and with lumps caused by flying missiles, but none had ever complained, and no one was absent on Saturday afternoons.

'Pah pah pah pon pom'... by jingo, Ned Bladdock was on form today, banging away on the big drum – stalwart Ned in a heavy belted overcoat and a tram conductor's hat. His gaze quickly moved to Cyril Chadwick, the only one to possess a tunic. Cyril loved his tunic, in fact he'd mentioned it several times in his letters to Betty Grable, and he knew that if ever she came to Grapplewick he only had to wear it and she'd spot him at once. He was lucky to inherit the tunic, because his father, being a vindictive man, had told him many times that, when he died, he was to be buried in it, and young Chadwick used to pray every night: 'Please, God, don't let him die.' But God works in mysterious ways, and one warm August night his father fell off the New Brighton ferry and his body was never recovered. The tunic was safe.

There was a smattering of applause, and a few ironic cheers greeted the end of 'Three Jolly Sailormen'. A halfpenny fell at Jack Puller's feet. He didn't deign to stoop and pick it up but put his foot on it – he'd have it later when no one was looking.

'Abide with Me,' said Mr Thurk, raising his arms. The lads looked round and shuffled uneasily.

The players were already back on the field, rubbing their hands and jumping up and down to get warm. A whistle blew, and the lads put down their instruments and made to leave the field.

'Stand fast the band,' barked Mr Thurk, and they milled uncertainly, just inside the touchline. The whistle blew again, this time more insistently. Mr Thurk ignored it and raised his baton. The linesmen grabbed at Jack Puller's arm and found himself in the second row of the stand. The crowd cheered.

The referee ran over to Mr Thurk and blew his whistle right into his face. 'Kindly leave the field,' he said.

The crowd were delighted with this. 'Off! off! off!' they chanted, and clapped in time.

' "Abide with Me" is traditional,' said Mr Thurk with dignity.

'Off,' said the referee.

'One more tune isn't going to hurt you, is it?' said Mr Thurk, wildly trying to find a face-saver.

'Very well.' The referee took out his little black notebook. 'Name?'

'One verse.'

'WHAT'S YOUR NAME?'

Over his shoulder Mr Thurk saw the band skulking off towards the exit. 'You know very well what my name is, Norman Taylor. We were in the same class at school.'

'Are you going to leave the field or not?'

Mr Thurk glared at him for a moment, then his resolve weakened. 'All right, I'll go. But you've never really grown up, have you?'

The referee blew a sharp blast at him and pointed to the exit.

'As long as you're in short pants, and sucking something, you're happy.'

The crowd cheered and clapped as he walked to the gate with head held high.

They were not forgotten, however. After Grapplewick went three more goals down, the crowd chanted, 'We want the band! We want the band!' But by this time most of the lads were back home.

Terence watched the performance thoughtfully. An idea

113

was already permeating his mind and he didn't notice the final whistle.

'Enjoy that?' said Elise.

Terence was jolted out of his reverie. 'What? Oh, yes, very much. Where do they practise?'

She laughed. 'Oh, I don't think they practise,' she said. 'They all have jobs to do. The goalkeeper is an undertaker, and Whittaker the right back is a milkman. . . .'

'No, no,' he said. 'I mean the band.'

'Oh, they practise every Thursday night over the Fire Station. Mr Thurk, the one who conducts them, is the Mayor.'

'Really?' said Terence, and they turned to shuffle towards the exit.

She stopped suddenly and he bumped into her. It was only her back, but it sent his temperature up several degrees – she put her mouth to his ear and he broke into a sweat. 'I've had a word with Mr Helliwell, and he said he wouldn't mind me having the evening off, as long as I don't make a habit of it.'

Terence shepherded his scattered thoughts. 'This evening?' He remembered he'd offered to take her out to dinner if she was free, but as much as he would have liked, and as much as his leg was twitching, he had other plans. In any case he felt that if they did go to dinner Fred would be sitting there to make up the party, and sod that for a game of shuttlecock. 'This evening,' he repeated. 'Oh, didn't I mention it? I have an important meeting tonight.'

Her face fell. 'On Saturday,' she said.

'Every day is a business day for me,' he said, but when he looked at her stricken face he was immediately thinking of excuses to get out of the meeting which he had just convened. Then he became resolute. 'I'm sorry, but I've quite a lot of money tied up in this venture.'

She was puzzled for a moment, then she nodded conspiratorially and began to edge along the row again. There'll be another time, thought Terence, but business first. His idea concerning the band was a stroke of genius, and the sooner he got the wheels in motion the better. Like all great inspiration, it was simple.

As Terence was making his thoughtful way home, Wilson Brown sat facing his flickering black and white television set. He'd hardly noticed the sport that afternoon, and he cared even less for the football results. What a way to spend a Saturday afternoon! Television wouldn't last long if that was the best they could do – the highlight was undoubtedly the interlude. Normally he would have spent the day at the Binglewood golf club, but he didn't have a car. Damn Terence, and why his sudden interest in football? Somewhere upstairs a door slammed, and he got up and switched the set off angrily.

Rembrandt came resolutely down the stairs with his ever clinking carrier bag. They were empties, but when he returned from the Weavers Arms the bag would be considerably heavier. He was looking forward to seeing Nellie again, and being Saturday there'd be a sing-song in the public bar. He never joined in, but if the Guinness was sitting well inside him he might be persuaded to render a chorus of 'The Wild Colonial Boy'. As he was crossing the hall he yelled, 'Oi'm goin' out, you silly old bag.' He never saw Mrs Farley, but he knew that somewhere she was watching his every move.

The drawing-room door opened and Wilson Brown eyed him with distaste.

Rembrandt stopped. 'Ah, der you are, just de man oi want to see,' and he brushed past him and shuffled to the fire.

Wilson Brown closed the door, waited for a moment, then opened it quickly, and his housekeeper almost fell into his arms. 'Do you want something, Mrs Farley?' he said stiffly.

'No sir, no.' She almost curtseyed in embarrassment, and he closed the door.

Rembrandt pointed to it. 'Dat woman is a menace,' he said.

Wilson Brown ignored him and moved over to the sideboard to pour himself a drink.

'Dat woman,' went on Rembrandt, still pointing to the

door, 'she took some empty bottles out of my room on Thursday, and der's money on dem.'

Wilson Brown settled down in the armchair and flapped open *The Times*.

Rembrandt came and stood directly in front of him. 'And she wiped off a half finished picture of Winston Churchill – she'd no right to do dat.'

A slight tremor of *The Times* was the only indication that Wilson Brown was listening. . . .

'Also de place stinks of disinfectant. It's worse dan de workhouse. It's a better stink in de workhouse, and dat's a fact.'

The paper still obscured Wilson Brown.

'An den dere's my shoes. What about my shoes? My good pair dat used to belong to a vicar – what about dem, eh?'

The newspaper didn't move.

'Oi leave dem out one morning to be cleaned, and she's gone and burnt them.'

Wilson Brown lowered the paper in order to take a drink, but his eyes never left the front page.

Rembrandt turned and went back to the fire. 'So on Monday oi'm 'aving a lock put on dat door of mine.'

This had the desired effect, and Wilson Brown looked at him as if he'd suddenly noticed his presence. 'You'll do nothing of the kind.' As soon as he spoke he was angry at himself for having been drawn.

Rembrandt picked up his carrier bag. 'Oh, no? You just watch me, dat's all. Wait till you see dat dirty great padlock oi'm tinking of. Yes, sorr, oi'm not having her pokin' round among my private tings.' He made his way to the door, and was almost knocked flat as Terence entered the room.

'A grand afternoon,' he said to no one in particular, shrugging out of Wilson Brown's black Crombie overcoat. 'And profitable, too. Aah, there's something about a good football match that stirs the blood.' He stood facing the fire and held out his hands to the warmth. 'It was cold, though. By the centre, it was cold. If it had gone on much longer, I'd have been drinking solid whisky.' He shivered and looked

116

over his shoulder at Rembrandt. 'Well, don't just stand there like a badly run jumble sale. A drink, man!'

Rembrandt stood firm, 'Oi'm just on my way out, sorr. Oi'm goin' to see my girlfriend,' he added.

Terence shook his head. 'Not tonight, you're not.'

Rembrandt was immovable. 'Oi promised oi'd see her at the pub and oi'm a man of me word,' he said stoutly.

'Never mind all that sanctimonious twaddle, go and pour me a large one.'

Rembrandt put down his carrier bag and walked over to the decanter. 'Oi'll pour you a drink, an den oi'm off.'

Terence lifted up the back of his jacket and warmed his rear end. 'And what have you been up to today, Joe? Been chasing Mrs Farley round the estate, have you?'

Wilson Brown didn't reply, but he folded his newspaper and laid it aside on the table.

Rembrandt handed Terence his drink. 'On the other hand, sorr, oi wouldn't mind stayin' in tonight. Oi don't mind at all.'

Terence watched him over the rim of his glass.

'Dat's a good idea about stayin' in, sorr. Oi'll just ring de pub and tell her to come up here.'

Wilson Brown slammed the arms of the chair and stood up. 'Oh no, you don't. I'm not having that slag Droopy Nellie in my house.'

Rembrandt turned to him. 'How did you know about Eleanor?' he asked, with much emphasis on the name.

Wilson Brown took his empty glass for a refill. 'There's not a lot goes on in this town that I don't get to hear about.' He looked at the little man in disgust. 'Droopy Nelly – that's about your mark, that is.'

Rembrandt leered knowingly. 'She told me about you, too,' he said. 'Oh, yes. She told me you fancied her. She told me she could have had you at de back of de washhouse once.'

'That'll be the day,' snorted Wilson Brown. 'But one thing is certain – she's not setting one foot on the Binglewood Estate. We don't want an epidemic.'

'She reckons you're a brown hatter.'

117

Terence felt it was time to intervene. 'For goodness sake, why don't you toss up for her?'

Wilson Brown shot him a look of annoyance. 'I'm warning you, if that woman comes within a mile of this place I'll have the police up here like a shot.'

Terence smiled indulgently. 'Now, Joe. We know you wouldn't do a silly thing like that. But for old times' sake I'll let him go down to the pub.'

Rembrandt moved to the door again. 'Oi'll give her your love,' he said.

In a flash Terence jerked him on to his toes by his lapels. 'Listen, Clark Gable, I don't want you to breathe a word to anybody about where you're staying. Is that clear?'

Rembrandt could barely speak, but he managed, 'Understood, sorr,' and Terence dropped him. 'Oi'll not say nuthin', sorr.' And he scuttled out before Terence changed his mind.

'I'll swing for that little bastard one day,' snarled Wilson Brown. 'He gets on my wick.'

'Yes, but he has his uses. Now sit down and listen to what I have to say.'

Wilson Brown, still seething, slumped into a chair.

Terence watched him for a moment. 'After a week's reconnaissance, and from conversations that have passed between us, I have decided that three houses on this estate deserve my undivided attention.'

Wilson Brown spluttered. 'Three houses?'

'Yes: Holmedene, The Beeches and Woodhaven East.'

Wilson Brown snickered. 'Well, I should forget The Beeches for a start. Burglar alarms, dogs . . . there's no chance. It's sewn up tighter than a Scotsman's purse. I should pick one of the others, if I were you.'

Terence eyed him coolly. 'I intend to visit all three.'

Wilson Brown tried to speak, but Terence held up his hand. 'All in one and the same night.'

Wilson Brown hooted. 'Hah, you've really gone round the twist, haven't you? How can you do them in one night?'

'That part of the plan doesn't concern you. In fact the less you know of it the better.'

The Commander frowned. 'Well, why are you telling me anything at all?'

'Because you can be useful.'

Wilson Brown stumped over to the sideboard and filled his glass. 'I don't like it,' he muttered.

'Well, don't drink it,' said Terence. It was wasted effort.

'I don't like it at all,' repeated Wilson Brown. He began to pace up and down.

'Supposing I just pick up the phone now, and make a clean breast of it to the Inspector – he's a pal of mine.'

'Because,' said Terence, 'we haven't done anything yet. The only thing to suffer would be your reputation, and that, dear Joe, is more precious to you than anything that could happen to me.' He tossed off his drink. 'And besides, you still owe them for the Chelmsford one. They know I didn't pull that job on my own.'

Wilson Brown returned to his chair and stared into his glass, then he tried again. 'Look, Terence, what's your price? How much for you to just pack up and disappear?'

Terence sighed. 'How can I ever make you understand? I'm a professional – I have my reputation to think of. Three houses in one night, and they'll know who's done it. Oh yes – but they won't be able to feel my collar because I'll have a cast iron alibi.'

In spite of himself, Wilson Brown was intrigued. 'I presume you're not telling me all this just to hear your own voice?'

'You presume correctly. Now you are, I believe, acquainted with the occupiers of the three houses?'

'You know I am. You've been asking questions about them all week.'

'Good. Well enough to exchange Christmas gifts?'

'Well, yes. What's wrong with that?'

'It's absolutely splendid, but this year I want you to play cagey. Drop hints that you've organised something rather special for them, a novel gift that you hope will be much appreciated.'

Wilson Brown was more than perplexed. 'Like what?'

'On Christmas Eve, your novel gift will be the Grapple-

119

wick Brass Band playing for them personally "Silent Night".'
He stood back like a conjuror producing something
impossible.

For a moment Wilson Brown stared open-mouthed, then
he sprang to his feet. 'That lot couldn't get a tune out of a
bloody gramophone.'

Terence smiled. 'As long as they're loud, that's all I care
about. Oh – and that they're capable of playing "Silent
Night".'

'There won't be much silence with that bunch, I'll tell you
that.' He gulped his whisky. 'And why "Silent Night"?
What's so special about "Silent Night"?'

'It's the only one I know,' said Terence smoothly, 'and
also it runs roughly five minutes, give or take a crochet,
and while they're doing their job I'll do mine.'

'Huh.' Wilson Brown was scornful. 'Five minutes isn't
long.'

'It's plenty if I know where to look.'

'And how will you get to know that?'

'I'll go through the houses beforehand. How else would
I find out – I'm not a bloody clairvoyant.'

Wilson Brown was thinking hard, sizing up the angles
and how it could affect him. Finally he shook his head. 'It
wouldn't work,' he said.

'Give me one good reason.'

'Well, for a start everyone knows I dislike the band. I've
been trying to get it scrapped for the last two years.'

'All the better,' said Terence. 'It will enhance the joke.
They'll be laughing about it for months.'

Wilson Brown thought again. 'Ah, yes, but how will you
get the band to go up there in the first place?'

'You try and stop 'em when I've finished with 'em.' He
chuckled. 'You should have seen them this afternoon – if
there hadn't been a football match they'd be playing yet.'

Wilson Brown didn't like it. He didn't like it at all. There
were a lot of ifs and buts and snags, but he couldn't think
of them at the moment. Nevertheless a warning bell was
sounding in the back of his mind. He finished off his drink.
'And when you've done this job you'll leave . . . I mean. . . .'

He stopped suddenly as one of the Ifs flashed into his mind. It was an enormous if and it staggered him. 'Just hold on a minute,' he said. 'If that damn band plays at these houses, supposedly on my recommendation, while at the same time they're being turned over, I'll be up to my neck in it . . . suspect number one, certainly as an accomplice.'

Terence nodded. 'Yes, I was afraid you'd spot that connection.'

'There you are, then,' said Wilson Brown triumphantly. 'No way am I getting involved.'

Terence studied him for a moment. 'But you are already involved, dear boy. I'm here, and that alone makes you a fully paid up member.'

Wilson Brown wasn't finished. He adopted a reasonable tone. 'Yes, but why must I inform these houses? Why not just have the band turn up and play?'

Terence shook his head. 'It's too chancy. The occupants wouldn't even get up from the dinner table . . . the butler would be despatched to send them packing the minute they started to blow . . . they'd set the dogs on them . . . or worse, they'd phone the police. No. The band has to be presented as a rather novel Christmas gift.' Wilson Brown snorted, but Terence ignored the interruption. 'Don't you see? People get socks for Christmas, they get ties and handkerchiefs, and they say, "Oh, isn't that lovely. Just what I wanted." And so it will be with the band. Everyone will gather to listen with fixed politeness until the last excruciating bar of music. Then perhaps – who knows – hot punch all round? A discreet fiver stuffed into one of the instruments? Psychology, old boy.'

Wilson Brown was unconvinced. 'It won't work,' he said flatly. 'Oh, I'll grant you there's a certain element of risk in having the band turn up unexpectedly, but I'm afraid that's a chance you'll have to take, because I'm certainly not going to have my name connected in any way.'

There was no reply, and he looked over his shoulder. Terence was at the little escritoire, scribbling on a small message pad. 'Got it,' he said, and tore off the paper, which

121

he took to Wilson Brown. 'There you are. Have that copied on nice greeting cards and sent.'

Wilson Brown studied the text. 'What's this?' he asked.

'Read it,' said Terence.

Wilson Brown flicked open his spectacles with one hand and put them on the end of his nose. 'To the occupants of Holmedene, The Beeches, Woodhaven East and Seven Seas.' Wilson Brown looked at Terence.

'Go on,' urged Terence, 'Read it.'

'At eight o'clock on Christmas Eve you will receive a novel gift, with the season's greetings, from a well-wisher.' He lowered the paper. 'Are you serious?' he asked, incredulous.

'Perfectly serious,' said Terence.

Wilson Brown skimmed the paper across at him. It settled on the rug. 'You don't know the people on this estate,' he said scornfully. 'Get a note like that and they'll tear it up straight away.'

Terence picked up the paper. 'Perhaps,' he said, 'but in any case you'll ring them up and ask if they've also received interesting Christmas cards. Be amused, play on their curiosity, tell them that in a strange way you're rather looking forward to it, whatever it is.' He propped the paper in front of the little clock on the mantelpiece.

'Better still, call round and compare cards. Two sherries and a biscuit, and with your undoubted charm Christmas Eve won't come quick enough.'

Wilson Brown lurched out of the chair and re-read the note. 'Bloody childish. It won't work.'

Terence was unruffled. 'Course it will, dear boy. Simplicity! And its precisely the childishness that will create the intrigue. Imagine it – when Christmas Eve comes, who can fail to be touched by the sound of "Silent Night", played personally by the whole band, in order to wish them the compliments of the season.' He spread his arms wide. 'The King does it at Buckingham Palace with the whole of the Grenadier Guards band.'

Wilson Brown snorted and moved from the fireplace to the whisky decanter.

Terence relaxed. He noted with satisfaction that Wilson Brown had stuffed the paper surreptitiously into his inside pocket. Bait taken. Terence sauntered over and held out his glass, but it was ignored. He shrugged and helped himself.

'My house is on your list.'

Terence nodded. 'Of course. Easiest way to allay suspicion – makes you one of the victims.'

'I know that,' said Wilson Brown irritably. 'What I would like to know is . . . am I to be turned over as well.'

Terence smiled. 'Would I do that to an old mate?'

Wilson Brown grunted. It was a politician's answer, and he made a mental note to place his valuables in the bank. This last thought brightened him considerably – every item locked away in a safe deposit could be claimed on the insurance as stolen. He began a quick mental assessment of the size of his claim, but his thoughts were interrupted by a discreet tap on the door, and Mrs Farley eased in.

'Ah, Mrs Farley,' said Terence cheerfully.

She ignored him and addressed her master. 'If you don't mind, sir, I'd like to go up to my room now.'

'Not well, Mrs Farley?' he asked solicitously, although he knew the answer. She was suffering from a severe case of Rembrandt.

'Off you go, then, Mrs Farley, and I hope you feel better tomorrow.'

'Thank you, sir. I've left some cold meat and salad in the dining-room.'

'Splendid, Mrs Farley,' said Terence.

He might not have been present. 'Will that be all right, sir?' she asked.

'It'll do, Mrs Farley, thank you. Now off you go and get a good night's rest.'

She bobbed slightly to Wilson Brown and glided out as if on wheels.

Terence squared his shoulders. 'That's the style, Joe,' he said. 'Always look after the lower decks.'

Wilson Brown grunted. 'Nothing wrong with her that your departure won't cure, and that goes for me too.' He settled back in his chair, then suddenly shot bolt upright as if the springs had broken through. 'Wait a minute,' he said. 'Mrs Farley knows you're here. She'll be questioned by the police. She'll have your descriptions, and it won't be too difficult to place two and two together – they'll soon trace the connections.'

Terence had already thought of this. 'She doesn't know who we are, does she?' He spread his arms reasonably. 'And at the time of the, er, incident, we will be in London, so why should we arouse suspicion?'

Wilson Brown's jaw dropped. 'But how will you be in London?' he asked stupidly.

'An express leaves Piccadilly Station, Manchester, about four on Christmas Eve. We'll be on it.' He looked intently into Wilson Brown's face, like a doctor trying to diagnose an ailment. 'Look, Joe, just do as you're told and leave the real thinking to me.'

Wilson Brown looked haggard. He had a feeling that somehow or other he was going to be left holding something nasty. He spoke in a small voice. 'I think I'll go up to my room.'

Terence patted him on the shoulder. 'Cheer up, Joe, there's nothing you can't get over except death.' He laughed. 'Tell you what – why don't you take the car and go into town and have a drink somewhere?'

Wilson Brown gave a mirthless laugh. 'You've had it so bloody often in the last fortnight they'll think I've stolen it.' He made his way slowly towards the door.

Terence called after him: 'Oh, by the way, you haven't got a record of "Silent Night" have you?'

SIXTEEN

Kenneth Sagbottom was a happy postman. He enjoyed delivering parcels in his little red van – he was an all-year-round Father Christmas – and when the day came to lay down his sack for the last time he had a pension to look forward to. He whistled as he knocked at number 46. While he waited he read the address on the parcel. Then he looked over his shoulder, but a grimy privet hedge hid his van from sight and he was unable to see the new Vauxhall creeping to a standstill behind it. He knocked again but there was no answer, so he walked round the back and tapped on the window. Old Mrs Buckley waved and got up to open the door.

'Mornin', Mrs Buckley. Parcel for you.'

'For me?' she said.

'Yes.'

'I wonder who it could be from?'

'It's from your son George – look.' He pointed to the sender's address.

She peered at it closely.

Kenneth waited patiently. She got a parcel every week from her son, but there was always the same performance. Once he'd wondered idly what George put in the parcels. Food? Magazines? But then again, knowing what a miserable devil George was, the most likely bet was his dirty laundry.

'It's from my son,' she said. 'He lives in Blackburn.'

'That's right. Would you just sign here, please?'

She did so, and he made his way round to the front, whistling. When he reached the gate his lips remained

125

pursed, but nothing came out . . . his van had gone. A knot of panic gripped his stomach. He craned sideways to look round the back of the new Vauxhall, but it wasn't there. He even stopped to look underneath. In a flash he saw his comfortable little world crumbling. The sun came out for a minute when the thought crossed his mind that he couldn't be held responsible if a gang had stolen his van, but the sky quickly darkened again. He was in the wrong for leaving the motor running. A flash of lightning brightened his eyes – it was old Mrs Buckley's fault, he thought childishly. If she had answered the front door like she should, he would have seen it go. But then again, he knew in his heart that she wasn't to blame. He decided to go home and tell his mother – she'd know what to do, she always did. But on this occasion she didn't.

She shook her head worriedly. 'Whatever possessed you to leave it standing in the road like that?'

He wrung his hands. 'I had to. I had to take a parcel round the back, Mam.'

Poor Kenneth, forty-two years old, and in moments of stress he still called her 'Mam'.

She stared into the fire. 'Well, I don't know what we can do. I don't. I mean, did you look properly?'

'Yes, Mam,' he said with a great sigh.

'Oh, Kenneth, you haven't an ounce of grey matter, have you? They'll make you pay for it, you know.'

He was biting his thumbnail. He'd already thought of that, but he still harboured a wild idea that she'd think of something.

'What will we do if you have to pay for it?' she asked petulantly.

He shrugged, his brain racing like an arthritic tortoise.

She tweaked her nose with a corner of her apron. 'I don't know, I don't.' She turned to address the fire: 'You slave and scrimp, to get 'em in the Post Office, and they no sooner get on the vans and they go and lose it.'

'It wasn't my fault, Mam,' he wailed.

She came to a decision. 'Never mind whose fault it is,' she said. 'Fetch me me shawl.'

126

'Where are we goin', Mam?' he asked anxiously.

'Where are we goin'? I'll tell you where we're goin'. You have while six o'clock before you report back to the Post Office, so we're goin' to look for it.'

He flapped his hands helplessly. 'Where will we look, Mam?' he asked plaintively.

'I don't know,' she said. 'But one thing I'm certain of, we won't find it sittin' on our backsides,' and she snatched the shawl from him.

In fact, the little red post van was chugging up the wide sweeping drive at Holmedene on the Binglewood Estate.

'Here we are, sorr, number one on de hit parade.'

Terence leaned forward in his seat to take in the magnificent old house. All he got was a blurred impression of something huge, but then he was wearing thick pebble glasses, which, with an enormous walrus moustache, completely altered his appearance. He spoke to Rembrandt as he lifted his glasses to examine the facade. 'Right! When we get in there, you keep your thieving hands to yourself, understand? Touch nothing – I don't care if it's a dog dropping, you don't touch it, right?'

Rembrandt sat there unmoved. 'Oi wouldn't touch one of dem. Oi don't like dogs, an dat's a fact.'

Terence heaved himself out of the van. 'Good. Get the tools and follow me.'

Rembrandt ignored him. 'Oi'll stay in here if der's a dog. Oi don't want nothin' to do wid a dog.'

Terence opened the door and hauled him outside like a sack of potatoes. 'How should I know if they have a dog?' he hissed. 'That's what we're here to find out. Now get the tools and follow me.'

Rembrandt did so and hurried after him, just in time to prevent Terence walking into an ornamental lily pond. 'The house is over dere, sorr.'

'I know where it is,' said Terence peevishly, and turned to walk towards the house with a confidence he didn't feel.

Rembrandt shuffled to the front door and watched patiently as Terence peremptorily knocked on the garage door.

Lifting his glasses, he glanced round to get his bearings, then joined Rembrandt in the front porch. 'They don't build garages like that any more,' he said in an offhand way.

Rembrandt wasn't fooled for a second. He avoided Terence's groping hand and hammered the door knocker.

Terence wondered whether the glasses were a mistake, but then again, nobody would connect this shortsighted stoop-shouldered menial with Commander Wilson Brown's suave, debonair house guest. Slowly the door opened, and Terence touched the peak of his cap to the tall, blurred shape of the manservant.

'Post Office engineers to check the telephones.'

'Tradesmen round the back,' intoned the dark mass, and closed the door.

'Round-the-back-sorr,' said Rembrandt with careful enunciation.

'It's only the glasses. I'm not deaf, you cretinous Guinness bag!'

Raising the glasses, he made his way round the rear of the house, making a careful mental note of the layout.

The manservant took even longer to open the back door. 'Yes?' he inquired.

'Post Office engineers to check the telephones.'

'The apparatus was in use not ten minutes ago, and it appeared perfectly functional then.' The door slammed, almost smashing Terence's brilliant disguise.

They looked at each other, but remained where they were. Terence pretended to examine his fingernails, although he couldn't have seen his hand, while Rembrandt stared at the woodwork. In less than five minutes the door was flung open and the manservant almost knocked them down.

'Ah, there you are,' he said, trying to regain some of his dignity. 'You're quite right, it doesn't appear to be working. Would you follow me?'

They nodded to each other knowingly. It's very difficult for a telephone to work if someone is dastardly enough to cut the wires.

The servant hovered around while they busied themselves. He watched in amazement and wondered how a man so afflicted with blindness could identify a fault in the complicated electrical circuit.

Terence turned in his direction. 'Bai gum. A wouldn't mind a cup of tea, if tha's doin' nowt,' he said in a dreadful parody of a Lancashire accent. He was quite safe: broad Lancashire at Holmedene was as foreign as Swahili.

'I am not the cook,' droned the servant.

'A didn't mean thee. I meant for thee to ask t'cuke.'

'Nor is this a restaurant.' He folded his arms and stood immovable, which was the last thing Terence wanted. 'Ast'a an extension?' He stood up.

'Certainly, they're in the bedrooms,' the man said.

'Well, if you wouldn't mind, like.' Terence gestured for him to show the way, which he reluctantly did, but he watched them even more closely – after all, it was the master's bedroom. Terence groped for the telephone and listened for a moment.

'Robin, lad, will you go t' van and get me t'circuit tester?'

Rembrandt turned to see who the dickens Robin was.

Terence grabbed him by the sleeve. 'I'm waiting, Robin.'

'Ah yes, sorr. Robin, dat's me. Oi'll go and get dat stuff, sorr.'

'Thank you, Robin. Mind you wipe tha feet, and close t'door after you.'

Rembrandt stood still for a moment, then, in a rare flash of intuition, he knew what was wanted. 'Oi'll close the door all right, sorr.' And he went.

Terence smiled ingratiatingly at where he thought the servant was. 'E's a one, is Robin. He dun't luke much, but e's a wizard with wires.'

There was no reply, and for a moment Terence thought he might be alone and wondered whether to chance taking his glasses off. Then a voice came from somewhere behind him. God – he hoped he hadn't smiled ingratiatingly at the wardrobe. He slowly turned towards the sound.

'How long do you propose to be? I have other duties to attend to.'

Terence pursed his lips. 'Well, if it's a contact tumbler, we have a replacement, but it might be the vibratory coil.' He

129

was about to elaborate but prudence shackled his tongue. Unable to see the effect of his words, he might be digging a pit for himself – he might even be talking to Marconi. 'Ah well,' he said, 'I'll mek a cup o' tea meself if you'll show me wher all t'stuff is.' He didn't expect a reply, but he had to play for time. Where was Rembrandt? Knowing the scrofulous idiot, he was probably scrabbling about in the back of the van searching for a circuit tester – whatever that may be. The silence began to unnerve Terence, but just as he was about to open his mouth to speak four faint thuds came from the bowels of the hall.

'Somebody's at the front door now,' clucked the servant, and Terence felt the whiff of brilliantine as he swept past him.

Quick as a flash Terence had the glasses in his pocket and was at the window behind the curtain, slipping the catch but leaving the window closed – if somebody latched it in the meantime, there were other ways. Then he made a swift inventory of the drawers and cupboards and went on into the next room. A bell sounded below and Terence froze in his tracks. Then he breathed again – full marks to Rembrandt: he'd been to the front, knowing full well he'd be ordered round the back, thus gaining a few more valuable seconds. Perhaps he had underestimated him. He didn't wait to examine the thought, for he had work to do, and by the time Rembrandt and the servant returned he was staring closely at the telephone.

'Oi couldn't find the – er – piece, sorr. Oi tink it's out on another job.'

'I'm not bothered now,' said Terence straightening. 'Ave found t'fault.'

The servant was impressed. 'Is it all right now?'

'Nay, it's not. It's a fault on t'line, I'll have to report it at t'depot.'

The servant's face fell.

'Is der any chance of a cup of tea before we go?' said Rembrandt.

'As I said before, this is not a café.' He shepherded them to the back door.

In the next couple of hours three more houses developed inexplicable telephone faults, but with an efficiency remarkable in the Post Office two engineers were on the spot almost immediately – useless, as it turned out, but willing.

Terence, a stickler for details, left the engine running in the little red van and settled himself in the new Vauxhall. 'Home, James, and don't spare the horses.'

Rembrandt released the handbrake, and once again they entered the gates of the Binglewood Estate, but before they put the car in the garage Terence, with the touch of a master, snipped the telephone wires in order to join the victims, and let himself in through the front door. Undoubtedly the covering of his tracks was a stroke of genius.

After finding the little red van exactly where he had left it, poor Kenneth Sagbottom dropped his mother home where she stood on a chair to box his ears. But, as he complained to his teddy that night: it wasn't a joke – somebody had taken it.

CHAPTER

SEVENTEEN

Due to its geographical situation, it was not uncommon for Grapplewick to be covered in a foot of snow while in nearby Blackburn and Bolton an overcoat was unnecessary. Conversely, this year December had slid into the town sunless but mild, and at the same time travellers from Blackburn were alighting at the depot wrapped up like overfed penguins, marvelling at the soft breeze. The workers clockered towards the mills, learning again to walk upright, and pleasant conversation about the weather dominated the morning. It was too good to last, however, and the hardy ones who had gone to work without even scarves scurried home cursing the fickleness of the elements. Most people relaxed in front of their fires th t evening, except those living in the vicinity of the Fire Station. It was Thursday – band practice night – and unless you were stone deaf it was a good night for the pictures or the pub.

Mr Thurk surveyed himself in the mirror and adjusted his cap. Then he gave his red sash a tweak – only a fraction, but it mattered. He was about to don his white gloves when there was a knock at the door. A flicker of annoyance crossed over his face, for he was a punctual man and he was already cutting it a bit fine. His brow cleared when he saw his visitor.

'Hello, Dorothy. This is a nice surprise.'

She edged past him towards the fire, and he popped his head out quickly to look up and down the street before closing the door. One or two curtains in the houses opposite fell back into place, and in any case there was Her Ladyship's unmistakable Daimler parked right outside. They'd all know who the visitor was and how long the visit lasted, but after all he was over twenty-one.

'Anthony, I know it's Thursday, but I have something to tell you and it may be important.'

'Oh?' He motioned to a chair but she shook her head, hardly able to contain herself.

'I went to see Mrs Helliwell this morning.'

He looked puzzled. 'Mrs Helliwell?'

'You know, Walter Helliwell's mother – he was at Dunkirk.'

'Ah yes, he fell under a train on his first leave.' He shuddered.

She allowed a moment's silence in respect, then she continued. 'That's what sparked me off. You see, Mrs Helliwell happened to be reading the press cuttings about it – they're all carefully pasted in a scrapbook. Poor dear, she's finding things very difficult since her husband died.'

He nodded in sympathy. No one realised the effect his son's tragic death had had on old Tommy Helliwell, until one freezing night in the cold winter of 1945 he polished his boots, put on his best suit and left the house. Nobody took much notice of the hole in the ice on the reservoir, and it wasn't until the thaw that they found him. Mr Thurk pulled himself together and glanced involuntarily at the clock.

'I'm sorry,' she said.

'No, no. That's all right, plenty of time.' The lie came easily, but he wished she'd sit down. His feet were killing him.

'I'll be as brief as I can,' she said, 'but I think it's important.'

'Take your time,' he said gently, and settled gratefully into the chair, gesturing towards the other.

'Thank you,' she said. 'After I left the Helliwells I started thinking, and decided to pay the *Grapplewick Chronicle* a visit, or to be more precise, Arthur Taylor. He's a neighbour of mine, as you know, and he kindly put the facilities of the newspaper at my disposal. He didn't ask me why, and I didn't tell him, but together with some of the staff I rummaged through the back numbers of the *Chronicle* covering the war years.' She stopped and looked at him.

'And?' He was beginning to get the drift, but how much had she discovered?

'Your brother,' she went on, 'Sergeant air gunner, quite a bit about him. Helliwell, Buckley, Waterhouse, who was at Arnhem, John Ashton and, er, whatsisname, er, young. . . .' She snapped her fingers for whatsisname's name.

'Yes, Dorothy, but I should say that nearly everyone local who was in the forces got in the paper some time, even if it was only for joining up.'

She leaned forward. 'Except Commander Wilson Brown.'

'Ah.' He sat back.

She was triumphant. 'Strange, don't you think?'

'Well, yes,' he said, flicking a speck of something off his trousers. 'But not having resided in Grapplewick for some years before the war, they may have overlooked him.'

She stood up. 'They may, but I'm not satisfied, and tomorrow I'm going to ring a friend of mine in the Admiralty.'

He rose wearily. 'Dorothy, please don't do that.'

Her eyes widened. 'But why not? We must find out.'

He sighed. 'I'll save you the trouble. Sit down.' They settled again. 'There won't be any reference to Commander Wilson Brown in the Navy lists, at least not our Wilson Brown.'

She rose to her feet. 'You mean he was never in the Navy?'

He looked at her. 'That's about the size of it.'

She slumped back in the chair. 'Are you positive about this?'

He spread his hands. 'I'm afraid so, Dorothy. I've known about it ever since he was elected to the Council.'

She stared at him for a moment. 'This is what you meant when you said you could get rid of him tomorrow?'

He nodded.

She looked at him incredulously. 'But why? I don't understand. If you've known all this time, why don't you get rid

134

of him? Well, for God's sake, Anthony, you know what he's doing – he's taking Grapplewick away from you.'

He stared into the banked coals. 'I may pull the rug from under him yet.'

She was exasperated. 'It may be too late! Why, oh why, didn't you act when you first found out?'

He shrugged. 'I was intrigued, and in the early days he was like a breath of fresh air in the Town Hall. He wasn't short of ideas. He was a driving force. He put a stiffening into the Council when it was flabby.' He looked down at his hands. 'But I suppose, most of all, I wanted to see where he was going.'

She leaned forward and tapped his knee urgently. 'But now we know where he's going. He wants Grapplewick, not your Grapplewick but a monstrous, soulless concrete desert – and incidentally, he wants to pile up a nice little fortune in the process.'

This time he stood and leaned his forehead on the mantelpiece. 'He has money, Dorothy,' he said to the fire, 'and I don't think his interest is purely financial.'

She sighed heavily. 'For heaven's sake, Anthony, at least go and see him and tell him what you know.'

He turned to face her. 'Dorothy, I couldn't do that. It would be blackmail.'

'I haven't noticed the Commander fighting with kid gloves on,' she said forcefully.

'I know, Dorothy, but to expose him will be a last resort.' He took her by the shoulders. 'Can't you see, Dorothy? We have all the cards, and I don't intend to turn them all face-up at this stage, simply to destroy a man.' She turned away and he gently took her chin until she was facing him again. 'But make no mistake,' he said earnestly, 'if I can be sure that you are right, and that he's using the town simply to fatten his bank account, I'll have him.'

She looked at him for a moment, then her shoulders sagged. 'All right, Anthony. I know that you'll do what's best.' Her eyes glistened. 'You're a good man, d'you know that?' She broke away to fumble in her handbag, and he laughed.

135

'That's not what the lads'll think when I turn up half an hour late.'

'I'm sorry,' she said. 'I've spent all this time trying to teach my grandmother to suck eggs.' She brightened. 'Come on I'll give you a lift.'

Again the curtains across the street fell back into place as he got in the car.

'They don't miss much round here, do they?' she said switching on the ignition.

'An unhealthy preoccupation,' he said. 'A black car in this street usually means a funeral.'

It was no distance to the fire station, and hardly worth getting into the car, but he enjoyed the luxury of the Daimler, and Dorothy wasn't a bad driver as long as there was little traffic and the road didn't bend. In less than four minutes they were there, and would have arrived sooner had she overtaken the cyclist.

'Well done, Dorothy,' he said, 'and thanks for coming to see me.' He patted her hand on the steering wheel. It was too dark to see her expression, but she suddenly leaned across and kissed him on the cheek. It startled him, and he looked quickly round to see if there was anybody about. But he needn't have bothered – on cold nights Grapplewick was like the inside of a pyramid. 'Well, er, thanks for the lift,' he said lamely, and got out. He bent towards the window to wave, but the car suddenly shot forward, as if Dorothy was embarrassed by her impulsive gesture. Grand girl, that, he thought as he watched the tail lights disappear.

It was then that he noticed the car parked opposite. It looked like Commander Wilson Brown's car, but it couldn't be – Wilson Brown would go a mile out of his way rather than pass the Station, let alone park right outside. He entered the yard and one of the Clydesdales in the stable snickered and stamped a great foot. He sighed: they were planning a new world that had no place for Ajax and Ramillies. . . .

He remembered the band practice and strode briskly into the Station. The lights, shining brightly, made the old tender gleam like a precious metal. Then he stopped – good grief, the ladder had gone now! He frowned: there was something else. He walked slowly round the old engine, then it hit him – it was on wood blocks. Right! He'd have it out with them tonight. They meant well, but dammit there were limits. If there was a fire in Grapplewick they'd be about as useful as an ashtray on a motor bike.

He strode over to the stairs leading up to the band room and flicked on the light switch, but there was nothing. He flicked it up and down but there was no light. Good grief – they're not flogging the bulbs as well, are they? At the back of his mind something else bothered him, and in a flash he knew what it was. No music. He should have been able to hear the band streets away, but apart from a desultory mumbling and shuffling from the room above all was quiet. He started up the stairs, but on the second step he stumbled over a helmet that had been strategically placed, and barely seconds after it had rolled to the floor the strains of 'Abide with Me' crashed out from the band room. Good God: they must think he'd fallen off a Christmas tree. When he entered the room there'd be no sign of the cards and football coupons, and music would be covering the magazines. He limped up the stairs trying to decide how to tackle several situations.

Ned Bladdock tapped the conductor's stand and the lads put down their instruments. 'Evening, Chief. It's coming. We've hammered out the passage from letter B, and it's nearly there.'

Mr Thurk nodded. 'I'm sorry I'm late, lads. Something urgent cropped up.' He squared his shoulders and stood resolutely in front of them. 'I've just been examining the tender, and I think I'm due some kind of explanation.'

Ned looked at his Chief and he knew that the kettle was about to boil, so he decided to turn down the gas. He jerked his head to the corner. 'Chief, have you got a minute?'

Mr Thurk followed him out of earshot of the band. 'What is it?' he asked testily.

Ned leaned to him and whispered, 'You've got lipstick on your face.'

Mr Thurk's hand shot to his cheek as if a mosquito had

crashed into it. 'Thank you, Ned,' he mumbled. 'Thank you.'

Ned strode back to his place behind the big drum.

Mr Thurk fronted the band again, but he was flustered. His resolution had gone. He spread his hands. 'Lads, lads,' he pleaded. 'You know what I'm on about.'

Ned relaxed. The bomb was defused.

Mr Thurk sighed. 'I'm only going to say one thing to you all. By the weekend I want to see that tender fully equipped again.'

The band eyed him sullenly, then Jack Puller spat into an empty bean can he always brought to rehearsals. 'If we've got to take all these instruments back, that'll be t'end of t'band.'

Mr Thurk shook his head. 'Not necessarily. I'll have a go at the Council again tomorrow.'

Jack spat again. 'That'll be like tryin' to get Ned here to buy a bloody drink,' he said.

Ned ignored him. 'What about allocating something from, say, the housing fund?'

'I'm afraid not,' said Mr Thurk sadly. 'Most of the housing fund goes to the upkeep of the park.'

Ned brightened. 'Well, there's a bandstand in the park. We should be entitled to something out of the park fund.' He looked round, and the band nodded.

'Impossible,' said Mr Thurk. 'The surplus from the park fund was swallowed up decorating the Town Hall.' He tapped his baton on the stand. 'Anyway, let's make the most of the instruments while we've got 'em: "Three Jolly Sailormen".' He raised his arms and waited until they sorted themselves out. 'Right, lads, Briskly now . . . one, two, three.'

The band responded with the briskness of a very old bull elephant making its way to the graveyard.

Terence, huddled in the car outside the Fire Station, winced. He'd never been a music lover, and what he was hearing tonight didn't tempt him to change his mind. He unscrewed the top of his whisky flask and took a deep pull. Oh, God, if only he had Elsie in the car with him. He felt sure her husband wouldn't mind him sharing the load. It was impossible tonight anyway – she fancied the reckless dashing Major Terence, and she would never have recognised the fat, doddering, white-haired old blimp. He considered for a moment nipping into the Dog and Partridge afterwards and giving, himself a build-up, but he dismissed the thought. He wasn't sure that his make-up would stand close scrutiny in the bright lights of the saloon bar.

An hour and twenty minutes later he was about to abandon the evening when in the gloom across the road a man emerged from the yard, and he realised that the band had packed it in some minutes ago. As the figure passed under the street lamp Terence recognised the band leader, who must be Mr Thurk. He struggled out of the car and called, 'Mr Thurk . . . I say, you there, is that Mr Thurk?'

The Mayor stopped and then approached him. 'Yes, I'm Mr Thurk. Can I help you?'

'I hope so, sir, I hope so,' said Terence fervently, in a passable imitation of an alcoholic Colonel in the Indian Army. 'Allow me to introduce myself. My name is Colonel Harper Warburton, ex 47th Punjab Regiment.'

Mr Thurk held out his hand tentatively. 'Pleased to meet you.'

Terence gave his padding an unobtrusive hitch and eased into the deep shadow. 'Firstly, let me congratulate you on your excellent band.'

Mr Thurk beamed. 'Really?' He didn't quite know how to accept the compliment – no one ever enthused about the band. It was as if George Washington's father had said, 'Thank God you got rid of that tree.'

Terence went on, 'I haven't heard music like that since we evacuated Cawnpore.'

'Really?' said Mr Thurk again, and cleared his throat in embarrassment. There must be something else he could say besides 'really'. 'Er, would you like to step into the Station . . . there's a cup of tea in there.' He made to take the Colonel's arm, but Terence shrank back into the shadows.

'I thank you kindly, sir, but no. I, er, have other rather pressing engagements, so I'll come straight to the point.'

'R. . . .' Mr Thurk closed his mouth in time to stop himself saying 'really' again.

'I know that your engagement book must be full, and time is short, but I would like to hire the band.'

Mr Thurk stared at him in amazement. 'Hire the band?' he said in a strangled voice.

'That's the idea,' said Terence briskly. 'I know that it may seem a strange request, but I would like them to play carols on Christmas Eve, or, to be more exact, one carol: "Silent Night".'

Mr Thurk was wallowing in uncharted waters. 'We've played carols before, yes, but er. . . .' He trailed off as Terence's shadowy form extracted something from an inside pocket.

'I trust you won't be offended, but I have here an envelope containing one hundred pounds.' Mr Thurk took a step back. 'One hundred pounds!' he gasped.

'I know this may seem to you an unorthodox manner of conducting business, but I'm a man of action . . . objective planning and execution – that's my motto.' He thrust the envelope at Mr Thurk as if it were a declaration of war, and there was little Mr Thurk could do but accept it.

His pride rebelled, however, and he held it out to the Colonel. 'I'm sorry, Colonel er. . . .'

'Warper Harburton,' beamed Terence.

Mr Thurk didn't notice the slip. 'I'm sorry, Colonel, but a hundred pounds seems a little extravagant for one carol.'

Terence ignored the envelope. 'This, of course, includes your transportation to the Binglewood Estate, plus the fact that I would require you to play the carol exactly at twenty hundred hours on Christmas Eve.'

'Eight o'clock in the evening?'

'Correct,' said Terence. 'Firstly in the driveway outside the house called Holmedene. After finishing the carol, you will proceed to The Beeches, and repeat your performance at Woodhaven East, then finally Seven Seas.'

Mr Thurk became wary. 'Did you say Seven Seas?' he asked.

'Correct,' said the badly stuffed Colonel. 'An old acquaintance of mine – Commander Wilson Brown.'

'Oh,' said Mr Thurk casually. 'Meet him during the war?'

It was too casual, and there were moments when the speed of Terence's brain amazed himself. 'God, no. Met him a couple of years ago in the Army and Navy Club.'

Mr Thurk relaxed visibly, and Terence sensed that he had avoided a rather nasty minefield. 'I must be honest with you,' said Mr Thurk. 'I don't think he'll appreciate us playing outside his house.' He laughed. 'He might even charge us with trespass and disturbing the peace.'

'Nonsense, old boy. I've already warned him I've planned something rather special. He'll be tickled pink . . . no fears on that score. If I know the old curmudgeon he'll accept anything that's free.' He was about to laugh heartily, then thought better of it – he wasn't all that securely put together. He patted his pockets and took out another envelope. 'Ah, here it is. Can't get used to these pockets in mufti, what?'

Mr Thurk, even more mystified, took it.

'In that envelope you'll find all the relevant information, plus a map of the Binglewood Estate.'

Mr Thurk gazed unseeingly at the envelope. 'I don't quite know what to say. I mean, it's all rather unusual.'

'Think nothing of it,' barked Terence. 'They're all acquaintances of mine, and it's a rather novel Christmas present, wouldn't you say?' He laughed heartily and saluted. 'Well, must be off.' He turned, then stopped. 'Oh, and if you wouldn't mind keeping this to yourself. Wouldn't want the surprise to be ruined, what?' And with that he bumbled across the road to the car, the darkness hiding the feathers that were escaping beneath his greatcoat.

Mr Thurk watched the rear lights disappearing round Horsedge Street; then he looked down at the two envelopes in his hands.

The lads sat round the band room. Conversation had been spasmodic since Mr Thurk's departure, and the feeling of discontent was almost tangible.

141

Jack Puller lifted his head. 'I say bugger 'im, if we hang on to these instruments what can 'e do? Tell me that, what can 'e do?'

Ned shook his head. 'It's no use talking like that, Jack. We've been ordered.'

Jack was unmoved. 'All right, then. What're we goin' to practise on? Band's done for, I'm tellin' you. If we have to wait for a grant from t'town we'll all be too bloody old to blow.'

Nobody had any other suggestions, but they were loath to leave – they needed each other's comfort.

Barmy stood against the wall with his hands behind his back. 'OK,' he grinned.

They ignored him.

He patted his stomach.

'All right,' said Helliwell. 'I'll nip out for some fish and chips.'

But before he reached the door it burst open and Mr Thurk strode in. All heads lifted – he was beaming. 'Don't forget, lads, first thing tomorrow morning I want you at Cowell and Bottisford's to reclaim our stuff.'

The lads moved restlessly. He hadn't come back to rub it in, had he? Mr Thurk strolled over to Ned and chucked the envelope in his lap. 'Any instruments you want, you can pay for out of that.' He smiled. 'Oh, and don't forget the change.' Then he turned and walked back to the door. 'And I'll want a full set of band parts for "Silent Night".' Then he was gone.

Silence followed him, then Ned slit open the envelope with his finger and drew out a wad of crisp fivers. 'Bai the bloody 'ell,' he said, 'he's a bloody miracle worker.'

Ned rose slowly. 'It's always darkest before the dawn.'

Jack grabbed the money. 'Never mind the bloody dawn,' he said gleefully. 'What about a pint before we go?'

Naturally Mr Bottisford was both relieved and delighted to return all the fire equipment. Lack of space had become an embarrassment – he even had parts of the appliance stuffed in his bedroom, and it had become something of an ordeal to make his way up and down stairs, so he hadn't

142

minded being roused in the early hours by a hung-over Fire Brigade to reclaim their equipment under cover of darkness. He was also delighted to put something in the till besides tunic buttons.

Half an hour later Grapplewick stirred itself to face a new day. There was considerably less clockering of the clogs in the direction of the factories – cotton was being manufactured more cheaply in other parts of the world. The Empire was dwindling, countries abroad were now competitors instead of easy markets, resources which were once accessible were now being used against Britain, and more workers were being laid off at the Monarch Mills, while next door at the Rutland they were already on short time. Fortunately the new Welfare State cushioned some of the despair that had gripped them in the thirties, and Christmas was on its way. The first fall of snow dazzled the early risers, but already, with a pale watery sun, the roads were a thin brown slush. It was a significant day, however. The whole Council was meeting to discuss the fate of Grapplewick. At best it would be a stay of execution, but more likely the bulldozers would be called in – in the warm spaces cold buildings would rise, and the bewildered townspeople would be housed but homeless.

Edward Helliwell made his way slowly up the Town Hall steps. Head down, he almost bumped into Wilson Brown, moving even more slowly.

'Sorry, Commander,' he said lifting a gloved hand to his hat.

Wilson Brown gave him a cursory glance and continued to negotiate the steps.

What's the matter with him these days, thought Helliwell. Probably still suffering from that do in the court room. However the news he had to impart would cheer the old bugger up. 'Oh, Commander. . . .'

Wilson Brown stopped and turned slowly, waiting.

'Oh, Commander, before you go in I have a little bit of information that might interest you.' He looked round, but they were alone, and fairly sheltered from the wind.

Nevertheless Wilson Brown turned his collar up, bleak

143

eyes staring at the war memorial opposite. 'Information?' he said off-handedly.

Helliwell wasn't put off. Wilson Brown would soon perk up when he heard what he had to say. 'About a week ago I was passing the Fire Station yard, and I noticed something odd.'

Wilson Brown looked down at his feet. 'Oh, yes?'

'Yes, something definitely wrong.' He looked over his shoulder again, and edged close. 'There was no bell, no ladder – in fact it was stripped down.'

The Commander studied him for a moment. 'It could be the equipment was in the Station.'

'Ah,' said Helliwell triumphantly. 'That's what *I* thought, but then I made some inquiries. I'm not without my sources, you know,' he added smugly.

The Commander surveyed the war memorial again. 'And?'

Helliwell touched his arm. 'The fact of the matter is, they have been trading the equipment to Cowell and Bottisford in return for musical instruments.'

Wilson Brown turned to him slowly. 'That's a very serious accusation.'

'It's true,' beamed Helliwell earnestly.

'Given that you are right, what do you intend to do about it?'

Helliwell was becoming exasperated at the lukewarm reaction. He hadn't expected a bouquet of flowers, but at least a light show of enthusiasm would have been in order. 'Don't you see . . . we've got him . . . the Mayor.'

'Oh.' Wilson Brown's eyebrows went up a shade.

'Well, he may not be directly involved,' went on Helliwell, 'but as Chief he must accept the ultimate responsibility.' He clucked his tongue sanctimoniously. 'If this became known, it could ruin him.'

Wilson Brown turned his head away. 'Is that what you want?'

Helliwell feigned indignation. 'Of course not. Nobody wants that to happen, but in any case nobody need ever know.' He dragged his hanky out and wiped his nose. 'Providing we have his vote for the slum clearance.'

Wilson Brown surveyed him with ill-disguised contempt. In a flash of insight he saw what his mind had been unwilling to accept. Mr Thurk was the only man for Grapplewick – a dedicated man, with no thought of personal gain. He felt a sudden surge of warmth for the man, which surprised him pleasantly. He looked steadily at Helliwell: what a miserable, jumped-up pipsqueak – oh, he'd get on all right, his sort always did. He turned away from the smug white face, hands clenched in his pockets.

Helliwell, misinterpreting the flash of anger in his eyes, nodded complacently. That'll teach him to underestimate me, he thought.

Councillor Pilkington hurried up the steps with a briefcase under his arm. 'Big day, eh?' He touched his hat, not waiting for a reply, and went inside.

Silly sod, always hurrying about with a briefcase under his arm. He'd hurry out of his office and scuttle along, then hurry back to the office to find out where he was supposed to be hurrying to. Never mind, he'd got it right today, and he was pretty certain to vote in the right direction. Helliwell cheered up. If the slum clearance went through, they'd have their high-rise flats, and he'd be out of Waterloo Street and domiciled on the Binglewood Estate before the scaffolding went up.

Across the street a bus pulled into the kerb and old deaf Crumpshaw got off. As usual he immediately began to cross the road, never looking right nor left, and he certainly couldn't hear. Wilson Brown watched, fascinated. How he'd survived so long was a mystery, but then he'd been crossing this road before motor cars were invented, which possibly gave him immunity. Wilson Brown turned to go inside when a movement caught the corner of his eye. A grocer's van was approaching too fast for comfort on the treacherous surface, and the driver, obviously seeing old Crumpshaw too late, clapped on his brakes. Skidding sideways to the other side of the road, it missed the old fellow by a whisker, to crash sickeningly into a lamp-post. At the same time a

145

Daimler travelling sedately in the opposite direction was forced to swerve, spinning in a complete circle before mounting the kerb in front of the Town Hall.

Oblivious of the chaos behind him, old Crumpshaw wheezed up the steps. He nodded to Wilson Brown. 'Cold this mornin', eh?' Then he disappeared into the big dark doorway.

'Silly old fool,' said Helliwell. 'He'll get himself killed one day.'

Wilson Brown ignored him. A small crowd had gathered round the van, but he noted with relief that the driver was on his feet, although someone was holding a cloth to his head. At the foot of the steps the Daimler eased forward off the kerb, and he heard the rasp of the brake. Lady Dorothy alighted as coolly as if she always parked in this fashion. As she approached, he doffed his hat.

'Good morning, Commander.' She smiled and swept past him in a cloud of expensive perfume.

He followed her with his eyes. Was it his imagination, or had she stressed the word 'Commander'? A cold hand clutched his heart. One way or another his world was falling to bits. He became aware that Helliwell was speaking. . . . 'Eh?' he said.

'Could have been nasty, that.'

'Oh yes, but I didn't actually see what happened – I was watching old Crumpshaw.' No way was he getting himself involved as a witness – any publicity at the present time was bad news. He turned to go inside, but Helliwell restrained him with a hand on his arm.

'What about Mr Thurk?'

'Ah . . . yes, Mr Thurk. What are you going to do about it?'

Helliwell was flustered. 'Well, I thought. . . .'

'Yes?' inquired Wilson Brown in a deceptively calm voice.

Helliwell spread his hands. 'Well, er,' he floundered. 'I rather thought it would carry more weight from *you*.'

Typical, thought Wilson Brown, they load the gun in secret, then push someone else into the firing line to pull

146

the trigger. He suddenly had an overwhelming urge to smash his fist into the snivelling white face.

Helliwell stepped back. For once he'd read the signs correctly.

The spell was broken by the distant clanging of the fire bell . . . then again, but closer this time. Helliwell gulped – it might be the ambulance for the poor wretch across the road, but a louder clang dashed his hopes. There was only one bell in Grapplewick that sounded like that, and it could only be attached to the fire engine. Ponderously the old juggernaut turned into the High Street and trundled lugubriously towards the Town Hall. Before it had come to a complete stop Mr Thurk relinquished the bell rope and stepped down. Ned Bladdock took his place next to the driver and rubbed his hands vigorously together before grasping the bell rope with joyous anticipation. Mr Thurk said something to the lads, and whatever it was, they laughed. Then with a shuddering roar and a deafening clamour the old engine lurched forward and made its way to wherever it was going.

Mr Thurk watched them for a moment, then turned and made his way up the steps.

'Morning, Helliwell. Morning, Commander.' He saluted as he passed, and disappeared into the Town Hall.

Wilson Brown's eyebrows rose, and he turned to Helliwell. For the first time in weeks he smiled happily. 'Any more bright ideas?'

Helliwell's face was priceless. Somebody had just chopped his Christmas tree down at the very moment he had got the coloured lights to work.

Most of the Councillors were already in the chamber. Some were standing in groups while others were already seated, fumbling with papers. It was going to be a big debate, probably the most important that any of them could remember.

Lady Dorothy was talking to one of the older members when Mr Thurk entered. Her eyes lit up, and she hurried over to meet him. 'Morning, Anthony.'

'Ah, good morning, Dorothy. First snow, eh?' He lugged out his great pocket watch.

She took his arm. 'Anthony, can we go into your room for a minute?'

'We haven't much time.' He smiled apologetically.

'It's important.'

He took out his watch again. 'OK, we have a few minutes.' They made their way along the corridor to the Mayor's Parlour. He closed the door quietly and turned to her. 'Dorothy, I think I know what you're going to say, and the answer is no.'

Her brows came together. 'But Anthony, if Wilson Brown goes against you it could be the end of Grapplewick. He carries a lot of weight.'

'So do I.'

Her mouth tightened in exasperation. 'Anthony, he's an imposter. He has no right to be here at all.'

He shrugged. 'That's my fault. Should have seen him off at the beginning, but now it's gone too far, and perhaps it may be that he's right and I'm wrong.'

Her eyes widened in amazement.

'Dorothy, if I do manage to stop them pulling down Grapplewick, it'll only be a temporary halt. The mills won't last forever, and what happens then? The young people are already drifting away ... the new generation won't be content to spend their life here. Modern technology will make Australia, America or the Far East as accessible to them as Accrington is to us. The *Grapplewick Chronicle* is just about managing to keep its head above water. Thanks to the new powers granted the Trade Unions, one more strike and this town won't have a newspaper – not because of conditions, but in many cases because of a blind backlash of revenge for the indignities of the thirties.'

She moved towards him. 'Anthony, I appreciate that you cannot halt progress, but there are still *people* in Grapplewick – middle-aged people, old people – you must fight for *them*. Remember the bellringers, the Fire Brigade, the Rose Queen Festival, the Good Friday procession.' She took his

148

hand. 'You are the last of the Thurks – don't you owe it to your family?'

Before he could reply, the Secretary popped his head round the door. 'They're waiting, Mr Mayor.'

'Thank you, Wilfred. Ask the attendant to pop in, will you?'

Dorothy smiled. 'Come on, Mr Mayor. Let t'battle commence.'

He laughed. 'OK, you go ahead. Just got to don my chain and I'll be in there.'

The great debate lived up to all expectations. It was unprecedented even by Grapplewick's unorthodox standards, the great surprise being a change of heart by Commander Wilson Brown, who spoke at length against the motion that he had been largely instrumental in composing. Most of the older Councillors were on the side of the Mayor, while the younger progressives were all geared to follow the Commander's banner, Helliwell, never a good speaker at the best of times, and without the backing of Wilson Brown quite weightless, babbled inconsequentially about our debt to the young, but floundered when he referred to babies yet unborn (he said 'stillborn'), and the laugh it provoked did nothing to steady him. He was nearing a breakdown. He had already been advanced a considerable sum of money on the understanding that the slum clearance would go through – he could return the diamond ring, his wife's Christmas present, but what about the deposit on White Pines? He'd already sold his own two up, two down. Through dry lips he mouthed meaningless clichés: progress . . . debt to society . . . he even mentioned the Parthenon. This ended what little support he might have expected. Limply he muttered, 'I beg to move,' and a voice from the public gallery broke the spell: 'Not before bloody time.'

Helliwell slumped back in his seat, acutely aware of the contemptuous gaze of Commander Wilson Brown. No one who valued his position could dare to ally himself with such a travesty of words, and the motion was defeated handsomely. Helliwell, panic-stricken, was frantically trying

149

to find the words to explain to his wife that they might soon have to move back to her mother's house.

Wilson Brown left the chamber feeling better than he had in months, while Lady Dorothy gazed at the Mayor as if he was indeed worshipful. Was it possible that he'd known all along that Wilson Brown would change his attack? And if he didn't know, how infinitely wise of him not to threaten him with blackmail. Mr Thurk sat in the great chair, astonished at his victory, but in his own mind he knew that the reprieve was only temporary. Mercifully he didn't know how brief, but in distant Whitehall, far removed from people, the death of Grapplewick was already on the agenda. He brightened with the thought that there was band practice again this evening: 'Silent Night' was coming along splendidly.

EIGHTEEN

Terence strode out of Heppleworth and Peabody's, one of the more fashionable of Blackburn's dress shops. What with clothes rationing, and a lack of luxury goods, he was pleased and rather surprised at the quality and inexpensiveness of the black silk underwear. At first, when he'd mentioned a present for his wife, a frantic, harassed assistant set out a display of bloomers and camiknickers. The bloomers could only have been Army surplus, dyed to various insipid colours, and the camiknickers looked as if they'd been tried on several times. He eyed them distastefully, and it was only when he mentioned the word 'Duchess' that things had begun to happen. Other shoppers, mostly middle-aged ladies in headscarves, who had been eyeing him with suspicion, stood back a pace in deference to Royalty, and he was received by a servile, dry-hand washing manager who ushered him into a private room. Over a cup of tea and a cigar he graciously accepted black silk underwear, obviously from a private privileged stock; the price was dismissed with a wave of the hand. As he was escorted to the door he wished he'd opted for a fur coat. He shook hands with the manager, who was looking up and down the street for the arrival of a great crested Rolls. Terence read the signs and was away as doubt began to replace the plastic smile. Once Elsie clapped eyes on the flimsies he'd be home and dry.

He didn't remember the drive back to Grapplewick – he was visualising her posing, showing off to him in the black silk. So vivid was the picture that he had to stop once and adjust himself. He even wound down the window to let the cold air revive him – only for a moment, though: he didn't fancy frostbite. Before he realised it he was back in Grapplewick High Street, bustling now with late shoppers, drifting from temptation to doubt, purses clutched tight – a pair of socks, a pipe, a half-crown Cadbury's selection box, a fountain pen perhaps, coloured lights, Christmas trees. He turned into Featherstall Road, a little darker and with not too many people, and pulled up outside the Fire Station. His brow darkened. All was quiet – he would have bet his bottom dollar they would be practising. Had they taken him for a patsy? He was just beginning to simmer when the opening bars of 'Silent Night' crashed out with such intensity that he flinched. God, he hoped they weren't going to play as loud as that – there'd be no point in making their way from house to house. One rendering, and as far away as Accrington people would be humming it. He decided that Colonel Harper Warburton would have to make a discreet visit, tactfully pointing out the proximity of the houses, and suggesting that a fortissimo rendering would ruin the surprise for the others.

Better still, there was a phone box just across the road and Terence was a man for prompt action. After a brief rehearsal, he dialled 999.

'Fire, Police or Ambulance?' asked the bored female voice.

'Fire, please,' bellowed Colonel Harper Warburton.

'Pardon?' said the voice.

'Fire, dammit. Fire!'

'Well,' said the voice. 'I can try them.' But she didn't sound hopeful.

Happy as always, Barmy slung a shovelful of coke into the red-hot stove. 'OK,' he said, blowing a droplet of sweat from the end of his nose. 'Phew,' he breathed, but it never occurred to him to take off his greatcoat. From the room above the band blasted through 'Silent Night', making a mockery of the title. Barmy nodded, satisfied, and strolled round the tender where it was fractionally cooler.

Deciding that a lie-down for a few minutes wouldn't do him any harm, he stretched himself and was about to yawn when he stopped. Something was different. He cocked his head to one side and there it was – under the crashing sound of the band he discerned a ringing, a tinny peevish insistent ringing. 'What's that?' he inquired to his teeth, but they just grinned back at him from the mug. He looked round him to find out the cause, but avoided the desk. In the deep cavern of his mind he knew it was the telephone, but he was loath to accept it. He could only remember it ringing once before, but then he hadn't been alone. Ned Bladdock had answered it, and even he'd had taken his cap off before speaking. Brrr, brrr. 'OK,' said Barmy, hopping round it, but never looking at it in case it was facing him. Panic-stricken, he skipped to the foot of the stairs and yelled, 'Brrr, brrr.' Hesitatingly the band broke off, and in the silence the telephone screamed. 'OK, OK,' yelled Barmy, petrified.

Mr Thurk hurried down the stairs, followed warily by the band. They bunched behind the tender as Mr Thurk made his way to the desk. Barmy hopped behind him, pointing an accusing finger at the telephone. 'Thank you, Mr Chronicle,' he said, picking up the apparatus. 'Grapplewick Fire Brigade speaking,' he said, but by that time Terence was getting out of the car in front of the Dog and Partridge.

Even before he reached the door of the saloon bar the sound of revelry hit him, and he frowned. In the past it was always a bit quiet at this hour, and he'd visualised strolling to the bar and ordering the usual. Then a little badinage, followed by a casual 'Oh by the way, I've got you a little something for Christmas.' Then perhaps a cigarette while she eagerly tore off the wrapping. But now that was another dream up the spout, he swore to himself as he opened the door.

The cacophony was almost physical – it was a bedlam reeking of sweat, cheap perfume and stale beer. Oh, bollocks! Why tonight of all nights? He stuffed the gift under his overcoat – he couldn't casually stroll to the bar and hand it over with this mob. It's hard to be nonchalant when you're being jostled by drunks. He correctly surmised it to be a Christmas office party – bosses, typists and secretaries all equal today with the levelling effect of alcohol. He

153

decided to stay by the door. He only had to catch Elsie's eye and she'd have a large whisky passed over to him like a shot, then they'd know he was Somebody. He craned and bobbed from side to side to get her attention, but it was hopeless – he could only get fleeting glances of the top of her head as she made her way from the pumps to the till to another cretinous customer. A sweating bore in front of him was in the middle of a story about a prostitute and a vicar. God, not that one. It was years old, and he hadn't thought it particularly funny then, although the prison chaplain wasn't a bad storyteller.

He moved to one side and found himself behind a tall girl. She was really tall – the label sticking out of the back of her blouse was on a level with his nose. He eased back half a pace to see if she was wearing high heels, but his eyes didn't get that far because a thin gnarled hand came round and clutched her backside.

'Don't, Mr Branwood,' she said, but she didn't move.

Terence eased round a little to see who was getting the action. Pathetic – a little old man with watery eyes was smiling up at her. 'Smile' was rather a generous description – it could have been that his feet were hurting.

'Oh, I know I may seem a bit harsh at times.' She cupped her ear with her hand. 'A bit harsh,' he repeated. 'I know I may seem a bit harsh, Doreen, but I've had my eye on you, you know.' He pointed his drink at her face. 'I've had my eye on you.'

She said something in reply that Terence didn't get, but the back of her neck was beginning to redden.

'And less of the "Mr Branwood", Doreen, *mumble mumble mumble* – call me Wilfred.'

She shook her head. 'I couldn't do that, Mr Branwood. It doesn't seem proper.'

He gulped some of his drink – it seemed to come out of his eyes. 'Wilfred,' he insisted.

God help her, thought Terence. If she walked into the office after the holiday and said 'Good morning, Wilfred,' she'd be at the Labour Exchange so fast she wouldn't have time to tuck her label in. He craned to the left and almost caught Elsie's eye, but she couldn't have seen him for she ducked out of sight. At the same time Mr Branwood was telling Doreen she'd been with the firm long enough for a move to the third floor . . . a burst of laughter greeted the prostitute/vicar story – it wasn't all that funny, but perhaps the Managing Director was telling it. He glanced back to the Doreen/Mr Branwood saga. Something was slightly different . . . then it struck him. Branwood was now clutching her with both hands . . . what the hell had happened to his drink? Clever girl, she was holding his glass as well – she'd make the third floor all right. But whether he'd be capable of claiming his prize was doubtful – he didn't look as if he'd see the New Year in.

Again Elsie's face came into view, and Terence stood on tiptoe and snapped his fingers in the air. In that mindless din it had about as much effect as breaking wind under Niagara Falls. A blast of cold air hit the back of his neck as other customers arrived – two large, beefy individuals who surveyed the scene for a moment, then crashed a path steadily through to the bar. There were a few half-hearted protests and drinks were slopped willy-nilly, and the noise subsided, but something about the pair discouraged confrontation. They leaned on the bar and spoke to Elsie, but he couldn't hear what they said – he only saw her head over the crowd make for the stairs and call for Mr Helliwell.

A sudden paralysis gripped Terence. He recognised the black bowler – it was Jimmy the Hat, it had to be. A half-turn and he saw a vivid scar down the left cheek. His worst fears were confirmed. Jimmy the Hat, a monster who'd break your leg just for the exercise. Terence started to shake and the parcel slipped from under his coat. It was unimportant now, and he trampled it in his panic to reach the door and the protection of the night. He flung himself into the car. Thank God he'd left the keys in the ignition – he was in no condition to find the right one, let alone insert it.

The car leaped forward, and a dog crossing the road took immediate evasive action, causing a cyclist to swerve into Buckley's family butchers. A long-dead turkey was dislodged from a hook by the door, and with a reflex action too quick

155

for the eye the dog had it and was halfway up Henshaw Street before Mr Buckley had taken his finger out of his nose.

With a squeal of tyres, Terence swerved left into the blackness of the Binglewood Estate. It was only then that he realised he'd been driving without lights. Quickly glancing in the mirror, he satisfied himself there was no pursuit before he switched them on just in time to prevent himself driving into the ditch. He wrenched the wheel over. How the hell had Jimmy the Hat found his way to Grapplewick? He took momentary comfort in the thought that Jimmy couldn't possibly have seen him, but the fact that he was in the vicinity was enough to double Terence's laundry bill.

By the time he let himself in through the front door he was shaking again. It wouldn't do. He took a few deep breaths to regain his composure. God, what a bombshell he was about to drop . . . he wondered briefly if Wilson Brown's heart would be strong enough to take it. He hung up his coat – a cigarette might help, but as he opened the case his palsied fingers scattered them all over the hall. He flung the case from him and took a few more deep breaths. Then his jaw dropped open – from the drawing-room he heard music: it was 'The Anniversary Waltz'. A wave of revulsion swept over him as he remembered the prison dances when he'd always had to dance 'The Anniversary Waltz' with Billy Big Knuckle. Billy never molested him or anything, he was just mad on dancing – thus Billy became his protector. It had been his own idea to put on scent and wear earrings. He shuddered now at his own sycophancy. He listened to a few bars with something akin to nostalgia. He hated 'La Cucaracha' – they always played that for the tango, and he had a rash on his cheek for three days afterwards. He wondered idly who Billy's partner was now. Then a sudden constriction of the bowels brought Jimmy the Hat back. Holy cow! What was he doing leaning back against the wall humming like a bloody great Deanna Durban?

He strode across the hall and flung open the door. He stopped as if he'd walked into a brick wall, and his mouth fell open. The carpet had been rolled up against the wall, and in the space Rembrandt was slowly gyrating in the arms of a dark-haired woman at least a foot taller. He didn't see Terence at the door – he couldn't see anything, for his face was pressed in between her enormous bosoms giving the impression that he was trying to see right through her. Terence raised his eyes to the ceiling, then crossed over to the radiogram and snatched the needle off the record. The woman stopped and turned her head, but Rembrandt couldn't possibly hear anything, cushioned as he was. Terence guessed rightly that this was Droopy Nellie. She looked at him questioningly, then held Rembrandt away from her. He blinked his eyes as if he'd just had five minutes. What a sight, thought Terence. If Wilson Brown's suits hadn't done a lot for him, they were an absolute travesty on Rembrandt. The shoulders sagged, his hands were invisible, and there was at least eighteen inches of trouser leg concertina-ed on the floor.

Rembrandt smoothed his sparse hair. 'Oh, it's you, sorr. Didn't see you come in.' He pointed to the woman, then looked down in embarrassment. 'We're engaged, sorr.'

Terence, conventionally delighted, was about to step forward and offer his congratulations when Jimmy the Hat sprang sickeningly into his mind. 'Never mind the nuts in May,' he snarled. 'Get rid of her.'

Rembrandt stood his ground. 'We're going to settle down here.'

'I don't care where you settle down – get rid of her. I have to talk to you.'

Nellie eased slightly behind him as he stepped forward and lifted her fiancé up by the lapels of Wilson Brown's jacket. Poor Rembrandt nearly slipped through. As it was, only his eyes were visible. Terence glared down at him. 'Now listen to me, Rudolph O'Valentin-bloody-O – .' He didn't get any further. Wallop! An excruciating pain at the back of his head, a blinding flash of white light, the ceiling spun over him, then there was nothing but blackness.

Rembrandt eased his head out of the jacket like a tortoise after a long hibernation. 'Dat'll bring tears to his eyes, oh yes.'

157

'Is that him?' she asked.

'Oh, dat's him all right. Dat's my partner,' he said proudly.

'Well, he's got a bloody funny way of showing it,' she replied, 'an' that's a fact.' She looked down at Terence and let out a short screech. 'Holy Mother of God, oi've scalped him.'

Rembrandt shook his head. 'Dat's only his wig,' he said, and shuffled over to the cocktail cabinet.

Terence groaned and tried to lift his head, but a sudden stab of pain forced him to abandon the attempt. Slowly he opened his eyes and panicked – he couldn't see. He was blind! His hands flew to his face, and he practically fainted with relief as his fingers touched the wig. Gingerly he lifted it up and squinted into the light. A blurred figure was approaching. He groaned again. Two identical Rembrandts knelt down and, supporting his head, put a glass of brandy to his lips. He gagged on it, but it cleared his vision. His first instinct was to lash out at the dull face above him, but he caught himself in time. Over Rembrandt's shoulder Nellie was hovering, and she was still holding the Guinness bottle. He heaved himself slowly and painfully to a sitting position, and with trembling, anxious fingers he explored the back of his head, but there was no blood – it was just mis-shapen. He blinked his eyes to eliminate one Rembrandt, and with some slight consolation he noted that they were merging. Lights swept across the room, and he heard the crunch of tyres on the gravel drive as a car pulled up. Rembrandt moved to the window and shaded his eyes, but it was too dark to see Wilson Brown paying off the taxi driver. He turned round but Terence was gone. He looked questioningly at Nellie, and she nodded her head to the bulge behind the trembling curtain.

Wilson Brown closed the front door behind him, and took off his hat. It had been a good day... the Grapplewick debate in the morning had given him a certain amount of satisfaction – the surprise on Mr Thurk's face, Lady Dorothy's astonishment (she had even thanked him before she left), and especially the humiliation of Helliwell. He had enjoyed that. The strange part was that, had Helliwell not attempted to co-opt him in that pathetic attempt at blackmail, he might well have gone against Mr Thurk. In the afternoon he'd taken a taxi to Blackburn to get a flight schedule from London Airport, details of sailings from Dover and Southampton and a train timetable (his Christmas present to Grapplewick). He unwound his scarf and was about to hang it up when he sensed that there was somebody in the drawing-room. It was their silence that aroused his curiosity. He made his way to the door and stopped in amazement as he surveyed the scene.

'What the devil's going on?' he asked. Terence's white face appeared round the heavy drapes and Wilson Brown's eyebrows shot up. 'Can anybody play?' he asked.

Terence emerged unsteadily. 'You'll laugh on the other side of your face when you hear what I have to tell you,' he snarled.

Wilson Brown giggled. 'How long has he been looking for you?' he said, jerking his head at Rembrandt. 'And God knows how he managed to count up to a hundred.' Then he noticed Nellie. He hadn't recognised her at first, because she looked different with her black hair in a bun. His face darkened. 'What did I tell you about her?' He took a step forward, but Terence held up his hand.

'That doesn't matter now,' he said. 'Ikey's mob's here.'

Wilson Brown froze, and his face paled like the moon coming out from behind a cloud. Rembrandt stared at Terence disbelievingly, hopping from one foot to the other, while Nellie backed away, startled by the sudden change in the atmosphere. They seemed to stand in silence for ages, broken only by what might have been Wilson Brown's stomach. He shook his head as if to deny what he had heard.

'Ikey's mob? Here?'

Terence nodded vigorously and wished he hadn't. He pointed vaguely. 'In Grapplewick.'

'In Grapplewick?' he echoed stupidly.

Terence was about to nod again but caught himself in time. 'I saw them in the Dog and Partridge.'

Wilson Brown was about to repeat it. Instead he glanced

around him wildly, searching for something different to say. It was like a lesson in basic English. 'Oh, my God,' he moaned, and staggered over to the sideboard to pour himself a large scotch. He dashed it down his throat, still holding on to the decanter. Terence snatched it from him, and attended to his own needs. Nellie handed Rembrandt a bottle of Guinness. Wilson Brown turned to Terence and held out his trembling glass for a refill. 'You couldn't be mistaken?' he asked, pleadingly.

Terence gulped down his drink and coughed. 'You can't mistake Jimmy the Hat.'

Wilson Brown stared at him aghast – his face wasn't just pale, it was a whitewashed lavatory wall. Terence topped himself up, then sloshed some to Wilson Brown's glass. He didn't seem to notice, but put it down and turned away. 'Oh, my God. Jimmy the Hat!'

Rembrandt crossed himself, and Nellie followed suit with a quick bob. Neither of them could remember the last time they'd attended mass, but it was insurance and it cost nothing.

Wilson Brown walked slowly across the bare floor and slumped into an armchair, eyes full of naked fear and bowels like a treacle factory. He calmed himself momentarily with the thought that he could always commit suicide – at least it could be quick and painless. He shuddered violently as he thought of one or two unfortunates who had got on the wrong side of Jimmy. Nobody deserved to end up as pig food, or – worse – cemented into the supports of one of those new motorways.

Terence, with the help of Glen Livet (God bless him) had managed to calm down somewhat. Indeed a slight tinge of watery sun was lightening the black cumulo-nimbus. Ikey had no quarrel with *him*. Prior to his release he'd handed over his tobacco concession in Block Four – it wasn't a big deal, but Ikey had appreciated it. 'You're a good boy, Raffles,' he had said, slapping him lightly on the cheek. Yes, he was now in possession of himself. He swaggered past a mirror, and shied away from his reflection. Dammit, his wig was on back to front. He looked like an ape badly in need of a haircut. He turned it round and patted it down. It would have to do for the moment.

Nellie put a protesting hand on Rembrandt's shoulder. 'An' what's the old divvil getting you into, my little darlin'?' She looked from one to the other. 'What's goin' on here dat oi don't know about?'

Terence stepped forward. 'Nothing to worry about, my dear. It's just someone who knew the Commander during the war.'

Wilson Brown looked at him sharply.

'Yes, the Commander had him court-martialled and . . . well, not to put too fine a point on it, the man don't like the Commander.'

She looked at Rembrandt, who shrugged. 'Not my pigeon. Oi don't know nothin' about de man. Dat man is a complete mystery to me, and dat's a fact.'

Terence nodded. 'Look, why don't you take your girl-friend down to the pub and buy her a drink?' He tried to take Rembrandt's arm, but the little man shrugged him off.

'No, sorr, not me. Oi'm not goin' in dat town on me own. Dat Jimmy is a pig of a man.'

Nellie put her hands on her hips. 'I thought you said you didn't know him?'

Rembrandt shook his head. 'Dat's right, oi don't know de man, but 'e might know me. Oh yes, an' oi wouldn't want to be gettin' into trouble at all.'

'OK,' said Terence. 'Take her up to your room and show her your etchings.'

'Dat's a good idea, sorr. Come on Nellie.' He took her arm, and reluctantly she left.

As soon as the door closed Wilson Brown was on his feet. 'Look, Terence, this isn't any good. I'm going to pack.'

Terence held him back. 'You're not going anywhere, Joe. I need you for Christmas Eve. After that you can dress up and join the *Folies Bergère* for all I care.'

Wilson Brown's mouth dropped open. 'You're not going through with that are you, not now?'

Terence spread his arms. 'Why not? Another day.'

Wilson Brown glared at him. 'Another five minutes is too long with Ikey's mob on our doorstep.'

Terence faced him squarely. 'Listen, I have a job for you on Christmas Eve to establish an alibi. Until then I'm not letting you out of my sight.'

Wilson Brown brushed past him and made for the door.

'Don't be silly, Joe. Come and sit down like a good little boy,' said Terence in a silky voice.

Wilson Brown knew that tone, and he stopped.

'You see,' Terence went on, 'if I don't clap eyes on you at least every five minutes, I'll get worried about you, and I may have to telephone.'

Wilson Brown turned towards him wide-eyed. 'You wouldn't shop an old mate?'

Terence went over to the decanter. 'There's only three places Jimmy the Hat would stay, and if you sloped off somewhere I'd need help.'

Wilson Brown sagged down into a chair. 'God, Terence. Prison's ruined you.'

NINETEEN

There was no stopping it. Once the twenty-third of December was out of the way, it was inevitably Christmas Eve, a day of happy anticipation, all the greater in Grapplewick because of the town's sense of Community. Most of the heavy Christmas shopping had been carried out in Blackburn and Bolton, but it was never quite finished. There were always last-minute additions to the list, knick knacks that were often better received than more expensive items, oranges for stockings, nuts, a yoyo, coloured pencils. Housewives adopted a harassed, anxious look as they scurried from one place to another, but it was a traditional mask, a badge, and most of them were happy to wear it. A hard frost through the night coated the town and its surroundings with a thin white patina, but the early morning clogs converging on the mills were vigorous rather than tentative. It would be an easy, short day – a couple of pints at dinnertime, mince pies, paper hats, jokes and outrageous mimes made necessary by the crashing noise of the machinery. The manager, the mule overlooker, boss of the card room would be all smiles. Who knows? Even they sometimes wore paper hats and traded kisses with the merry knees-up operatives, but this year the festivities would be tempered with unease, not quite a false gaiety, but not as relaxed as when the future, although never bright, was fairly predictable.

While it was not yet light, the cotton workers were already safely inside the great mills and there was peace once more on the white streets, a sheet of newspaper danced along on a sudden gust of wind, pausing at a lamp-post as if for breath. The stillness was shattered by the quavering notes of a cornet playing 'Silent Night'. After a few notes a dog barked and the cornet broke off . . . tentatively the cornet sounded once more, and the dog immediately joined in. Once again the cornet ceased and a voice shouted: 'Prince, 'old yer bloody noise.' There was a momentary pause, then 'Silent Night' began again. The dog, perhaps not fully understanding what was required, broke into a plaintive howl. The melody increased in volume and the dog, not to be outdone, howled even louder.

Jack Puller snatched the cornet away from his lips in exasperation. 'Prince!' he yelled. 'Prince, you great stupid sod . . . here, Prince.'

Prince cocked his head on one side, then scratched on the lavatory door.

Jack leaned forward, clicked the latch, and the dog bundled in, tail wagging from the neck down, and nuzzled his bare knees.

'Down, boy . . . down.' He lifted the instrument and wet his lips, but before he could take breath the dog yowled again. He lowered the cornet resignedly and broke wind instead. 'Florrie!' he shouted plaintively. It was half-hearted and he knew his wife couldn't hear him. Bloody typical, she wouldn't let him practise in the house, and when he came down here she let the bloody dog out.

Prince sat and watched him earnestly. Jack shook his head and, clutching the cornet and his trousers in one great fist, he took the dog's collar and half dragged the animal up the yard, opened the door and slung it in.

'How long you goin' to be down there?' queried his wife from the gloom within.

'Give us a flippin' chance,' he shouted through the small gap in the door. 'I've only just got sat on.' He eased the door shut, so as not to take off Prince's nose, then made his way carefully back down the yard to his cold brick practice room. . . .

Two doors further up Ned Bladdock heard the strains of the cornet and shook his head sadly. Poor old Jack, he thought. Fancy having to practise in that draught in the middle of winter. He shuddered and settled back in his overstuffed armchair. There was a great similarity between the two – food rationing never bothered him, nor indeed any other member of the brigade. He was full of bacon and eggs – he would in fact have liked two more eggs, but he always felt a little guilty about others who were not so well off. Half an hour yet before he would have to make his way to the Station. He leaned his head back, the heat of the fire stabbing at his moist chins. His eyes wandered over the mantelpiece with its green velvet cloth and watched the fire dancing on the bobbles as they hung down, and had done for many Bladdocks before him. A piece of coal spat, and he moved his eyes to see if a cinder had fallen onto the rug. He couldn't see the rug for the mound of his belly, and he almost raised his head, but the effort was too much, so he made a mental note to have a periodic sniff for the first sign of smouldering.

He felt a draught on his left arm as the door opened, and the windows rattled as his wife padded in from the front room. She knelt in front of the fire to do something to the grate, all the while humming 'Rock of Ages'. He smiled happily to himself. He hoped she'd be pleased – he'd bought her a new carpet sweeper for Christmas and everybody said that Ewbanks were pretty good. The clock wheezed through its chimes and scattered his thoughts.

'Bai heck,' he said to no one in particular. 'I'll be late for band practice.'

'Rock of Ages' stopped immediately and she eased back on her heels. 'Band practice, in t'middle o' t'day?' she said, brushing a wisp of hair from her face with the back of a large red hand.

'Aye,' he said, heaving himself to his feet. 'We've got a show tonight on 't'Binglewood Estate.'

She put down the hand brush. 'Tonight?' she said, watching his retreating back. 'It's Christmas Eve. I told Emmie and Joe we'd meet them at the Star tonight.'

Ned reappeared from the front room, lugging his big drum with him. 'I'll be there as soon as I can.'

'We always go to t'Star on Christmas Eve,' she moaned.

Ned didn't appear to have heard – he was shrugging into

165

his overcoat. 'I'll see thee at dinnertime,' he called, and with a swirl of curtains and a gebloom-berdoom he was gone.

Fireman Cyril Chadwick was already at the Station, a glazed look on his face as he rat-tat-a-panned away on his kettle drum. Barmy watched him proudly, eyebrows going up and down every time Cyril lifted his drumsticks on a level with his nose, something he'd been practising ever since he saw the band of the Royal Marines on the newsreel. It was brisk and nothing to do with the carol that evening, but there were no band parts in 'Silent Night' for kettle drums. He stopped suddenly as the thought occurred to him. They didn't really need his drum on the Binglewood Estate tonight, although Mr Thurk had meant it kindly when he'd said: 'Don't look so disappointed, Cyril. Somebody has to carry the lantern.' He perked up, however, at the thought that Betty Grable would have received his Christmas card by now. Then just as quickly he perked down again – just his luck if Betty happened by some gigantic coincidence to be a guest at one of the houses tonight, and him standing there with a candle in a jam jar.

On Featherstall Road some kids caught up with Mr Thurk as he made his way gingerly along the treacherous pavement. From a safe distance they chanted: 'Station's on fire and the band's on parade, send for the Manchester Fire Brigade'. He lurched towards them with a mock ferocity and they scattered, shrieking with delight at their own daring.

Old Norman Winterbottom who was busy putting down salt from his front door to the bus stop glared at him. 'Cheeky young buggers,' he muttered.

Mr Thurk smiled. 'Oh, kids were singing that at my father and his father before him.'

Winterbottom nodded darkly. 'Aye, but thy father would have fetched 'em one.'

'Ah, well,' said Mr Thurk. 'A Merry Christmas.'

He was about to move on when he saw the pony and trap in the distance. Winterbottom turned with him, and they watched its approach. Dr McBride was on his way home, and there was always curiosity to know where he'd been, who he'd been treating and what they'd got. At a steady trot the pony clip-clopped towards them, and as it drew level Mr Thurk smiled.

'Good morning, Dr McBride.'

His greeting was ignored, and the pony continued a further twenty yards or so where it stopped at the doctor's surgery, steam rising from its flank. McBride remained where he was, and the pony looked back and fidgeted.

Winterbottom turned to Mr Thurk. 'Fast asleep, I'll bet. I 'eard 'im leave, just turned five this mornin'.' He sniffed in disapproval. ''E should let young Dr Bedford do them sort of calls.'

A knot of apprehension gripped Mr Thurk. There was something unnatural about the way Dr McBride was sitting. In a flash he knew what it was – one didn't fall asleep with a straight back and head upright. He hurried towards the trap, calling Dr McBride's name, but now he was sure it was wasted effort. Dr McBride was dead – there was no hurry now. Mr Thurk stared up at the austere face, small icicles hanging from his white moustache, eyes looking out on a Christmas they would never see. Mr Thurk took off his hat, and Winterbottom, who was at his elbow, followed suit. Already there was a knot of people standing round, and doors were opening all the way along the street. Mr Thurk collected himself and stepped up into the trap in order to close the dead eyes, but he would have needed a hammer and chisel. The poor doctor was frozen solid, and they had to carry him into the surgery in a sitting position.

Young Dr Bedford, in an effort to assert himself, smiled cheerfully. 'Ah, well. We all have to go some time.'

Mr Thurk turned slowly away and let himself out.

How trite an epitaph. How shallow a sentiment. But then shallowness was becoming socially acceptable. There wouldn't be any more Dr McBrides. Somewhere in the last few decades they'd lost the mould – integrity was now derided as naivety, dedication was for fools, and truth was to be applied only when advantageous to a lie. Dr McBride had possessed all the qualities of a man, and sadly they would be buried with him. Most of the people of Grapplewick had been brought kicking and scowling into the world by the caring hands of Dr McBride – indeed he *was* Grapplewick, and now he was gone. Mr Thurk's eyes pricked with tears as he looked at the old, worn trap. He ran his hand lovingly over the cracked leather seat, and he knew in his heart that Grapplewick was sitting up there in place of Dr McBride, but that the end was perilously close.

Barmy greeted him at the Fire Station with a steaming mug of tea. 'OK?' he grinned.

'Yes thanks, Mr Chronicle.' He climbed the stairs heavily and broke the news to the lads. Those with caps took them off, and they all stared at the floor.

It was Jack Puller who broke the spell. He raised his cornet to his lips and started 'Abide with Me'. One by one the band took up their instruments and joined in the hymn. Mr Thurk didn't conduct – for once it was unnecessary. It was as if God had taken over his baton.

By 12.30 the Dog and Partridge was already packed with early Christmas revellers, their babbling voices, laughter and shrieks punctuated by the steady jingling of the till. Helliwell, the proprietor, should have been pleased but he wasn't. He had had to take on three extra staff, but even so his main asset, or rather his two main assets – Elsie – wanted time off. Angrily he pulled a pint of best Threlfall's, shouting over his shoulder to where she was adjusting her little hat in the mirror behind the bar.

'Your mother isn't that poorly that she can't wait while three o'clock.'

'Eh?' said Elsie to the mirror.

He banged the slopping pint on the bar next to the glasses. 'That'll be three and six in all.'

The man screwed up his face to block out the noise. 'Ow much?'

'Three an' six,' yelled Helliwell.

Elsie opened the flap in the bar. 'I'm off,' she mouthed, pointing to herself, then the door.

Helliwell scrabbled in the till for one and six change. 'Don't forget tonight,' he shouted. 'We're open while midnight.' But she was already pushing her way through the leering drinkers.

Old Dobson took off his cap and opened the door of his ancient taxi. Elsie got in, pleased when he spread a plaid rug over her knees. He settled himself in the front seat, and as they pulled away from the kerb he half turned towards her. 'Dr McBride died this morning,' he said over his shoulder. 'Delivered a baby at Sagbottom Farm, got back in 'is cart, and 'e were dead when 'e got back.'

She leaned forward. 'Oh, I am sorry. Me mother 'll be upset.'

'Ay, 'appen.' A couple of miles went by. 'How is your mother?'

Elsie, startled out of a daydream, was about to tell him she was shopping in Accrington but said instead, 'She hasn't been too well lately. Well, she's had a bad leg for about two years now.' He nodded, 'Ay, a know.'

Panic gripped her stomach, then she relaxed. Old Dobson was a teetotaller, so there was very little chance of Helliwell getting to know she was on her way to the Grand Hotel, Manchester. She looked out of the window, but didn't see the sheep-dotted moors flashing past. What a strange man the Major was . . . fancy sending a taxi to bring her all the way from Grapplewick just to have a Christmas dinner she would have walked. She wasn't entirely besotted – more accurately she was flattered by his attention, stimulated by his manner – but having been brought up in an atmosphere of strict North Country orthodoxy bed never entered her thoughts. Well . . . fleetingly, but to be dismissed immediately – there was enough guilt in her merely having lunch with him in Manchester, but then how could she refuse? She wasn't, however, so naive as to imagine that he desired her company purely for her mental agility. She'd noticed that, though his eyes were pointing at her face, they were actually looking down the neck of her blouse. But then he was too much of a gentleman for a quick feel and a slobbery kiss – he'd seen too much, done too much . . . a film producer, and God! What he must have gone through during the war – dropped at Arnhem, last off the beach at Dunkirk, first on

169

at Normandy, and, according to his scruffy Irish batman, was even awarded the VC but sent it back. The rasp of the brake brought her out of her reverie.

'Here we are, Elsie,' old Dobson wheezed out and opened the door for her.

'Thanks, Mr Dobson,' she said. 'That was quick.' She fiddled in her purse.

'Nay, that's all right, lass . . . it's all been taken care of.'

She smiled her thanks.

'Ah well, I'd best be getting back now while it's daylight.'

Gingerly he got back into the driving seat, apprehensive of the traffic, although a Mancunian would have been surprised at the lack of it.

Elsie was even more terrified when she entered the Grand Hotel. She hovered uncertainly by the reception desk, awed by the tired opulence of the foyer and the men and women who looked so self-assured as they made their way in and out.

'Can I help you, miss?' a large man in blue uniform and brass buttons inquired.

'Yes . . . er, I'm, er, having lunch with Major . . . erm.' She stopped, blushing – she didn't even know the Major's name.

'Oh, yes,' said the large man a trifle coldly, and Elsie blushed again. He must think she was one of *those* women.

She looked round wildly and was about to dash for the door when she felt a hand on her elbow. She turned, panic-stricken, thinking for one split second that she was about to be forcibly ejected, but it was Terence.

'Ah, my dear. We were beginning to think you'd got lost.'

She smiled feebly, and the commissionaire dry-washed his hands and bowed up and down with a humility that was sickening.

'Thank you and Merry Christmas,' said Terence, and a fiver passed from one hand to the other with a smoothness mastered only by long-serving commissionaires.

If the foyer had unnerved her, the dining-room was a paralysing experience with glittering chandeliers, a steady hubbub of conversation, the rattle of crockery, tailcoated waiters, spotty boy apprentices in short Eton jackets, waitresses in black with white aprons and frilly white caps – all moving purposefully among the tables. Elsie was accustomed to admiring glances, but here she was embarrassed. She was only fractionally relieved at the table when she saw her fellow guests. Commander Wilson Brown rose and held a chair out for her, but the scruffy little Irishman just nodded and continued to stare at the tablecloth. Elsie smiled tentatively at the large woman sitting next to him, and felt slightly more at ease. Droopy Nellie had done her best with make-up, but she was unused to it and the result was a gaudy ship's figurehead. Terence seated himself with a great self-satisfied sigh.

'Pleasant trip?' he asked.

'Yes, thanks. Mr Helliwell wasn't too pleased. I told him. . . .'

Terence leaned back and snapped his fingers. A waiter glided alongside. 'We'll have the wine now.' The waiter bowed and backed off. Terence smiled at Elsie. 'I took the liberty of ordering for you, my dear. Saves time, and we have a train to catch.' He lit a cigarette. . . . 'Oh, so sorry. I interrupted you, my dear.'

She shrugged. 'No, it's all right.'

The Commander raised an eyebrow and glanced disinterestedly round the room.

Elsie looked down at her plate, hands clasped under the table. She could almost feel the hostility round her. Terence, lounging back in his chair, was tapping idly with his fork. From the corner of her eye she noticed that Rembrandt and Nellie were also staring fixedly at the table, although they could have been saying grace.

'What time's your train?' she asked in an effort to break the spell.

'What?' Terence pulled himself back from wherever he was. 'Oh – train,' he sighed. 'Yes, sadly we must get back to London tonight. We were looking forward to spending Christmas in Grapplewick but . . . ah.' He broke off as the stooping wine waiter returned.

Elsie watched the Major in admiration as he examined the label on the bottle and nodded. The waiter withdrew the

171

cork, and this too was given close scrutiny. Then the wine
– Terence held it up to the light, then he sipped, head to
one side as he savoured the bouquet. The wine waiter
watched him with a certain amount of trepidation. Finally
Terence swallowed and nodded.

'Excellent,' he said.

'Bloody fool,' thought the wine waiter, who was rather
good at his job.

When all the glasses were charged Terence raised his; he
proposed a toast to Grapplewick and hoped they would
return soon. 'To Grapplewick!' They all sipped and pretended to enjoy the wine except Rembrandt. He didn't touch
it but had a surreptitious swig of Guinness from the bottle
he had been holding under the table. The Commander glared
at him in disgust, but Rembrandt just grinned back at him
and had another swig. The soup arrived to rescue the situation, and conversation was then impossible until
Rembrandt had finished. Nellie looked round the guests
apologetically but Rembrandt was oblivious. He sighed contentedly and another bottle of Guinness appeared from
under the table.

Slices of turkey were carved next and distributed expertly
onto the plates. A waitress hovered round with the vegetables, and the various stuffings were delegated to one of
the spotty apprentices. This provided the only light relief –
so busy was he endeavouring to see down Elsie's blouse that
he slammed a large dollop of sage and onion on
Rembrandt's lap. The Commander looked away in disgust
and when he looked back Rembrandt had eaten it.

Elsie had hardly noticed the meal – in fact she would
gladly have got stuck into boiled alligator just to be done
with it. The whole group seemed preoccupied and only
smiled at the waiters. Why the Major invited her at all was
a mystery.

Terence knew, though – her presence was vital, and he
complimented himself once again on the brilliance of his
plan. He leaned towards her. 'Something else, my dear?' But
before she could decline politely, he was already placing five
pound notes on top of the bill.

'Thank you, sir,' said the waiter, hesitating just long enough for Terence to wave a deprecating hand to the change.

The Commander rose quickly to his feet. 'Come along, then. We'll see these two off at the station, then I'll take you, er . . . ladies home.' He spoke with false sincerity, like an actor who notices people leaving their seats, but he *was* acting and he knew roughly what he would have to say during the next hour. Terence noted with satisfaction that London Road Station was crowded, but not too many people had arrived yet for the London train. It was early . . . again it had all been carefully pre-planned. They stood awkwardly at the barrier as people will when goodbyes are in order and there's no common ground. Rembrandt opened a bottle of Guinness and proffered it to Nellie, but she shook her head, unable to speak as black mascara tears flowed through the rouge. Wilson Brown turned away in disgust. . . .

Terence took off his hat carefully – he didn't want his wig to come with it. 'Well, my dear,' he said, 'no point in hanging around.' Elsie looked at the station clock, wondering if he might kiss her. Terence was also wondering whether he should. There was a quick movement by him and Rembrandt was snatched into Nellie's great bosom, black tears splashing his cap.

'Oi'll be waitin' for you, my little darlin', that you are.' Then she released him.

Rembrandt nodded. 'Oi'll be back. Yes, sorr. Don't you worry, oi'll be back.'

Terence smiled at Elsie. 'Don't worry, we'll be back, and if I pull off this deal we may have another lunch at the Grand,' he chuckled. 'Better still, I might buy the hotel for you.' He held out his hand and Elsie shook it, wondering why she'd bothered – bath, hairdo, clean underwear.

'Don't leave it too long.' She smiled and turned to go, but the Commander restrained her.

'Might as well see them safely aboard.'

Terence held out his ticket, and turned back to Elsie. 'Oh, and a Merry Christmas.'

'Same to you,' she called.

'It's in,' grunted the ticket collector.

'Thanks,' said Terence. 'Pity you have to work on Christmas Eve.'

'Oh, it's only the London bound, then I'm finished.'

'Oh well, anyway, have a Christmas drink on me,' and he slipped a fiver into the man's hand.

'Well, that's very nice of you, sir. Thank you.' He hadn't seen what the note was, but by the feel he knew it was a fiver.

Terence raised his hat again so that the man could get a good look at him – it was essential. 'And a Happy New Year.'

'And to you, sir.' By God, he thought, if only there were more like that – this little ratbag holding out his ticket wouldn't give you the end off a cork-tipped cigarette. First-class, too – must have nicked it.

Commander Wilson Brown and the two girls waved. Terence waved back and then pulled up the window and moved down the train.

'Ah, well,' said the Commander, 'let's get you two back.'

They walked slowly towards the exit, Nellie still blubbering. It was embarrassing, to say the least. She'd tried to repair the damage with a minute handkerchief. It would have been better if she hadn't, because she looked like a Black and White Minstrel doing a show in the rain.

'Here we are.' He opened the car door and they got in the back. Elsie was anxious and decided she'd go straight round to her mother's before Fred did. He had still been in bed when she left, and he might not have seen her note about her mother being ill. On the other hand he might have seen the note and gone round to check – he'd do anything rather than cook a meal himself.

'Damn.' Wilson Brown was pressing furiously on the starter but there was no life in the engine. The girls weren't worldly enough to notice that it wasn't even switched on. 'Oh, blast,' he muttered. 'It's broken down again. I'll have to leave it and get Hepworth's to pick it up.' So they all alighted, but before they walked over to the taxi rank he leaned into the car and surreptitiously dropped the keys on the seat.

On platform two the guard held up his flag and blew sharply on his whistle. The last train to London eased out of the station – the big one had gone bang on time. Fifteen minutes later the door to the gents opened, and a hump-backed man with a curly white beard, accompanied by a scruffy little man, made their way cautiously to the exit. The elderly humpback was obviously on the critical list, and the new man at the barrier helped him into his Vauxhall that was parked outside. Five minutes later Terence and Rembrandt were on their way back to Grapplewick, ostensibly speeding towards London – at least four excellent witnesses would testify to this if necessary. Stage one was complete.

At about 6.30 Rembrandt eased the car into Grapplewick High Street.

'Nearly there, sorr,' he called over his shoulder.

There was no reply. Terence was crouched on the floor in the back with a rug over him. Jimmy the Hat was some-where in the vicinity, and he'd be watching the cars. He wasn't sure how well Jimmy knew Rembrandt, but to be on the safe side he'd lent the scruffy little man a moustache – it was an old one anyway. He lurched as the car turned, and rightly assumed that they were now going up Feathers-tall Road, which, thank God, would be considerably darker than the High Street. Slowly he raised himself and peered furtively out, noticing with satisfaction the lights in the Fire Station and a knot of dark shapes milling in the yard, then blackness as they sped past the gate.

Mr Thurk, happening to glance towards the road at that moment, subconsciously registered what appeared to be Wilson Brown's car, but immediately dismissed the thought – there was a white labrador in the back looking out of the window. Jack Puller went up and down the scale on his cornet, then again, and Mr Thurk turned his attention to the band.

'Once more, lads,' he called. Cigarettes were pinched out. Mr Thurk nodded to the Station. 'Lights, Mr Chronicle,' and Barmy, quivering with self-importance, clicked off the three switches. The sudden darkness was almost tangible. 'Form up on the beacon,' said Mr Thurk smartly but softly. Cyril lifted the jam jar containing the candle high above his head, and the lads scurried into columns, each man holding onto the belt of the man in front of him. When the jostling had ceased Mr Thurk almost whispered, 'By the left, quiiiick march.'

They followed the pathetic pinprick of light to the end of the yard, then round and back, and once again, until Mr Thurk called, 'Baaaand, Halt.' They stopped smartly and there was a shuffling and clink of metal as they adjusted their instruments. A couple of coughs and they were ready. Mr Thurk squeezed Cyril's arm, and the little jam jar waved twice and then was lowered. Mr Thurk called 'One, two a three,' and they eased into 'Silent Night'.

With head bowed he listened, and it wasn't bad. In fact, considering the short time they'd had to rehearse, it was quite moving. He sighed. Perhaps they were better when he didn't conduct. He squared his shoulders. To hell with it! He was proud of them all. First they'd had to learn it by heart, which not one man had failed to do. Then the practising in the band room, each man blindfolded to accustom him to the dark. Even Barmy had stood to attention with his eyes slightly shut. 'Sleeeep in heavenly peace.' The carol came to an end and all was silent. It was an emotionally charged moment. Mr Thurk, glad of the dark, wiped his nose.

'Lights, Mr Chronicle,' and the Station burst into light, which had them all squinting and turning away. 'Splendid lads, we'll take a fifteen-minute break. Thank you.' The lads jostled about putting down their instruments, and one or two sloped off towards the gate to down a couple of pints before boarding the bus which was to take them to the Binglewood Estate. Some of the lads were disappointed not to be using Aggie, but, as Mr Thurk pointed out, it was really a private engagement and to utilise Corporation transport (i.e. the fire engine) without proper authorisation would

176

have been out of order. Hence the hire of a bus – a double-decker to accommodate the smokers.

Unwittingly Lady Dorothy had become an accessory. Anthony had confided in her, apprehensive as to how they would be received, but she assured him that it would be a splendid surprise and the Bendlethorpes would be tickled pink. However, she took the precaution of being at Holme-dene at 7.30. Lord Bendlethorpe was a large, self-made man who had risen from a modest tinned meat manufacturer to the nobility, thanks to the healthy appetites of the Allied forces, and was now in the process of buying up large chunks of bombed-out buildings in Manchester. He helped himself to a large whisky and soda.

'Oh, come on, Dorothy,' he said, 'give us a clue.'

She smiled. 'All right, Jack. For a man who's got every-thing, this is something different . . . anyway, you'll know in half an hour.'

He looked at her shrewdly, juggling the loose change in his trouser pocket. By jingo, if she only knew – £200,000 tucked away in his wall safe upstairs, a cash deal he would exchange for a large piece of Piccadilly.

His small daughter's eyes widened. 'I know,' she lisped. 'It's somebody going to come down the chimney.'

Lady Dorothy winked at her. 'Who knows?'

The tall manservant circulating with the decanter of sherry glanced at the roaring fire. 'If somebody does,' he thought, 'he'll get his arse burnt.'

Terence and Rembrandt, in black polo neck sweaters, black trousers and plimsolls, crouched in the drainage ditch on the East Road. Terence peered at the fingers on his luminous watch. Dammit, were they going to be late? He rested his forehead on the bank in front of him – he was sweating even thought it was near to freezing. Bile rose in his throat – it had always been thus. He tried not to look at his watch again. It must have been like this during the First World War – Sergeant coming along behind him; 'Steady, lad. You'll 'ear the whistle any minute. Then over over the top, lad.' A soft, cold breeze rustled the trees and the wind died, but the rustling continued. He realised it wasn't the trees – it was Rembrandt having another pee. On a night like this it was enough to waken the dead. He was about to give him a rollicking when he caught sight of the tiny firefly bouncing towards them, then he heard the sound of marching feet.

'Put your cock away,' he hissed. 'They're coming.'

The band approached in good order, and outside the gates of Holmedene the command was given to halt. Terence heard the scrape of a match, and there was a flare of light as someone bent down to examine the name plate. Something was whispered, the great gates squealed open, and the band crunched down the drive to form up in front of the house. The lighted jam jar waved twice, then the band broke into 'Silent Night'. Almost immediately lights went on in the front of the house, and the great oak door opened. Taking advantage of the strident music, Terence and Rembrandt hurried round the back, lugging the ladder between them.

Jack Bendlethorpe didn't know whether to be pleased or disappointed. He dragged on a huge cigar. Ah well, it's different – bloody awful, but different. He leaned towards his manservant scowling in the background.

'Bring out the whisky and some glasses.'

The manservant faded indoors. Lady Dorothy glanced apprehensively at him, but it was a success. His little daughter was standing mesmerised. This would undoubtedly be the highlight of her pampered Christmas.

Terence, knowing exactly where the safe was, couldn't hear the band – a doctor's stethoscope blocked out all the noise except the click of the tumblers. Rembrandt, with one ear on the music, was stuffing anything that sparkled into a black bag. Two very expensive furs went flying out of the window. He glanced at Terence, then stopped. Terence was staring into the safe.

'What's up, sorr?' he said.

There was no need to whisper. Terry whistled and grabbed inside, bringing out wads of new crisp Treasury notes. 'We've come to the wrong place, old fruit. This is bloody Barclay's.'

178

Quickly they began to transfer the booty, so wrapped up that they didn't notice the band had finished. They need not have worried, however. There was more noise now, as the band enjoyed a Christmas libation with the householders. Finally, all the empty glasses were replaced on the tray, and the band formed up to repeat the performance at the other houses, unnecessary now because Terence was satisfied. As the band marched along towards the Beeches, they followed at a respectable distance carrying the loot between them, Rembrandt loaded with the two fur coats. Any drunk would have sworn that he'd seen a tall man walking down East Road with a polar bear. The band turned left towards The Beeches but Terence and Rembrandt carried on to Seven Seas. They had enough for one night.

Wilson Brown didn't hear them come in, and when they entered the drawing-room he actually shrieked. Terence went quickly to the sideboard – as always the aftermath left him shaking. Wilson Brown was beside him.

'What's happened? Chickened out? Why are you back? Are they still coming here?'

Terence knocked back his drink in one quick gulp, then poured another. 'Is the car in the garage?' he asked.

Wilson Brown nodded.

'All tanked up?'

Wilson Brown nodded again. 'Why are you back so early?' he asked.

Terence jerked his head at Rembrandt. 'Go and get changed. I'll fix the stuff.'

Rembrandt hurried away. He had some Guinness upstairs.

Terence took his glass to a chair and settled down, stretching his legs before him. 'I've only done Holmedene,' he said to the fire, 'so don't go commiserating with the other two houses.'

'What happened?' squeaked Wilson Brown.

'I'm getting old, I think,' he sighed. 'Anyway, it wasn't a bad night's pay. No point in risking the lot.' He sipped his drink. No way was he going to tell his old mate just how successful it had been. He was still in a state of shock himself – good grief, if anybody had any inkling of the size

179

of that wad, they'd all be on his back. He hauled himself to his feet. 'I'm going to get changed.' He put his glass down and left.

Wilson Brown shook his head. Poor old devil, his nerve had gone. All this preparation and planning, and when it finally came to it he hadn't the balls. The noise of the band interrupted his thoughts. Oh God! He had this lot to contend with now.

Mr Thurk was happy. He felt that the evening had been a success, apart from Wilson Brown. The Commander had seemed preoccupied and hadn't even invited them in for a drink afterwards. Still, at least he did hear them out. The bus trundled them back to the Fire Station. One or two of the lads were already a bit over the top and wouldn't see midnight, but as was customary they had a couple in the Star on Christmas Eve, nipping across to the Station every now and again to take Barmy a drink. Barmy just grinned and poured whatever it was into the great dixie of tea.

At Seven Seas Wilson Brown quickly and expertly disarranged his bedroom. He remembered exactly how Terence worked, and this job had to be a replica of the one at Holmedene. He tilted a couple of pictures off-centre, then he took down the reproduction of Constable's *Haywain* and opened the safe, the contents of which were deposited securely at Lloyd's Bank. Lastly he opened one of the windows clumsily with his pocket knife. Satisfied, he picked up the phone.

Detective Inspector Waterhouse was gulping down a mug of sweet black coffee in an effort to steady the room. He wasn't completely drunk, but he'd been working at it. He jammed a battered brown trilby on his head and was about to leave when the phone rang. His wife answered.

'If it's for me tell 'em I left ten minutes ago,' he hissed.

She covered the mouthpiece. 'It's Commander Wilson Brown.'

He frowned, hesitated for a moment, then took the phone from her. 'Hello, Commander. Bill here.'

His wife hovered like a sheepdog waiting for a whistle.

'Another one!' he exploded, but the effect was better than

a gallon of black coffee. He turned to his wife and raised his eyes despairingly. 'No, the station's been on to me. I was just about to make my way to Holmedene. There's been a break-in there.' He listened for a while, grunting now and again. Whatever happened, his Christmas was up the spout. He nodded. 'OK, Commander, you know the drill. Don't touch anything, and I'll be up there with a couple of the lads.' He nodded again. 'I'll alert Blackburn, we'll need reinforcements . . . well, it's Christmas Eve. I mean it couldn't have happened at a worse time . . . OK.' He put the phone down. 'There's been a break-in at the Commander's house as well.'

She put her hand to her mouth in dismay.

'When d'you reckon you'll be back?'

He shrugged. 'God knows.' Then he smiled thinly. 'Anyway, a Merry Christmas.' He kissed her on the cheek and hurried to the door, then he turned. 'God knows,' he repeated. 'But just in case, a Happy New Year.'

Wilson Brown settled himself in a large armchair and stretched his legs towards the fire. At least Terence and that stunted walking peatbog were off his back. He sipped his whisky contentedly – just the one, there'd be plenty more when he'd finished with the police. He laid his head back and stared at the ceiling. The insurance on his valuables alone was worth £25,000, and when that was safely gathered in he knew a fence in the East End who would buy the stuff off him for at least another £15,000. The house was already in the hands of the estate agents, and they'd assured him of a quick sale for this most desirable residence. Yes, in a month or so he could stash it all in a suitcase and head for the Antipodes. He shook his head ruefully, wondering why he hadn't thought of it in the first place instead of burying himself in Grapplewick. A heavy knock on the door scattered his thoughts. He heaved himself out of the chair and hurried towards the hall, composing his face into what he felt to be an expression of perplexed outrage. 'God, Inspector! What do we pay the police for?' He smiled to himself. No, that was a bit strong. No good

181

alienating them. Another heavy knock, and he opened the door.

''Ello, Joe,' leered Jimmy the Hat.

TWENTY

Commander Wilson Brown staggered back a pace, clutching his heart – a mistake: it was the seat of his trousers he should have gone for.

Jimmy the Hat jerked his head and his companion hurried back to the car.

'How did you find me?' he asked stupidly.

Jimmy smiled, but it didn't touch his eyes. 'A bit of paper, Joe. There's always something on a bit of paper. *Grapplewick Chronicle*. Know it, eh? You standing up the Cenotaph there in a sailor suit. Oo's been a naughty boy, eh, eh?'

Wilson Brown struggled to collect himself. He spoke awkwardly because there was no moisture in his mouth. 'Please, Jimmy, we used to meet in the old days. How much? You name it Jimmy. How much?'

The smile left Jimmy's face. 'Ikey wants you,' he snarled, 'and if you don't want to freeze to death, get your coat on.'

The other man pushed past and skipped up the stairs two at a time, carrying a five gallon petrol can.

Wilson Brown watched him, then turned to Jimmy. 'What's he up to?' he bleated.

'Don't ask,' said Jimmy, 'and get your coat on. You can walk to the car or you can 'obble with a broken leg.'

Wilson Brown hesitated for a second, then grabbed his overcoat from the hallstand. Out of the corner of his eye he noticed the other guy sloshing petrol on the stairs as he backed down.

'What's the point of that?' he squeaked.

Jimmy nodded. The tall man lit a cigarette and flicked it

over the banisters. Wilson Brown finally lost control of his bowels as the stairs exploded in a seething mass of flame.

The new Vauxhall passed smoothly through Royton. In another twenty minutes or so Manchester would be navigated for the second time that day, then south to London. There wasn't much traffic about – in fact they'd only seen two other vehicles mobile; the others were parked every so often outside the noisy watering places a-glitter with lights. Terence glanced sideways at Rembrandt, glugging away at another Guinness bottle. God, not another one. When they stopped for a pee he made a mental note to park on a hill, otherwise they'd be swamped.

Rembrandt belched. 'Dat was a good job we just did. Yes, sorr, dat was class.'

Terence smiled. They were the first words that Rembrandt had uttered since they'd left the Binglewood Estate, and Terence had had a bet with himself that that's exactly what the little ratbag would say. It was just like old times. A cold wind slapped his face as Rembrandt opened the window and jettisoned another dead man. Terence grunted. Bloody fool was laying a fine trail – a smashed Guinness bottle every three miles or so. Hope to God he hadn't got too many left. He pulled up dutifully at the end of the Broadway, then turned right into Oldham Road, and his heart all but stopped. Thirty yards ahead was a police road block, and they were already going past another car which was pulled into the side.

With reflexes too quick for his brain, Terence jammed his foot on the brake, and almost immediately another car ran into him. The back of his head jerked forward, but even as it did he noticed two policemen coming towards him, torches swaying as they ran. Again purely reflex, but when he straightened up – and it couldn't have been more than two seconds – he was wearing a large walrus moustache. As the police reached the car Rembrandt stepped out and leaned into Terence.

'Tanks for de lift, guvnor, oi live just round de corner.'

And he was trudging down towards the bright lights of Manchester as if he hadn't seen his old mother for years.

Terence rolled down his window, and one of the policemen stuck his head in. 'You all right, sir?' Terence nodded resignedly.

The other policeman came to the other door, and addressed his companion across Terence. 'The one behind's being sick . . . he's drunk as a fiddler's bitch.'

The policeman looked back towards the retching in disgust, then turned back. 'Bit of luck we happened to be on the spot, eh?'

Terence tried to smile – no licence, no insurance: they were about as welcome as piles on a Grand National jockey.

Another car joined the queue, and the policeman straightened. 'Any road, we've got more important things to do.' He flashed his torch over the back seat and the floor. 'Would you mind stepping out and opening the boot, please.'

Terence pulled himself together. Way in the distance he spotted Rembrandt scurrying through the light of a street lamp, and a flush of anger swept over him. 'Constable,' he said in his best browbeating manner, 'at ten o'clock tomorrow I have a very important meeting in London.'

The policemen looked at each other over the top of the car. 'It's Christmas Day tomorrow,' said one of them, then stopped as Terence let himself out of the car. He stepped back a pace as Terence faced him squarely.

'The affairs of the nation do not stop just because it's Christmas,' he said quietly. He took a little black notebook from his inside pocket. 'May I have your name and number, Constable?'

The policeman frowned.

'Nothing to worry about,' Terence assured him. 'I can tell you, however, that the meeting tomorrow is vital, and if I'm late the cabin . . .' he pulled himself up, 'er, the people with whom I am meeting will require reasons and corroboration.'

Another car joined the line-up, and the policeman looked anxiously at his watch. His colleague moved to the rear of the car, and while Terence jotted down the particulars he was struggling with the boot. The policeman volunteered his name and number.

'Thank you,' said Terence.

'The boot's jammed,' called the other policeman. They joined him and examined the boot lid.

'May I try the key, sir?'

Terence took his keys from the ignition. 'May I ask why you wish me to open it?'

'Just a routine check, sir.'

'On Christmas Eve?'

'Well, sir, like you we don't stop just because it's Christmas.' He tried to sound jocular, but a glance at Terence unnerved him. 'There's been a series of robberies in the north, and we're stopping all cars.'

Terence was about to insert the key when the other constable straightened up. 'You'll never get this open without tools,' he said. 'It's buckled, Jack.' Jack came round and bent down, trying to peer into a one-inch gap. 'Made a bit of a mess of your car, sir.'

Terence smiled. 'There's plenty more in the motor pool.' He walked round and settled down in the driving seat.

The policeman got out his notebook and was about to ask for Terence's licence, etc., when there was a loud groan and the driver in the car behind slid sideways out of his seat and sprawled messily in the road. The policeman stuffed the notebook back in his pocket and moved to the drunk. Grabbing both legs like a wheelbarrow, he started to drag him towards the pavement. The new Vauxhall roared into life, and with a wave Terence was off.

'Hey,' shouted one of the policemen half-heartedly.

'Did you get his number?' said the other one.

'What number?' said his companion, feigning innocence.

'Bloody Lord Fauntleroys . . . that car.'

'I never saw a car,' said the older one, dropping the drunk's legs. 'All I saw was this silly bugger run into a wall.'

Terence watched the receding knot of people in his mirror, then breathed easily. There seemed to be no move to get into the police car and give chase. He made up his mind, however, to switch transport as soon as the opportunity

186

occurred. He was so wrapped up in his thoughts that he almost knocked down the scruffy figure ahead thumbing a lift. He just managed to swerve in time, then pulled up. In his rear view mirror Rembrandt was scuttling towards him, and for one fleeting moment he was tempted to put his foot down and leave the stupid sod to his Guinness.

'Nasty moment that, sorr,' puffed Rembrandt, settling back.

'Thanks for your help,' said Terence icily.

'Dat's OK, sorr,' replied Rembrandt, happily taking the top off another bottle. They didn't speak again until after Manchester. . . .

'Dey didn't look in the boot, then, sorr?'

Terence glanced at him. 'Why should they look in the boot?'

'Dat's what they're looking for, isn't it?'

'My dear Hibernian dropout, you don't think I'd trust our friend Helliwell to that extent, do you?'

'Oi don't follow dat, sorr.'

Terence shook his head slowly. 'I suspected that he might chicken out, and have a reception committee somewhere along the route.' He chuckled. 'He always did tend to underestimate me.'

'I taut you said dat de stuff was all packed?'

'I did, but not in the boot. Oh no, my poor leprechaun, the goods are safely locked away in Helliwell's house.'

Rembrandt's mouth fell open in admiration. He took advantage of this to insert the neck of another bottle, then he wiped his lips. 'Dat's good thinkin', sorr. Dat's amazin' thinkin', sorr.' He swigged again. 'Oi wish you'd told me earlier, sorr. Oi've been wetting me pants every time we passed another car, and dat's a fact.'

Terence pulled into the kerb.

'What's up, sorr?'

Terence nodded towards a phone box across the road. 'I'm just going to wish Joe a Happy Christmas, and I suggest you empty your trousers over the hedge now.'

Rembrandt bundled out. 'Does he know dat de stuff's in his house?' he inquired.

187

Terence shook his head. 'No, but he will.' He was about to add a witty remark but Rembrandt, head down against the hedge, was already enveloped in a cloud of his own steam.

Wilson Brown watched hypnotised as a billow of smoke crept along the ceiling like a malevolent plague. Jimmy the Hat watched as a voyeur might view a stripper, then he pulled himself together. 'Let's go.' He grabbed Wilson Brown's arm and, just as they were about to leave, the telephone rang. They all turned. The bell still had the power to summon people peremptorily.

'Let's go,' said Jimmy again, and as they bustled him up the drive to the car Wilson Brown could still hear the waspish ringing punctuating the crackle and roar of the fire.

Police car Zulu Baker One pulled up outside the Bingle-wood Estate and a constable nipped smartly out and hauled the big gates shut. His mate pressed his mike: 'Zulu Baker One in position, South Ridge Gate.'

His colleague climbed in and slammed the door. 'Bloody waste of time, this. Talk about locking t'stable bloody door. He pushed his cap back, and was about to light up when he craned forward. ''Ello, 'ello?'

Two pinpoints of light were approaching fast down South Ridge.

Jimmy the Hat peered over the driver's shoulder. 'Wot's the game? They've closed the gates.' The car slowed, and it was then that the police car chose to put on full headlights.

Jimmy, blinded, thumped his mate on the shoulder. 'Quick! Turn left down 'ere.'

The car accelerated, skidding into a left turn down Wimpers Lane, and Wilson Brown caught a fleeting glimpse of a policeman running to open the gate. The car screeched left again at the end just as the tiny beams of the police car bent round into Wimpers Lane behind them.

'Where does this lead?' yelled Jimmy.

'Up to the golf club,' replied Wilson Brown, white-faced and holding tightly onto the strap.

They rounded a curve in the road and drove straight

through a large brick gateway. The headlamps swept across the building in front of them, then stabbed out into the darkness. The car followed them over the practice putting green and down the slight bank to the eighteenth green.

'God,' thought Wilson Brown inconsequentially, 'the secretary won't like this.'

Leaping and bouncing, the car raced along the eighteenth fairway, all three heads banging against the roof of the car. It couldn't be the fairway – the fool was in the rough. Bouncing up and down some way behind them were the beams of the police car, and they seemed to be drawing closer. Wilson Brown didn't care any more. If his spine didn't snap his head would surely go through the roof. The beams of the car behind were flashing up and down, lighting up the driver's back intermittently, getting brighter. Then suddenly all was blackness – there was no pursuit. The driver pulled up slowly and they all looked back. Only Wilson Brown knew that the police car had gone into the deep bunker on the sixteenth. Jimmy tapped the driver on the shoulder, and without lights they cautiously felt their way over the rough ground, still bumping and lurching round the back nine. A clump of trees loomed to the right.

'OK, stop 'ere,' said Jimmy. The driver applied the brake. 'Now get out and 'ave a shufti round, see if you can find a flat bit of somewhere.'

'We're on the practice ground,' said Wilson Brown.

'I'm not asking you,' snarled Jimmy.

About a hundred yards to the left the headlights of a car raced by.

'That's what I want,' said Jimmy, and as he did so the driver returned. 'OK, OK. I saw it,' said Jimmy. 'Give it half an hour and we'll be off.'

He lit a cigarette, then cupped it quickly in his hands as another car flashed by in the opposite direction. Wilson Brown followed it with his eyes. The lights disappeared, leaving a thicker blackness behind, but even so he could just discern the red glow over the tops of the trees.

'Come on,' shouted Jim Cork over the cacophony in the

Star. 'Let's have a sing-song.' And in an unsteady voice he began, 'I took my wife for a ramble, a ramble.' He broke off. 'Come on, lads.' He waved his arms: 'Singing High Jig A Jig. . . .'

'Give over, Jim,' said Ned Bladdock. 'There's ladies present.'

'Bloody 'ell, Ned, it's Christmas,' he wheedled.

A crash of glass came through from the snug and the noise stopped, then a great cheer went up.

Jim Cork tried again. 'Took my wife for a ramble. . . .' But the song degenerated into an incoherent mumble, and he staggered out to the back. As he opened the door he was jostled by PC Jellicoe coming in.

He was a Grapplewick lad, but new to the police. His face puckered as he tried to pierce the heavy, smoke-laden atmosphere. He took a step forward and looked round uncertainly. The noise dribbled away as they became aware of his presence.

The landlord looked up. 'It's OK, lad. We 'ave an extension while midnight.'

The young constable nodded, embarrassed like a man who has just walked into the ladies by mistake.

'Oh, bless 'im,' said Mrs Dyson, and gave him a smacking kiss. A ragged cheer went up.

Ned Bladdock proffered a glass of rum. 'Get that down you, lad. It'll do you more good than she will.'

Young Jellicoe shook his head. 'Not just now. I'm on duty, thanks.' He craned round the room again. 'You haven't seen Mr Thurk, have you?'

Ned took his arm. 'Chief's over yonder in t'corner.' He pointed his glass across the room, but Mr Thurk was already pushing his way towards him.

'What's up, Constable?' he asked.

Jellicoe pushed back his helmet, relieved. 'Ah, Mr Thurk. I've been looking all over for you. There's a fire.'

Mr Thurk looked at him stupidly. He wasn't a drinking man but it would have been churlish of him to refuse the hospitality of the Binglewood householders, and his eyes and brain were heavy. 'Fire?' he repeated, as if it was a clue in a quiz game.

'Yes. Sorry I couldn't reach you before, sir, but I was on my own at the station. They're all out on the robberies.'

'Robberies?' asked Mr Thurk, although he was still struggling with the word 'fire'.

'I telephoned the Fire Station, but there was no reply,' went on Jellicoe, 'so I nipped over, but I couldn't get any sense out of the man in there.'

'That'll be Barmy,' said Ned, helpfully.

'Well, I couldn't get any information out of him as to your whereabouts. He just handed me a mug of tea.'

Mr Thurk nodded. 'Yes, he would.' Then the full realisation of what the policeman was saying hit him. 'Fire?' he squeaked. He slammed his glass on a table. 'Fire Brigade outside!' he yelled.

'Fire,' shouted Ned. 'Come on. Chop, chop.'

They stared at him for a moment, then drinks were downed quickly and the lads of the Brigade lurched and staggered outside. The wives and some of the more sober customers crowded the door as they watched them stagger up the street towards the Fire Station.

The landlord, stretching to look over their heads, muttered, 'They're in no condition to go to a bloody fire. They're all inflammable as it is.' He laughed at his own joke, but it fell flat.

The wives turned to him. 'It's thanks to our lads you can sleep safe in your bed,' hissed Mrs Bladdock, and wrapping her coat round her she made her way to the gates to watch their departure.

The night was shattered by the roar of the engine, then there was a vigorous clamballang and the old engine trundled towards the gate. PC Jellicoe stood in the middle of the road, hand up to stop all traffic, although there was nothing mobile for miles. He waved them on, but Jack applied the brake. Mr Thurk, adjusting the strap of his helmet, looked at him inquiringly.

Jack shrugged. 'I'm not a bloody mindreader,' he said, 'where's the soddin' fire?'

'Sorry, sir.' He took out his notebook. 'Seven Seas, a house on the Binglewood Estate, it's on the. . . .'

'I know where it is,' broke in Mr Thurk. 'Binglewood Estate,' he shouted to Jack, and with a great shuddering roar the engine leaped forward, scattering the onlookers. Fireman Harper fell off, but they couldn't wait for one man, so after being helped to his feet he made his way sheepishly to the bus stop.

Eyes streaming with the wind, Mr Thurk jerked fiercely at the bell. Ned Bladdock, behind him, risking life and limb, leaned over his shoulder to point ahead to the red glow of their destination. Two of the lads were hanging onto Jim Cork, who appeared to have passed out. It was a hairy drive. Jack Puller at the wheel was swerving round objects in the road that only he could see and which in fact were the product of a mind pickled in alcohol.

Tragically he didn't see the car coming towards him at high speed – hardly Jack's fault, because the car was travelling on sidelights only. As it closed with the fire engine the driver put on his headlights, blinding them all. Instinctively Jack stamped on the brake, but Lyndhurst Road is narrow, with an abnormally high kerb, and the driver of the oncoming car had no chance. The headlights veered away from them, then suddenly jerked back as the car hit the pavement. The lights swept over them all again at sickening speed, and the rear of the car slammed in to the offside front wheel of the fire tender.

Firemen flew off in all directions, although Jack and Mr Thurk managed to hold on, but the car slid along for thirty yards or more in a shower of sparks, to the scream of tortured metal. Shakily Mr Thurk got down and made his way towards the car. Some of the lads were already struggling with the door, and as he reached them they had extricated the driver, although it was obvious he'd never see the New Year in. The other two were alive, but just how barely it was impossible to tell. Mr Thurk was about to make his way back to the tender when he stopped. God Almighty! It couldn't be – he turned and bent over one of the moaning figures. It was, though, – it was Commander

Wilson Brown. Shocked, he tried to identify the others, but they were strangers, one of them with a livid scar on his cheek.

He glanced impatiently towards the red glow in the sky, then at the bodies – he couldn't leave them here. On the other hand he had a duty to the Fire Brigade. Luckily a police car screeched up and matters were taken out of his hands. 'Quick, lads, mount up.' The lads got shakily onto the engine. They were sober now, but all their guts had been knocked out of them. Jack was heaving at the front mud-guard where it had buckled onto the tyre. He stepped back, wiping his sweating forehead.

'Well, don't just bloody sit there,' he gasped. 'Give us a hand with this.'

Ned and a couple of others got down, but it was hard work. Old Aggie was built like a Sherman tank – thank God, because any other vehicle would have been knocked back into Grapplewick. Mr Thurk fretted. Was it in his imagination, or had the red glow died down? He joggled the bell rope with impatience, and the great juggernaut moved off.

Seven Seas was gutted. The blaze had been so severe and so sudden that it was almost hopeless. By the time the Blackburn Brigade arrived all they could do was contain it, and make sure the woods didn't catch. A tender from Manchester joined them, and together they brought what was left of it under control.

Quite a few sightseers clustered round, huddled in coats and scarves, but now the show was over they were beginning to disperse. Smoke-blackened firemen rolled up the hoses and gathered their equipment together. Some stood in a group having hot tea kindly supplied by one of the neigh-bours. The two fire chiefs, conspicuous by their white helmets, conferred quietly.

'What a bloody way to spend Christmas Eve,' one of them remarked. His opposite number nodded glumly. Then both their heads turned at the sound of a fire bell. They looked at each other, puzzled, then the Manchester Chief relaxed.

'Well, I'll go to our house and back.'

His colleague shook his head. 'I don't believe it! The Grapplewick lads have arrived – we're saved.'

On approaching, Mr Thurk spotted 'Manchester Fire Brigade' lettered on the side of the sleek gleaming tender. As the weary firemen paused in their duties to greet the new arrival Mr Thurk's head shrank into his collar in embarrassment. This would fuel another generation of derisory stories. They drew up alongside the Blackburn tender and the crowd raised a ragged cheer. One of the Blackburn Brigade sauntered over.

'Don't tell me,' he sniggered, 'one of the 'orses dropped dead.'

The trial was more of local interest than nationwide. Robberies were ten a penny, and too much was happening elsewhere in the world – for which Wilson Brown was grateful. He'd had a remarkable escape in the car smash, suffering mild concussion and a broken ankle. Jimmy the Hat was unfortunately injured rather badly, and as soon as he was able he was transported by ambulance to attend the court, his arm still splinted, one leg shorter than the other, and a heavy bandage round his head. A famous neurologist diagnosed brain damage, which in Jimmy's case was rather complimentary. However, the fates smiled again on Wilson Brown, as Jimmy could recollect nothing of the evening in question, nor, for that matter, the events leading up to it, which left a clear field for Wilson Brown's flights of fancy. Indeed he made a very imposing figure as he hobbled to the witness stand supported by a stout stick. His evidence was lucid and to the point, and the judge was impressed.

It transpired that, after he had reported the robbery, the two villains returned to his house, having inadvertently left some of the stolen goods upstairs. Modestly the Commander went on to describe how he had tackled them, but the odds were too great. Why they fired the house was open to conjecture. Vandalism? Revenge? Still dazed, he had been forced into their car, presumably as a hostage. The court knew the rest. The police were still making inquiries as

194

to the whereabouts of their accomplice, a Colonel Harper Warburton, but so far with little success. It didn't affect the outcome. Jimmy the Hat was ordered to be removed to a prison hospital, and thereafter for several years hard labour – harsh justice, but in his case an occupational hazard.

Some weeks later a popular women's magazine hit on the idea of a series entitled 'Heroes are born, not made'. Commander Wilson Brown was to be the subject of the first article, and a writer was despatched for an interview, but despite all efforts she was unable to trace the whereabouts of the gallant Commander. In the course of her research, however, a number of discrepancies came to light and she notified the police. Inside a week the story was headlined in a national newspaper, but it was a one-day wonder. Thankfully the *Daily Express* was not delivered in Tocumwal, a small town in New South Wales, Australia.

There weren't many applicants for the post of golf secretary, but as soon as he walked before the committee they knew he was the right man. Two days later Brigadier Wilson Baverstock limped to his desk and took up his post.

Twelve thousand miles away the black police van pulled into the archway of one of His Majesty's prisons. Jimmy the Hat looked out of the little barred window and sighed. His arm was still in splints and he still couldn't understand what he was supposed to have done. His last view of the outside world was a number 11 bus. It pulled up at the stop across the road. A little man in a scruffy raincoat was squatting on the pavement chalking a picture on the pavement.

The bus driver leaned out of his cab. 'I've got a job all planned,' he said.

Rembrandt didn't even look up. 'Oi've retired.'

Terence snarled, 'Next time round you be on this bus or I'll push a bottle of Guinness where it hurts.'

Ting-ting-ting. He glared at the black conductress, then released the brake.

The little man concentrated once again on his masterpiece. With a piece of charcoal he sketched smoke coming out of the two factory chimneys. Then he sat back to survey the scene, and it occurred to him that there hadn't been any smoke coming from the chimneys. To hell with it – artistic licence.

Some years later . . .

The Greater Crime of Grapplewick

Mr Thurk stared out of the window of his sixth-floor flat. The sight of the moors crisscrossed with black dry stone walls still gave him comfort, and the two tall factory chimneys remained, though the mills were derelict now. He leaned his forehead against the cold glass pane and felt the vibration as traffic spiralled round the circular road slightly above his eye level. The road was part of the many complex whorls of the spaghetti junction feeding the industrial towns of the north-west.

When Grapplewick first came to the notice of the planners in Whitehall they found it was ideally suited for their purpose, but the town itself had come as a shock. Research discovered it possessed no parliamentary candidate – not Tory, Labour, Liberal, nor indeed any other. Grapplewick in fact didn't officially exist, but a town in exactly the same location called Gwick did, although forms and letters addressed to it had for years been returned marked 'Not known'. After a humorous debate in cabinet Attlee sarcastically inquired if it was indeed British. Therefore, with no possibility of lost votes, the Town Council and the townsfolk were ignored, and almost before they could grasp the full import of the tragedy the bulldozers were eating into the town. Protests were swept aside, and a delegation to London was shunted from a junior minister to even more junior menials, while all the time concrete was spewing into the town centre.

Now, years later, the Attlee government was gone. Most of the original planners were either dead or else ennobled, diligently scribbling their memoirs to ensure themselves a place in history as the founders of a new, caring society.

Mr Thurk looked over his shoulder at the clock on the wall. In half an hour he would be catching his usual bus to the infirmary in Blackburn. Being a hospital porter didn't carry as much responsibility as his occupations of old had done. It should have been a satisfying vocation, but it wasn't. He could quite easily complete his day's work in one hour, and he was actually embarrassed at the ludicrous overtime, spent mainly in the hospital kitchens drinking tea: skiving was not only acceptable – it was compulsory.

Sadly, the new Gwick didn't warrant a Town Council, nor even a Fire Brigade. His gaze wandered down to the tandoori restaurant where the old Fire Station used to be, and as always he sighed. He remembered how he'd held up the demolition while he and Ned searched for Barmy. It was useless – Barmy had disappeared. Later, when the contractors were clearing the rubble, they found him. The Fire Station had been his home and during the search he had managed to remain hidden somewhere known only to himself. Poor Barmy! A grin had remained on his face even in death, a pair of dentures clutched in his right hand. Some two years later Ned passed away. Jack Puller still worked at Hepworth's Garage, but it wasn't the same Jack. A few years ago half a dozen kids on motorbikes had driven up, squirting petrol from the pumps haphazardly, pulling over the cigarette machine and starting to smash the windows. It was too much for Jack. He went into the garage and came out with a crowbar. Before they realised what was happening he was amongst them, and it was a massacre. Three of the bikes were wrecked, one of the yobbees received a fractured skull and another had his leg broken before the police arrived. The youths were given suspended sentences and ordered to pay for the damage, but Jack was sentenced to six months for assault. He came out a bitter, broken man.

The ghosts of Grapplewick crowded Mr Thurk's mind – the lads in the band, Dr McBride, old deaf Crumpshaw, even the vicar. He looked down at the church. St Mary's had been spared, but he very rarely went in now. He couldn't accept a clergyman who wore a pair of blue denims.

The door bell rang. Visitors were rare. He opened the door: 'Ah, it's you, Dorothy.' He stood aside to let her enter.

'I'm off to Blackburn myself,' she said, 'so I thought I'd offer you a lift.'

'Yes, that'll be fine . . . hang on while I get my coat.'

Lady Dorothy walked to the window, as she invariably did. 'If there's a strike next week,' she asked over her shoulder, 'will you come out with them?'

He shrugged into his coat. 'Oh, I don't think there'll be a strike. It's just a lot of hot air.'

She frowned. 'But if they do call a strike, what will happen to the patients?'

He smiled and took her arm. 'Exactly,' he said firmly. 'For that reason they'll call it off. They wouldn't just drop everything and leave the patients to suffer.' He laughed. 'It's unthinkable.'

They got into the lift, which always embarrassed him. Twice he'd painted it himself, but it was only a fresh background for even more graffiti. He was relieved when they stepped out of the main door. 'Cheer up, Dorothy,' he said. 'There's always a bright side.' He realised that she wasn't listening, and when he followed her gaze his heart sank – all the tyres on her car had been slashed.